"HEY THERE, MISS LORETTA!" DREW CALLED OUT FROM THE BUGGY. "I HAVE AN ERRAND TO RUN. WANT TO COME ALONG?"

For a moment, Loretta felt lower than a worm, but she couldn't allow Will to believe he could take up where they'd left off. He hadn't heard a word she'd said as she'd gently countered his suggestions. Loretta nipped her lip, glancing apologetically at the handsome young man who'd gone through such an ordeal these past several months. Without a word, she hurried down the porch steps and across the front yard toward Drew Detweiler.

Grinning, Drew dropped down from the buggy. As he clasped Loretta's hand and escorted her to the other side of his open vehicle, she wondered if he was leading her down a path riskier than Will's, and far more dangerous. A path more daring . . . and passionate. When Drew placed his hands on either side of her waist, he paused before lifting her up.

Loretta's heart went wild. Drew's sapphire eyes held secrets and intentions she couldn't decipher, and he brought to mind a fox in the henhouse cornering his tasty prey. Effortlessly he lifted her into his buggy and then hopped in on the other side. "Hope I wasn't interrupting anything important," he said as he took up the lines. "If I'm not mistaken, Gingerich looks like a man come courting."

A
SIMPLE WISH

Charlotte Hubbard

ZEBRA BOOKS
KENSINGTON PUBLISHING CORP.
http://www.kensingtonbooks.com

ZEBRA BOOKS are published by

Kensington Publishing Corp.
119 West 40th Street
New York, NY 10018

All Kensington titles, imprints, and distributed lines are available at special quantity discounts for bulk purchases for sales promotion, premiums, fund-raising, educational, or institutional use.

Special book excerpts or customized printings can also be created to fit specific needs. For details, write or phone the office of the Kensington Sales Manager: Attn.: Sales Department. Kensington Publishing Corp., 119 West 40th Street, New York, NY 10018. Phone: 1-800-221-2647.

Zebra and the Z logo Reg. U.S. Pat. & TM Off.

First Printing: October 2017
ISBN-13: 978-1-4201-3871-9
ISBN-10: 1-4201-3871-5

eISBN-13: 978-1-4201-3872-6
eISBN-10: 1-4201-3872-3

10 9 8 7 6 5 4 3 2 1

Printed in the United States of America

Chapter One

Ordinarily, the shaded front porch was the coolest place to spend an August afternoon, but the sweat trickling down Loretta Riehl's back had nothing to do with Missouri's heat and humidity. Will Gingerich, her former fiancé, sat on the other end of the porch swing from her, and his back-and-forth motion was becoming so quick and jerky that she could barely guide her homemade toothbrush needle through the loose knots of the rag rug she was making.

"The biggest mistake I ever made was to let your *dat* end our engagement, Loretta," Will said urgently. "I should've stood my ground. I should've believed that our love was strong enough to withstand my losing the farm to my brothers."

Loretta swallowed hard, fearful of where this conversation was leading. She'd been devastated when Dat had come between her and Will a couple of years ago, but she'd accepted it as her father's will—which was second only to God's. "Who among us has ever stood up to Dat and won?" she asked in a tight voice. Her hands were trembling as she drew the strip of sage green fabric through the next rug knot with her needle. "I cried my eyes out and pleaded with him again and again, but he was convinced you weren't *gut* enough—that you could never provide me a home."

"He was wrong!" Will declared. "I should've insisted that you and I could live at your place—back when we were in Rosewood—the way a lot of newlyweds do until they have the money for a home of their own."

Loretta stifled a sigh. Why was Will thinking this way, when they both knew they would've been miserable living under Dat's roof after Mamm had died? Even with her sisters, Edith and Rosalyn, to encourage them, their marriage would've gotten off to a rocky start.

"And the other monumental mistake I made," Will continued fervently, "was latching on to Molly Ropp too quickly after your *dat* severed my relationship with you. Why didn't I realize Molly's parents were too *eager* to get us married?"

"How could you have known Molly was pregnant?" Loretta pointed out. "We don't like to believe that young Amish women would succumb to temptation— or keep such secrets—"

"And how was Molly supposed to know that it was Drew Detweiler who fathered her twins rather than Asa?" Will demanded. As he raked his light brown hair back with his fingers, he appeared lost in his own world, not really seeming to hear anything Loretta said. "Molly was deceived. *I* was deceived—"

"You paid dearly for that, Will. But that episode's behind us now—although I sense you're still mourning Molly's passing," Loretta put in quietly. She rested her hands in her lap, no longer able to concentrate on her rug. "Still, God saw to it that some *gut* came of your trials and tribulations, ain't so? Little Leroy and Louisa are a joy to us all. And once Drew confessed and apologized to everyone for masquerading as his brother, he became an accepted, forgiven member of our church district and the Willow Ridge business community. That's real progress, to my way of thinking."

When Loretta looked across the road, she noticed that one of the Detweiler brothers was coming out of the stable in an open buggy pulled by a tall black Percheron. Asa and Drew, identical twins, owned matching horses, so it was impossible to tell which one of them was heading down the long lane toward the road.

She held her breath. Was it her imagination, or was the driver of that buggy looking right at her?

"I—I've never forgiven myself for turning my back on the love we shared, Loretta," Will said again. He stopped the swing so suddenly that Loretta's long, loose strips of rug fabric fluttered to the porch floor. "We both knew we had a love that would have seen us through a lifetime together. I was so upset about your *dat* splitting us up that I didn't realize Molly was coming on to me too fast, too soon," he lamented, gazing at her with the soft brown eyes of a begging dog. "I am so sorry, Loretta."

Loretta was feeling more unsettled by the second, because Will's soul-baring was leading her down a path she no longer wanted to follow. How could she tell him she wasn't interested in rekindling their relationship? It would break his heart and depress him further while he still mourned the death of his wife and their misguided marriage.

Sighing, she chose her words carefully. "God has a

reason for everything He does—every stumbling block He places in our paths—"

"But I see the world so clearly now!" Will blurted out. "I've prayed over these things night and day since Molly died and left me with her six-month-old twins. And while I never wished her ill, once she was gone I began to hope that you and I could—"

Loretta stood up, dropping her unfinished rug onto the swing between them. As the Detweiler buggy approached the road, coming toward her, she realized that Drew surely must be driving, because Asa and her sister Edith were inseparable—they went everywhere together and took the twins they'd adopted with them, in their baskets. Her pulse quickened. Drew was gazing right at her, pulling out of the Detweilers' lane and stopping the buggy on the roadside in front of her house.

"Loretta, I've got a *gut* steady job now, farming for Luke and Ira Hooley," Will was saying, oblivious to the buggy. "Soon I'll be planting a vineyard for them—can you imagine that? And I'll be asking the Brenneman brothers to build us a house—"

"Hey there, Miss Loretta!" Drew called out from the buggy. "I have an errand to run. Want to come along?"

For a moment, Loretta felt lower than a worm, but she couldn't allow Will to believe he could take up where they'd left off. He hadn't heard a word she'd said as she'd gently countered his suggestions. Loretta nipped her lip, glancing apologetically at the handsome young man who'd gone through such an ordeal these past several months. Without a word, she hurried down the porch steps and across the front yard toward Drew Detweiler.

Grinning, Drew dropped down from the buggy. As

he clasped Loretta's hand and escorted her to the other side of his open vehicle, she wondered if he was leading her down a path riskier than Will's, and far more dangerous. A path more daring . . . and passionate. When Drew placed his hands on either side of her waist, he paused before lifting her up.

Loretta's heart went wild. Drew's sapphire eyes held secrets and intentions she couldn't decipher, and he brought to mind a fox in the henhouse cornering his tasty prey. Effortlessly he lifted her into his buggy and then hopped in on the other side. "Hope I wasn't interrupting anything important," he said as he took up the lines. "If I'm not mistaken, Gingerich looks like a man come courting."

Feeling downright wicked—yet too flummoxed to look over at Will on the porch—Loretta let out the breath she'd been holding. "You saved me from a really embarrassing scene," she murmured as the buggy lurched into motion. "Once upon a time I loved Will with all my heart, but after Dat broke us up and Will latched on to Molly so fast—well, I had second thoughts about his . . . sincerity. His true feelings for me. And now, well—"

Loretta faltered. The man beside her had lied to Molly about who he was when he'd gotten her in the family way, before poor deluded Will had married her. Everyone in town had officially forgiven Drew for deceiving Molly, but Drew was still a mysterious newcomer who played his cards close to his vest.

If Dat saw whom you were riding off with, he'd be even more upset than when he made you break up with Will.

It was true, yet Loretta didn't regret what she was doing. For the first time in months, she felt breathlessly alive. *Anything* might happen when she was with the Detweiler who had such a checkered past, and Loretta welcomed the sense of adventure that filled her.

"You and I have a lot in common, Loretta." Drew scooted so close to her that their thighs brushed with the rhythm of the buggy. "I was head over heels for Molly, the way you were for Will. I admit that it was wrong to tell her I was Asa," he went on with a shake of his head. "But she ripped my heart out and stomped on it, as though bearing my children meant nothing to her—as though she wouldn't so much as give me the time of day. She up and married Gingerich without even telling me she was pregnant. That still stinks!"

Waves of Drew's regret and hurt carried Loretta along on the tide of his emotions. She felt bad for him. His brother and Edith were now adopting Leroy and Louisa, but Drew hadn't had a chance to make good with Molly, because she'd died from cancer before he'd learned the little twins were his. Loretta admired Drew for assisting with the twins' expenses— and for agreeing that they were better off growing up with a mother and a father who had married and were able to put their welfare first.

Drew halted the wagon near the big windbreak of evergreens just down the road from the house. He turned to face her, drinking her in with his midnight gaze. "What say you and I put the past behind us, Loretta?" he whispered. "I'm betting I can make you forget all about Gingerich, and I think you're the kind of girl who can put Molly's memory to rest for me. Know what I'm saying?"

Before she could answer, Drew framed her face with his large, pleasantly calloused hands. His kiss, earnest and probing, took Loretta to a place she'd never been. She poured all of her being into making the kiss go on and on, reveling in the feel of Drew's embrace even as she felt Will watching them from her front porch. She hadn't intended to snub her former fiancé quite so brazenly . . .

But Drew made her feel so daring—so free—that she wasn't sorry.

Will choked on a sob, wishing he could stop staring at Loretta. He'd loved her for so long, it nearly killed him to see the way she was responding to Detweiler's kiss . . . as though she'd shared his affections many times before.

Could this be true? Has she been sneaking around with that con artist, only pretending to listen to me? The way Molly did? Am I the biggest fool on the face of the earth?

Will turned and bounded down the porch steps. He cut around behind the house, jogging alongside the Riehls' thriving vegetable garden and past the large fenced section of yard where their chickens pecked at the ground. The rooster's crow mocked him. As he picked up speed behind the Grill N Skillet Café and Zook's Market, he was nearly blinded by anger. Loretta's betrayal ranked right up there with Molly's crying out her love for another man on her deathbed—the moment he'd learned that Leroy and Louisa were not his children. Even after Molly's parents had kicked him off their farm, he hadn't felt this destitute. This desperate.

Just ahead, the big wheel of the Hooleys' gristmill slowly turned, splashing the Missouri River's surface, but the scene's beauty was lost on him. Now that Ira was married and living in the new white house behind the mill, Will was renting the bachelor apartment in the mill's upper level. Unfortunately, the stairs to his new home were inside, so he had to pass through the mill store—and when he burst through the door, Luke and his redheaded wife, Nora, were lip-locked, sharing a clinch behind the checkout counter.

Luke had the presence of mind to ease away, cradling Nora to his chest as he smiled at Will. "Oops," he teased. "Guess we should save this mushy stuff for after we get home, *jah?*"

Will's breath escaped him in a rush. He looked doggedly around at the shelves of bagged flour and cereals, and the refrigerator case filled with local eggs, butter, and goat cheese—anything to avoid watching yet another couple pouring their hearts into a kiss.

"Will, what's wrong?" Nora asked softly. "You look like you've seen a ghost."

Jah, the ghost of my hopes and dreams for Loretta Riehl.

Will coughed nervously. Luke was his employer more than his friend, and he hesitated to reveal too much about his love life—or lack of it. But Nora's concerned expression touched him. From what he'd heard, she had endured more than her share of rejection and upheaval when she'd moved back to Willow Ridge to be with the family who'd shunned her, so maybe she would understand. Maybe she could empathize with his degradation and shame.

"Loretta just left me for that lying cheat of a *Detweiler*," he spat. "That dog had the nerve to *kiss* her, right there on the road, knowing I'd see him at it."

Nora's mouth dropped open as she came out from behind the counter. "Will, I'm so sorry," she murmured.

"*Jah*, well, *sorry* doesn't begin to cover it for me,"

he blurted. "I was practically on my knees as she and I talked on her porch swing, saying I'd been wrong not to marry her back when her *dat* came between us—"

"*Gut* luck going against Cornelius," Luke muttered as he joined them.

"—but I might as well have been talking to the wall," Will continued miserably. "One look at Detweiler as he pulled his buggy across the road, and Loretta was his—hook, line, and sinker. No doubt in my mind that before the day's out, he'll ruin her reputation. Ruin *her*."

Luke cleared his throat. "I can understand why you feel Loretta kicked you to the curb—kicked you where it hurts most," he said, "but she's fully aware of Drew's earlier deceptions. And she's old enough to know what she's getting herself into."

"Loretta has no idea what he's capable of!" Will countered hotly. "She's led a sheltered, quiet life with her sisters, keeping the household running since their *mamm*'s passing. *Jah*, Cornelius is a piece of work, but Drew Detweiler passed himself off as his twin brother with not one but *two* other women!"

Nora held his gaze with her tranquil hazel eyes—eyes similar to Loretta's, except that they were windows to a much wiser, more compassionate soul. "Well, he came clean after you exposed him during Edith and Asa's wedding," she pointed out. "None of us could imagine the *nerve* it took for Drew to feed Asa sleeping pills and then stand in as Edith's would-be husband, but Edith was the first to forgive Drew."

"Edith's a saint. Loretta—" Will looked away, hoping the Hooleys didn't see the tears in his eyes. "Loretta is sweet and loving and—and unable to comprehend the concept of such evil temptation. She doesn't stand a chance against the likes of Detweiler."

Luke gave Will's shoulder a brief squeeze. "I understand why Drew's advances have upset you—but I understand this situation from Detweiler's perspective, as well."

Will scowled, backing away. "What do you mean by that? Are you taking his side?"

Luke shook his head good-naturedly, smiling at his wife. "Before Nora caught my eye and held me accountable for my actions, I took great pleasure in running the roads with Annie Mae Knepp—the bishop's daughter," he replied. "Why was I sneaking her out of the house at night, making the tongues wag about how I, at thirty, was ruining a seventeen-year-old girl? I did it because I *could*—because I got a kick out of breaking the rules. And Annie Mae was rebel enough to enjoy it as much as I did."

Before Will could stop himself, he blurted, "So you—you took advantage of her? You took her because you *could*?"

"Absolutely not." Luke leveled his gaze at Will. "We appeared to be lovers, but appearances can be deceiving—"

"What he's not telling you," Nora put in, "is that his brother was along for most of those rides. Ira was seeing my daughter Millie—who, *jah*, was entirely too young to be dating a fellow nearly twelve years older than she was. But the four of them kept each other honorable, and now they're all responsible, married adults—"

"*Happily* married adults," Luke insisted as he slung his arm around Nora's shoulders. "What I'm saying, Will, is that maybe Drew's coming on to Loretta to irritate *you*. Maybe he's just rubbing your nose in it without any intention of leading Loretta astray."

"You think it wasn't enough that he got Molly pregnant?" Will demanded. "I'm saying history could repeat itself—sooner rather than later—"

"And what can you do about that?" Luke asked softly. "The more worked up you get, the more Drew will enjoy stepping out with Loretta—and the more control he'll have over your mindset. Just sayin'."

Nora rolled her eyes. "Spoken like a guy," she remarked. Her sigh sounded apologetic. "Sorry to say this, but if you were talking about marriage again, maybe Loretta wasn't ready to listen—"

"But she loves me! Back before Cornelius butted in and—"

"Things change, Will. People change." Nora gazed at him apologetically. "You're not the same man she was courting before her *dat* stepped in. You've been married, and you were widowed by a terrible disease. Your life took a direction neither you nor Loretta wanted or could've predicted."

Will sagged like a balloon losing its air. Would his short, ill-fated marriage with Molly color the rest of his life? What if Loretta—or any other young woman he met—found him unattractive because he was used goods . . . or because he'd caved in to need and desperation when he'd married Molly on the rebound?

"*Denki* for listening," he muttered. "I'd appreciate it if you didn't spread this around, all right?"

"Wouldn't dream of it. We've all been dragged behind the wagon at one time or another," Luke said. "I hope Loretta realizes what a fine, reliable man you are and comes to her senses. And if she doesn't, I hope you'll find a way to move beyond your hurt feelings." Luke smiled at him. "Either way, Will, I'm mighty glad you've come to work for me. You're an excellent farmer, and together we'll make a go of that new vineyard."

"If there's anything we can do, just say the word," Nora added kindly.

But what could anyone else do for him? He'd had Loretta's complete attention—or had thought he had—until Detweiler drove up in front of the Riehl place with his dubious intentions and come-hither smile.

Will started for the stairway at the back of the store. "*Denki* for your kindness, but this is between me and Loretta."

Except Loretta left. Without so much as a backward glance.

His footsteps in the stairwell sounded as hollow as he felt. When Will opened the door to the upstairs apartment, he sighed loudly. The place was sunny and reasonably clean, but if the Hooley brothers hadn't left their furniture, it would be almost empty—and that was a kick in the head. He'd lost the farm he'd grown up on when his two older brothers had taken it over—and then, after Molly had died, he'd been evicted from the farm her parents had let them rent. Will had come to Willow Ridge with nothing but some clothes and a few personal effects to show for being a widower of twenty-seven.

Not much to offer a bride, his thoughts taunted him.

Will leaned against the windowsill in the small kitchen, staring out over the narrow ribbon of the Missouri River. From this vantage point, he could see the back of Nora's white house and the red barn that housed her Simple Gifts store . . . a well-kept orchard . . . Bishop Tom's herd of grazing Holsteins and the chicken house behind the Reihl home—and beyond that, the new metal shop building, where Detweiler kept an upstairs apartment because he didn't want to live in the main house with Asa and Edith.

Detweiler's no better off than I am. What does Loretta see in him?

Cursing under his breath, Will stepped away from the window. Until he had some answers, there was no sense in torturing himself with more painful questions.

Chapter Two

On Monday morning, as Nora was setting up a new pottery display in the front of her gift store, she couldn't help smiling. Last weekend's special Hot for August sale had decimated her wares, so she'd called her crafters with a plea for more of their handmade items. Her Simple Gifts shop had become a bigger win-win than she'd anticipated when she'd opened it last year: her Amish and Mennonite suppliers were earning a steady income from consigning their crafts to her, and she was making a nice profit from the English folks who loved to buy their quilts, furniture, dishes, and other unique, handmade items in her store. She felt she was empowering a lot of Plain ladies by allowing them to earn money that supplemented their husbands' incomes while they worked at home.

After Nora dusted the handsome walnut bookcase the Brenneman brothers had brought in, she carefully arranged Amanda Brubaker's tan and blue plates, bowls, and serving pieces on its shelves. A number of quilts were ready to be hung from her upstairs display poles, the result of a quilting contest the

Schrocks had held in their quilt shop down the road—and one of them would cover the new sleigh bed that matched the Brennemans' walnut bookcase, along with a fresh set of embroidered sheets Nellie Knepp had brought in. Nora was pleased that Annie Mae's younger sister—another of ex-bishop Hiram's daughters—was finding her way after her infamous *dat*'s crimes had claimed his life and rocked the foundations of Willow Ridge. There was great healing to be found in the community of women who expressed themselves in their handwork.

When a clock across the shop struck eight and played "Jesus Loves Me," she thought of Cornelius Riehl, the clockmaker who'd moved to town with his three daughters this past spring. Sternly traditional and autocratic, he'd quickly realized that displaying his new and refurbished clocks in Simple Gifts brought in a lot more money than leaving them on his workbench at the house—and he was grudgingly allowing his girls to consign their baskets, rugs, and wreaths as well. Nora was hoping Edith would still have time to make baskets now that she was a wife and the mother of little Leroy and Louisa, and she believed Loretta could sell every rag rug she had time to make—

She can't make rugs while she's running the roads with Drew Detweiler.

Nora laughed at this thought. After their conversation with Will, she and Luke had agreed to stay out of the sticky situation bubbling up between him and Loretta and Drew. Young love was known to blow east one day and west the next—but she felt sorry for Will. Seemed he'd been left with no love at all after his unfortunate marriage to a deceptive young woman had ended with her death.

Loretta, on the other hand, was probably getting herself in over her pretty head when it came to spending time with the elusive Drew Detweiler. Nora chuckled. She knew exactly why the middle Riehl daughter was so drawn in by Drew's charisma: every *gut* and dutiful daughter longed for a bad boy to steal her away from her predictable life. Luke's rebellious refusal to conform to the Old Order had been among the first of his traits to attract Nora, after all.

When the bell above the door jangled, Nora laughed. "Loretta! I was just thinking about you," she called over to the young woman.

Loretta's face was rosy with excitement, her hazel eyes alight with secrets as she carried a large rolled rag rug to where Nora sat. "Your thoughts were all *gut* ones, I hope," she teased as she unrolled the multi-colored rug on the floor beside the sleigh bed. "I've decided to work in your store, Nora—even teach rug-making classes, if you still want me to."

Nora's eyes widened. "What's your *dat* saying about that? Last I knew, he'd forbidden you to work here among my English customers."

"Dat's gone to Kansas City for clock supplies today, so I'm feeling bold." Loretta planted a fist on her hip and raised one eyebrow. "He doesn't listen to me when I tell him it'd be faster and cheaper to order his supplies from a catalog and have them shipped, so why should I feel bound by his restrictions?"

Loretta's new attitude set off alarms in Nora's mind. She, too, had suggested that Cornelius order his parts from a catalog—and she thought it was highly suspicious that he hired a driver to take him into the city so often—but it wasn't like Loretta to throw caution to the winds when it came to dealing with her *dat*. "I'd be delighted if you worked for me," she said carefully. "And we've talked about what a perfect teacher you'd be for ladies who'd like to make rugs—"

"*But?*" Loretta challenged with a grin. "But you think Dat will storm in during one of my classes and order me to go home, ain't so?"

"The image has crossed my mind, *jah.*"

Loretta rolled her eyes. "The way I see it, Edith defied Dat by dating Asa against his wishes—then by marrying him despite all the hullabaloo Drew caused on their wedding day," she said confidently. "If Edith found her happily-ever-after by following her heart instead of Dat's orders, that's what I'm going to do, too. Life's too short to spend so much of it under my father's thumb."

Part of her was cheering for Loretta's independent streak, because Nora had defied everything her father, Preacher Gabe Glick, had stood for back in the day. But Nora knew Loretta would encounter some serious consequences for upsetting the Old Order ways—and her father, who was the deacon of Willow Ridge. She hated to see this young woman's dreams get deadheaded before they could even bloom.

Nora moved closer to Loretta's rug, smoothing the oval rows of purple, pink, and cream so it would lie flatter. "How did you know that this new rug would look so perfect alongside the set of pink sheets Nellie embroidered?" she asked lightly. "I have to wonder, though, what—or who—compelled you to declare your independence."

Loretta's cheeks turned pink. "Rosalyn and I have talked a lot since Edith married and left home, and we've made a pact. We've both decided to look for men to court and marry, rather than feeling so sorry for Dat that we remain at home forever taking care of him—as he hopes at least one of us will do. We deserve our own lives and families, don't you think?"

"I do," Nora said without hesitation. "I didn't know your mother, but I'm sure she never intended for you to be stay-at-home daughters after she passed on. No doubt she—like most folks—figured your *dat* would remarry someday."

"As if that's going to happen," Loretta said with a sigh. "Every time we mention that subject, Dat accuses us of dishonoring our *mamm*'s memory. So Rosalyn and I have sworn to stand up to him the way Edith did, instead of living timidly in his shadow."

Nora moved the pile of quilts from the sleigh bed to a nearby table. It was time to be quiet so Loretta would fill the silence with the rest of her story. As she shook out the pink fitted sheet, Loretta grabbed the end closest to her and walked to the opposite side of the bed. After they'd slipped the bottom sheet over the box that served as a display mattress, the younger woman smiled at the row of pink and purple flowers across the top sheet.

"Nellie did a nice job. Look at her tiny, perfect stitches on these lilacs and lilies," Loretta said as they smoothed the sheet. Her expression became more thoughtful as Nora chose a double wedding ring quilt in the same colors for the bed, and they folded the top of the sheet down over it so the embroidered flowers would show. "Nellie's still a kid—not even a teenager yet—and she's got to find her way without a mother just like we're doing, except for a lot longer time," Loretta remarked wistfully. "It's so kind of you, Nora, to encourage all us girls. You don't just provide a place for our crafts; you really *listen* to us."

Deeply touched, Nora clasped Loretta's hand

across the bed. "I was cast out of Willow Ridge for something that wasn't my fault," she murmured. "I know a little bit about surviving on the sheer refusal to believe I was as unredeemable as folks told me I was. I made it back—made *gut* on God's plan for me—so I hope I can help you girls do the same."

They were silent as they stuffed pillows into Nellie's embroidered pillowcases and then plumped them against the curved walnut headboard. Nora's heart thrummed as she listened between the lines, wondering if Loretta was about to confide more.

"Wow, this bed looks like something out of a fairy tale," Loretta whispered. She took a deep breath, her lips twitching with a smile. "These past couple of days, I've been imagining Drew Detweiler as my handsome prince, dreaming about the day we'll ride away on his big black horse to find our happily-ever-after."

Nora smiled. Didn't every young woman fall in love with a man she believed would relieve the tedium of dirty dishes and solve her family problems—all the while making her giddy with his perfect affection? It was no time to burst Loretta's rose-colored bubble by asking where Will Gingerich fit into this idyllic picture.

"Drew's a fascinating fellow," Nora said. "At twenty-seven, he's lived through more, um, *challenging* situations than most men twice his age."

"One kiss, and I was hooked," Loretta murmured dreamily. "Well, really he had me from the moment he drove his buggy in front of the house and asked me to ride with him. I just couldn't say no."

Nora smiled to herself. Change out the buggy for a shiny new Lexus, and the story could be about the day her ex-husband, Tanner Landwehr, had first asked her out on a date. "Drew impresses me as the charismatic sort," she said. "Some guys are magic. They know exactly what to say and do . . . exactly how to kiss you and hold you. The trick is to know if they're just pretty words—all smoke and mirrors—or if they really do have a rabbit in their hat, and if it's a rabbit you want to live with for the rest of your life."

When Loretta appeared confused, Nora realized that she probably wasn't familiar with stage magicians. Proper Old Order Amish girls didn't watch television or indulge in the hocus-pocus games along the midway of the county fair.

"Be sure Drew's actions match up with his words," Nora explained gently. "Once you get beyond the thrill of running the roads and letting him kiss you silly, ask yourself if he sincerely likes and respects you, or if he's making a game of it."

Loretta sucked in her breath. "Drew would never—why do you think he would take advantage of me?" she demanded. "And why do you think I can't handle any tricks he might try to pull?"

Because you're a sheltered young Amish woman and you don't understand the way men think.

Nora smiled patiently. "I thought I was pretty savvy at your age, too—and I was already married to that English guy by then, lost in love with him," she replied. "So lost I didn't see it coming when he left me for somebody more *sophisticated* and interesting. I'd been working as a housekeeper in one of his family's big hotels, so I was living out my own Cinderella story when the boss's son married me—until he didn't want me anymore."

Loretta's eyes widened as she thought about Nora's story. "But—but you ended up with Luke," she said. "And he's just *perfect*."

Nora laughed. "*Jah*, he is now. But when I first met

Luke, he was convinced that my red convertible and shorts meant I was easy prey," she elaborated. "He believed he was so suave and handsome and persuasive that I couldn't possibly refuse him. *Puh!*"

Loretta giggled. "So you had to polish him up and smooth off some rough edges? It's that way with Drew, too. He's pretty impressed with himself sometimes . . . But wow," she whispered. "He makes me feel really special. Absolutely beautiful."

"Just be sure you know who you are and what you expect," Nora suggested. "Don't sell yourself short—or give yourself away. If he walks off, you'll still be Loretta Riehl, who has her life to live, instead of being Drew's castoff. And if you want to work in my store and teach rug-making classes," she added purposefully, "you'll have an even better foundation for this independence you're growing into."

Loretta's eyes lit up with gratitude. "You know, lots of Amish girls my age are already married—like Edith, who's only nineteen," she pointed out. "But at twenty-three, I still want to have some *fun.* I want to try new things and visit places I've never been—and so does Drew. And I want to work in your beautiful store, Nora! Am I being selfish or wicked, wanting to enjoy my life before I settle down with my handsome prince?"

Nora stepped over and wrapped her arms around Loretta. "I understand perfectly, even though some of what you're wanting goes against Amish tradition," she replied. "But you've done the responsible thing—you've joined the church and committed your life to following God's plan—so *jah*, allow yourself time to figure out what His plan for you is, sweetie."

Loretta hugged her tightly. "I am *so* glad you're my friend, Nora. I can't tell Dat *any* of this stuff—and he'll be furious that I've come to work for you after he's told me I couldn't," she admitted. "But I want to give it a shot. Plenty of time to follow the rules after I'm an old married lady, *jah*?"

Nora laughed, steering Loretta toward her office in the back of the shop. "*Jah*, we girls all figure we'll settle down when we're old—just as we tell ourselves we'll never *be* old," she agreed. "Let's talk about your new job while we enjoy some lemonade with a couple of Lena Witmer's cute cookies. She's another one who stumbled and fell a few times before she found the life God intended for her and Josiah to share. And now the Grill N Skillet he runs with his sister Savilla is hugely successful."

They paused at the checkout counter, where a large, flat basket of decorated sugar cookies tempted customers. "I've sampled more than my share of Lena's cookies, and they're awesome," Loretta said as she studied them. She snatched up a colorful butterfly, as well as a flower-shaped cookie with a smiley face in its center. "Here I am—as happy as this flower and as light and free as this butterfly!"

Nora smiled. *Help Loretta grow into her freedom and remain as sweet and fresh—and unbroken—as these cookies, Lord. She's got it bad, so You and I need to watch out for her.*

Chapter Three

Later that afternoon—much later than she'd figured on—Loretta hurried into the kitchen through the back door. Her sister Rosalyn looked up from dredging chicken pieces in flour and arranging them in a skillet that bubbled and crackled with hot oil. "Where've you been, missy?" she asked softly. "Dat just got home. He's in a dither because you weren't here, and supper wasn't ready, and all manner of other things he found to grouse about."

Loretta let out an exasperated sigh, sorry she'd left her sister to deal with Dat's nasty mood. "Nora hired me!" she explained as she washed her hands at the sink. "And we talked about holding a class for ladies who want to learn how to make toothbrush rugs. I didn't mean to stay so late, Rosalyn. I'm really sorry."

"Time flies when you're having fun," her sister quipped kindly. "I'm happy for you, Loretta—but I suggest you don't bring this up at supper. Edith and Asa are coming over, which is one reason we're running later than Dat prefers." Rosalyn's eyebrows rose playfully. "Hope it's all right that I told them to bring Drew along."

Loretta sucked in her breath as she measured flour into a mixing bowl for biscuits. There was no time to change her dress, and she could only hope her hair was still tidily tucked up into her *kapp*. "Has Dat said anything about Drew and me going for that ride Saturday night?" she asked as she went to the fridge.

"No, but I certainly want to hear about it now, Loretta," her father replied tersely from behind them. "Where have you been, young lady?"

Loretta dropped the egg she'd gotten out and watched it spread wetly over the kitchen floor. How long had Dat been standing in the doorway, listening to their conversation? *Remember what you told Nora? About how you weren't going to cower in Dat's shadow anymore?*

Bracing herself for whatever her father might say, Loretta plucked another egg from the bin in the refrigerator before carefully stepping over the one she'd dropped. It was a toss-up, which of his topics to address first, so she chose the one that seemed the least likely to further stir him up. "I took my finished rug over to Simple Gifts," she replied. "Nora's gotten in a lot of new items, so I was helping her arrange them while we talked. How was your trip to Kansas City, Dat?"

"Don't change the subject!" Dat's chair scraped against the floor as he pulled it out and sat down at the table. "Why were you doing Nora's work when you should've been here at home helping Rosalyn with supper?"

Rosalyn shot her a sympathetic look. "We didn't know what time you'd be home, Dat," she pointed out, "so we didn't want to start cooking the chicken until—"

"Your sister is perfectly capable of answering, Rosalyn. If I want your opinion, I'll ask for it."

Loretta cringed, praying for patience as she cleaned up the egg. Had Dat already overheard her talking about working at Simple Gifts? Was he testing her? Years of experience had taught her that a direct answer was better than dancing around the issue— even though the answer would make her father even angrier than he already was.

And why is that? Why would a trip to Kansas City to buy clock parts upset him?

Loretta placed the sloppy egg in the pan where they collected scraps for the compost pile. Taking a deep breath, she turned to face her father. "I was helping Nora because I've taken a job in her store," she said in the bravest voice she could manage. "I started this afternoon, matter of fact, and in a couple of weeks I'll be teaching a class on—"

"Loretta, I forbade you to work there, *matter of fact*," Dat interrupted testily. "Tomorrow when Nora opens the store, you'll be going over to apologize for acting rashly today and to tell her you'll be making your rugs from home, as you and I agreed upon earlier."

Her knees shook beneath her calf-length dress. A knot clogged her throat, and for a moment Loretta wondered if she'd choke on it. But if she was to become independent, she couldn't knuckle under every time Dat told her what to do. "No, Dat," she said nervously, "tomorrow—on Tuesdays, Thursdays, and Saturdays—I'm working for Nora. I'm doing this so I can buy dress fabric, shoes, and—and other things I need, because you've told us money is tight."

Dat's face turned redder. "You know full well that

the Bible commands you to honor your father and your mother," he stated so softly she could barely hear him. "If you continue to defy me—"

"*Gut* evening!" Edith called out as she came through the front room carrying a foil-covered casserole. "Asa was hungry for mac and cheese, so that's what I've brought. How is everybody?"

Loretta gazed gratefully at her younger sister, whose expression told her Edith had overheard the difficult conversation she and Dat were having. "We're glad you brought a *big* pan of your mac and cheese, Edith," she replied. "Those two fellows behind you can really tuck that stuff away."

"And Edith's homemade version is so much better than the boxed kind Drew and I subsisted on as bachelors," Asa chimed in. He smiled down at the twins in their baskets, which he set on the nearest countertop. "Won't be long until these two are devouring their *mamm*'s mac and cheese, the way they're growing."

"How are you, Cornelius?" Drew asked as he entered the kitchen behind the others. He set a large tossed salad on the table. "Saw you heading off with a driver about the time I was shaving this morning. *Gut* trip, I hope?"

Loretta nipped her lip. Was Dat scowling at the casual way Drew had spoken to him—or had his trip been troublesome? It seemed that on some days, there were no right words to say and no best way to say them because her father took offense at every little thing.

Dat's eyes narrowed as he gazed up at Drew. "A little bird told me you took Loretta out for a ride on Saturday. Don't think for one minute that you're going to pull any more stunts like you did the day Edith and Asa were originally to get married. I will never forget that you fed Asa sleeping pills and tried to marry my daughter in his place."

Drew, looking perfectly composed, pulled out the chair to Dat's right and sat down. "That's all behind me now, Cornelius," he replied. "Associating with your family has cured me of any inclination to stray from salvation's path."

"Don't you dare mock me—or the faith that saves us," Dat muttered.

Drew looked him in the eye. "I wouldn't dream of it, sir," he said softly. "If it weren't for your family's compassion and forgiveness, I'd still be living a lie. *Denki* again for giving me a chance to start fresh in Willow Ridge."

Loretta's heart thudded proudly. Drew sounded sincerely repentant of his former ways, yet he wasn't kowtowing to Dat's unpleasant mood. While Asa recounted the sales he and Drew had made from their new furniture-refurbishing shop today, she quickly stirred up a batch of biscuits, rolled and cut them, and slid them into the oven. Rosalyn was placing the lid on the cast-iron skillet of frying chicken while Edith set plates on the table. For a few precious moments, Loretta could catch her breath. As she cooed at the babies, she hoped her date with Drew and her new job at Nora's wouldn't again become heated topics.

Dat, however, was like a dog gnawing a bone when his questions went unanswered. As Rosalyn positioned the platter of fragrant fried chicken on the table next to Edith's casserole, everyone took a seat— leaving Mamm's chair at Dat's left empty, as they had since she'd passed. They bowed their heads in anticipation of their silent grace, but Dat ignored them. "Loretta, before we can give thanks, I must have your assurance that you'll not be working at Nora's store," he said in the rolling voice with which he read the Scriptures at church.

Loretta's breath escaped in a frustrated rush, and her cheeks burned. How dare her father postpone their prayer until she gave in to him! As several long moments of tense silence filled the hot kitchen, she kept her head bowed and her eyes closed tightly, pleading with God for a response that would satisfy both her *dat* and her needs.

"Heavenly Father, we thank You for the family gathered at this table, for the food You've provided us, and for all of Your *gut* and perfect gifts," one of the Detweiler brothers prayed aloud. "We ask it in Jesus' name. Amen."

Loretta nearly choked when she caught Drew's cat-like smile from across the table. He'd dared to say the blessing, trying to get her off the hook, and she was grateful beyond words. When the acrid aroma of burning food reached her, however, she sprang from her chair to rescue the biscuits. Rosalyn rose to wave a towel and dispel the smoke in a room overheated by the oven and the August humidity—and by Dat's foul mood.

But there was no saving the biscuits. Loretta blinked back tears as she lifted them with a spatula and saw that every last one of them was burned on the bottom. If only she hadn't been so distracted by Dat's angry words. If only she'd paid closer attention to the time this afternoon.

"Haste makes waste," her father remarked as Loretta brought the basket of biscuits to the table. "If you'd been home instead of working at Nora's, you wouldn't have had to rush with supper. Your mother, bless her soul, never burned a biscuit or ruined a meal in her entire married life."

Edith and Rosalyn's eyebrows rose, for they recalled a time or two when meals hadn't been as picture-perfect as Dat was describing. But they said nothing as they began passing the food.

"Cornelius, has it been a rough day?" Asa asked gently. "You seem . . . agitated."

Dat glared at him, but before he could reply, Drew spoke up.

"I'll have three of those biscuits, please," he remarked as he accepted the basket from his brother. "Truth be told, when our *mamm* lost track of what was in the oven, we boys ate every bite. After you cut off the bottoms, butter and jelly go a long way toward fixing scorched biscuits—but I suspect it'll take more than that to cure whatever's ailing you, Cornelius. Confession's *gut* for the soul, you know."

Loretta appreciated the way the young men across the table were trying to help her out of this difficult spot, but she suddenly felt like a boiling teakettle about to whistle with its buildup of steam. Slapping the table, she stood up, despite the tears that were running down her hot cheeks. "It's been five years, Dat," she blurted in a quavering voice. "For five long years we've all been missing Mamm something awful—and you know full well that we girls will never take her place. When will you move beyond your grief so the rest of us can as well?" she demanded as she held his startled gaze. "I wish—I just *wish* we could all live in a happy, peaceful home again. Is that too much to ask?"

The stunned silence nearly swallowed her. Somehow, Loretta's knees didn't buckle, nor did a bolt of lightning strike her down, for speaking in such a tone to her father. It was such a simple wish, yet it was one she feared would never come true. The grandfather clock in the front room struck six. The twins squirmed in their baskets, but otherwise nobody moved or said anything.

Finally Rosalyn stood up, slipping her arm around Loretta's shoulders. "Amen, sister," she murmured. "I am so tired of the way your grief and depression fill this house like storm clouds, Dat. And—and I wish you'd get some help for it," she added sadly. "We're really worried about you."

Across the table, Edith stood up with them. "Truth be told, Mamm would be appalled at the constant tension and unhappiness here, which squeeze out any chance for growth or a fresh start," she murmured. "Maybe, Dat, you should consider the possibility that Loretta wants to work at Nora's store to spend time with folks who have a more positive frame of mind. I was hoping we could leave your grief behind in Roseville so you'd have a chance to feel better, but that didn't happen."

"It's your decision, Cornelius," Asa put in gently. "If you don't find a doctor or a counselor who can help you, I suspect you'll become even more depressed—and you'll drive your family away in the process."

Dat rose from his chair so suddenly that it clattered backward against the floor. "Feel free to leave anytime," he snapped as he glared at each of them. "Don't let the doorknob hit you in the butt."

The babies began to wail, startled by the chair's noise and Dat's loud voice. As their father left the table and clomped down the basement steps to his workroom, Asa rose to comfort the twins. Loretta glanced nervously at her sisters. "Maybe I shouldn't have—"

"You said what Edith and I have been thinking for years," Rosalyn assured her. "There's just no living with that man, tiptoeing on eggshells all the time."

"In the short time I've been across the road, I've begun to feel so much more relaxed," Edith said, taking Leroy from her husband. "Guess I didn't realize how unbearable Dat's moods had become until I got away from them."

"You girls are welcome to stay at our place anytime you need a break," Asa added, swaying from side to side with Louisa. "I suspect that with Edith gone, you two are shouldering even more of his frustration and—"

"Sarcasm," Drew put in matter-of-factly. "And let's not leave out manipulation and intimidation. I'm sorry you have to live in a state of constant confrontation— and I intend to do all I can to stop it."

Loretta's pulse pounded in her temples. Did Drew have any idea what he was letting himself in for, trying to alter Dat's personality? She gave him the brightest smile she could manage, and after the babies were quiet again, the five of them sat down to eat. It was a meal she wasn't hungry for anymore, but she ate a piece of chicken and some of Edith's mac and cheese, grateful for the comfort food her sisters had prepared—and somewhat amazed that Asa and Drew were devouring their third biscuits.

"You fellows don't have to eat those just to make me feel better," she said softly.

The two brothers, so exactly alike in appearance, looked up at the same moment, wearing the same expression. "That's not the way it is," Asa insisted as he spooned apple butter on the buttered biscuit on his plate.

"I never eat anything to make somebody else feel better," Drew teased with a shake of his head. "When it comes to food, it's all about me and what I want, Loretta. But I do want you to feel better, sugar."

Loretta's heart thudded hopefully. *Sugar*, he'd called her, as he had the other night—it sounded especially exotic because he pronounced it *shugah*. Once she cut off the burned bottom of a biscuit and slathered butter and strawberry jam on it, she discovered that the Detweiler brothers had it right: the biscuits had risen high and light, so there was still plenty about them to enjoy. "Seems Dat was wrong," she whispered as a giggle escaped her. "Imagine that!"

Rosalyn and Edith looked at her and began to chuckle as well. "He's missing out on a yummy supper," Edith remarked. "And just so you sisters know, Drew made the salad on his own, without anybody suggesting he bring something."

"It's crisp and fresh," Rosalyn said as she took another helping of the greens. "I don't even care that you slipped over to our garden for your ingredients, Drew. You're welcome to anything you find there."

"Uh-oh, I've been caught," Drew replied with a mischievous grin. He held Loretta's gaze. "How about if you and I pick all those green beans out there after we're finished eating? Since you ladies'll be firing up the canners and filling jars soon, helping you pick them is the least I can do . . . because truth be told, I've helped myself to your garden before."

"You're on," Loretta replied happily.

"You two are excused from kitchen cleanup," Rosalyn declared.

"We should have a snapping frolic," Edith suggested. "Asa, if you help with the picking, it'll go faster—and then the five of us can sit on the porch and snap them. I'll be over to help you girls can them tomorrow, or whenever you're ready."

Asa nodded, looking at his brother. "We're pickers from way back, because Mamm didn't have girls to help her with the garden. Used to have races to see who could fill his basket the fastest."

"Last one out there's a rotten egg," Drew challenged as he rose from his chair. "I'm guessing your baskets are in the—"

"I'll get them," Loretta said as she stepped away from the table. "Wouldn't want you fellows to miss a single minute of picking. See you out there!"

With a light heart and a smile on her face, she hurried through the mudroom just ahead of Asa and Drew. What a relief to be surrounded by family members who sided with her and who made the summer chores fun by working together as a team. As she reached the stable, where they stored the garden tools, Loretta wondered briefly when Dat would emerge from his cave and what he'd eat for supper.

He's a grown man. He'd better figure it out, because someday he'll be home alone.

Chapter Four

Drew repeatedly held a bean bush aside, tugged on handfuls of the long, sturdy green beans, and dropped them into his basket. He was a few feet farther along his two rows than Asa was, which felt exhilarating in a boyish sort of way—but it was even more gratifying to glance up at Loretta's backside now and again. She'd gotten a slightly later start, and she was picking wax beans, which were more scattered on the plants, so she wasn't keeping up with him. The view of her bare feet in the damp, dark soil, along with her shapely calves and the swell of her bottom beneath her green cape dress, fed Drew's imagination as he picked.

"Say, Drew—I'm seeing several beans left hanging on the rows you've picked," Asa remarked as he backed up and shifted his basket to a new position. "Loretta might make you start all over and do it *right*. Like Mamm did."

Loretta's laughter made him tingle. "Our *mamm* did the same thing when we girls were distracted," she called out.

Distracted didn't halfway describe the way Drew was feeling. He was somewhat sorry Edith had sent Asa out here to help, because he'd had visions of sharing flirtatious banter with Loretta, just the two of them out here working. Somehow he'd keep his hands to himself, but by the time they finished snapping all these beans he'd be ravenous for direct contact with her. If he had his way, he and Loretta would share a long, late evening together somewhere the darkness would hide them from intruders and interruptions. He did *not* want Cornelius finding them and delivering another mean-spirited lecture.

Something happened today while he was gone. Something that's eating at him, and that he can't talk about, so he's taking out his frustration on his girls. And that's just wrong.

When he reached the end of his two rows, Drew stood with his arms raised like goalposts. "I win!" he boasted.

Asa stood up, arching with his hands on his hips to stretch his back. "So now you'll do the honorable thing and pick those stragglers you missed, *jah?* Now that our race is over, it's all about quality."

Drew grabbed his basket and strode between the two rows he'd picked, stooping when he reached Loretta. "No, it's really about making you smile, Loretta," he murmured—and when she turned her face, he gently caught her head in his hand and kissed her. "You and me. Later. *Jah?*"

When her eyes lit up, Drew felt ten feet tall . . . and suddenly needy. So he kissed her again, knowing it would only whet his appetite rather than appease it.

"*Jah,*" she whispered eagerly. "Think of a *gut* place—"

"Two little lovebirds sittin' in a tree," Rosalyn teased through the kitchen window.

"K-I-S-S-I-N-G!" Edith sang along.

When a door slammed in the kitchen, Drew instinctively eased away from Loretta and went to the beginning of the rows he'd already picked. It rankled when he heard Cornelius demand his supper, and he was pleasantly surprised to hear Edith point out that the mac and cheese and chicken were on the counter, so he could help himself. His brother's new wife surprised him sometimes. Edith was a fresh-faced pixie of a woman, but she was bolder than she appeared—and Drew hoped the Riehl sisters would continue standing up for one another when their *dat* behaved unreasonably.

He wasn't surprised that Cornelius didn't join the five of them on the porch to snap the green beans, and he certainly wasn't sorry. As dusk fell, Rosalyn hung a couple lanterns so they could see to pick out any bad spots. They all chatted amiably as the subtle *snap . . . snap . . . snap* punctuated their conversation and their bowls filled with crisp bean sections. Edith and Asa took time out to give the twins their evening bottles, and by the time they finished snapping, a pleasant breeze was blowing, and fireflies were winking out on the lawn.

As Drew helped carry their bowls of snapped beans inside, he noticed that the only sign of Cornelius was the cheese-smeared dinner plate he'd left in the sink. He was grateful when Asa and Edith started across the road with their sleeping babies and when Rosalyn silently waved him and Loretta toward the mudroom. Who knew where their *dat* might be hiding, listening to whatever they might say about him—or about where Drew was taking Loretta?

With his hand on the small of Loretta's back, he steered her outside and silently closed the back door. Reasoning that Cornelius couldn't possibly see them, Drew walked to the space between the two low basement windows and pressed Loretta against the house to claim the kiss he'd been yearning for all day. Her eager response made him flare inside and kiss her more insistently. "Loretta," he whispered against the velvety skin of her neck. "Loretta . . ."

"Dat's bedroom—and his shop window—are on the front of the house," she whispered, "but he might step out the sliding glass door over there, looking for us. The sooner we get across the street and behind the windbreak of pine trees, the better the chance he won't spot us."

Drew admired the way she grabbed his hand and started around the side of the house. The moon was a pale fingernail clipping in the sky, not shining much light, although Drew felt so electric, he might be emitting a glow visible for miles as he crossed the road with Loretta. Anyone standing outside whose eyes were accustomed to the darkness—say, Bishop Tom, or perhaps the Brennemans—might spot two lithe figures stealing behind the dense evergreens. But he was beyond caring.

And what can anyone do to us? We're slipping out of sight as Amish folks of courting age have done forever.

When Loretta opened her arms, Drew pulled her close and kissed her hungrily. He reminded himself to be cautious. Although he'd followed passion's course where Molly Ropp had led him, Loretta wasn't that sort of young woman. She was sweet and innocent and had no idea how her eager embrace inflamed him. After a few delectably dangerous moments, he eased away from her. "Wow," he murmured.

"More," Loretta whimpered. "I haven't been able to stop thinking about you since Saturday."

Drew held her close again, carefully placing his head against hers rather than succumbing to another kiss. "Same here. Let's, um, walk for a bit, shall we?"

With a sigh, Loretta relented. "I can't thank you enough for taking my part—and for saying the prayer!—at dinner, Drew," she said as they walked along the windbreak. "The expression on Dat's face was priceless. Nobody's ever stolen his thunder that way."

He considered what he wanted to discuss with her, hoping the topic wouldn't spoil their walk. "What he did to you was just *wrong*, Loretta—trying to force you to quit your job before we could say grace and eat," he began. "Why do I suspect that he behaved that way before your *mamm* passed, but that it's gotten worse lately?"

Loretta gazed at him, her mouth dropping open. "H-how did you know that?" she whispered. "Oh, Drew, even though we moved here from Roseville without much warning earlier this year, it hasn't helped his moods. I thought leaving the house where Mamm had lived would make things easier, but he's gotten so impatient. So intolerant."

"And he's holding her death over your heads, placing her high on a pedestal as though she were a saint—beyond reproach or ordinary mistakes." He considered what she'd said about their move to Willow Ridge. "Any particular reason you left Roseville?"

She shrugged, clinging to his hand. "Dat's cousin Reuben moved to Roseville to help take care of his widowed *mamm*, who lived just down the road from us," she explained. "He and Dat agreed it would be advantageous to just swap houses, even up, so we brought our clothes, the furniture—and Mamm's things, of course. We got Reuben's chickens as part of the deal because he didn't want to move them."

Drew thought about this. "Did your *dat* ever act as though he'd gotten the short end of the swap?"

Loretta's brow puckered endearingly. "Not that I know of. The houses are about the same size—and because Reuben was the deacon for Willow Ridge and Dat had served the Roseville church district as deacon, it seemed like a *gut* move for both towns, because their church leadership wouldn't be interrupted."

Why does this sound a little too convenient? A little too easy? Drew tried to dismiss his misgivings about Cornelius being the man in charge of church finances, but maybe he was just suspicious because Loretta's *dat* was always so disagreeable.

It's more than that. Cornelius is too secretive. Downright slippery. But he couldn't say this to Loretta. Her heart was already fragile from her father's verbal abuse.

"What are you thinking?" she asked sweetly. They'd almost reached the end of the windbreak, and she stopped to face him. "You don't like my *dat* much, do you?"

Drew had no intention of answering that question, so he placed his hands lightly on Loretta's shoulders. "I don't like the way he treats you," he replied. "It was such a simple wish you made, wanting your home to be happy—free of constant conflict. Every family has its quarrels, but overall I'd say most other folks take your wish for granted. And that's sad," he added quietly. "I want better for you, Loretta."

When she hung her head, he wished he'd been a bit less honest. Then again, keeping secrets and being deceptive had gotten him in trouble when Molly had believed he was Asa, and again when he'd tried to pass himself off as Asa at his brother and Edith's wedding. Perhaps because he'd become so adept at deception, he was more aware of that trait in other folks. Namely Cornelius.

Drew held Loretta close, nuzzling her neck until she kissed him again. He eased away with a smile, holding her hands. "If you're working for Nora tomorrow, we should get you home for some sleep," he suggested. "Can't have you nodding off on one of those beds displayed in her store."

She chuckled. "I feel bad, leaving the canning to Rosalyn and Edith," she admitted.

"But you didn't know we'd be picking all those beans after supper," he pointed out. "And I suspect your sisters are cheering you on for taking that job, so they'll be happy to tackle tomorrow's canning without you."

"*Jah*, you're probably right. I'll whip together a casserole or two before I leave tomorrow," she said, planning aloud. "Only fair to prepare their meals when they'll have such a busy day. And maybe I'll go home over my lunch break—Nora and I haven't yet talked about how long that will be."

"It'll be an exciting day," Drew said as they walked back the way they'd come. "I'll be thinking about you." *Even though I'll be imagining you're with me instead of in Nora's store.*

Will's fists clenched at his sides as he stared out the window. Unable to sleep, he'd been pacing his dark apartment—just as two shadowy figures emerged from behind the evergreen windbreak to stride across the road toward the Riehl place.

"Really?" he whispered in exasperation. Wasn't it enough that Drew had hidden behind those trees when Will had accused Asa of fathering Molly's twins—the day this whole fiasco involving Drew Detweiler had come to light? It couldn't bode well for Loretta's reputation that she'd been back there with him. Will knew from plowing the nearby field that the thick grass bordering the windbreak was tall and lush . . . much softer, cooler, and more enticing than hay in the loft of a barn on an August night.

The thought of that dog Detweiler rolling in the grass with his Loretta made Will's face tingle and burn. He had to confront Loretta about this—because if he didn't watch out for her, who would?

Chapter Five

On Tuesday morning Loretta stepped inside the Simple Gifts store and inhaled the pleasant fragrance of the potpourri Nora kept in bowls around the store. As she took in the beautiful displays of quilts and pottery, the Brennemans' furniture, Matthias Wagler's saddles, Preacher Ben's ornamental metal gates, Bishop Tom's carved Nativity sets—not to mention Nora's three-dimensional quilted hangings in the upper level—her sense of perspective returned. She'd felt a little guilty leaving Rosalyn and Edith stirring steaming pots of green beans on the stove, but she'd felt only relief at leaving Dat. His lecture this morning had stung her soul, and it had taken all her strength to arrive at Nora's store with dry eyes.

Your mother—and Jesus—are shaking their heads, weeping for your wayward soul, daughter. The black marks beside your name in God's Book of Life are adding up to a disastrous day of reckoning unless you repent your rebellious ways.

"*Gut* morning, Loretta!" Nora called out from her

office. "It's wonderful to see you, sweetie, and I'm looking forward to your first day in my store!"

Like a bee to nectar, Loretta passed between the displays toward the friend—now her employer—whose encouraging words turned her mood from darkness to light. For the next few hours she would observe and listen carefully as Nora showed her how to tag new items that had come in, as well as how to ring up sales and record them in the blue notebook alongside crafters' consignment numbers. She and her sisters had played store as children, but working at Simple Gifts felt like much more of an adventure than their game, because she was working with real items that Plain folks were being paid for. And she would soon be teaching a rug-making class! It amazed her how confident Nora seemed in her own abilities, even though she'd never worked in a store before she'd opened Simple Gifts.

"First, let's set a date and time for your rug classes and figure the cost of materials and your time so we can post a sign-up sheet," Nora suggested. Her auburn hair was tucked up into a bun beneath her small, circular Mennonite *kapp*, and her pink and tan geometric print dress accentuated the sprinkling of freckles across her nose. But it was Nora's smile that revealed her true beauty. "I'll also include a sign-up form in an email newsletter I'll send to my customers. I've taken photos of a couple of your rugs so they'll know what sort of item they'll be working on," she explained. "This is so exciting, Loretta! You'll be the first of my crafters to teach a class—and I think we should set up two different times, for starters."

Loretta's head was swimming with joy. She had no idea what an email newsletter was, but if Nora was sending it out, it had to be good. She threw her arms around the storekeeper, laughing nervously. "If you really think I can pull this off, Nora, I'll give it my very best shot."

"No doubt in my mind," Nora said as she gave Loretta a squeeze. "I think if we offer one in the morning and another in the afternoon of a different day—maybe one of those on a Saturday—we'll allow for our potential students' schedules. And who knows? We may have so many ladies responding that we'll need to arrange for a third class!"

They decided on Thursday afternoon the twenty-fifth and Saturday morning the twenty-seventh. As Nora did the math to cover the cost of fabric and a two-hour lesson, Loretta's heart thrummed. She watched in amazement as Nora opened her laptop and put together her email newsletter with a headline and rug photographs and a few paragraphs of information, along with a simple response form. Somehow—computer magic, most likely—when Nora hit the Send button, her hundreds of customers would all receive this message, and they could reply to it without having to call or come to the store.

"That's awesome," Loretta murmured.

"It is," Nora agreed. "And while I understand why the Amish faith doesn't allow folks to own computers, I can honestly say that my store wouldn't be doing half so well if I couldn't advertise online with my website and send newsletters to my customers."

Nora's honey-colored eyes lit up.

"You'll meet Rebecca Oliveri this afternoon when she comes to discuss some updates on my website. She's one of Miriam Hooley's triplet daughters, a sister to Rachel Brenneman and Rhoda Leitner," she explained, "but when she was wee little she was washed away in the flood of nineteen ninety-three.

After a couple in New Haven found her, they raised her English," Nora continued with a smile. "Rebecca came back to find her birth mother, Miriam, after her English mother passed. She recently built a new home down the road—and she's been a huge asset to all of us in Willow Ridge ever since she returned."

Loretta considered this. "So . . . she's Miriam's daughter, but she's not Amish anymore? And Miriam's okay with that?"

Nora's smile crinkled the skin around her eyes. "Miriam was so overjoyed that Rebecca hadn't drowned in the flood, she doesn't mind that her long-lost daughter plans to remain English," she replied. "Sometimes, for weddings or other occasions, Rebecca dresses Amish with her sisters, but you'll usually see her in jeans. She has an office for her computer design work above Andy Leitner's clinic, and she's his receptionist several mornings a week."

"Wow. That's an unusual arrangement," Loretta remarked after she thought about what Nora had told her. "If something like this happened in Roseville, I'm not sure the daughter would be so welcome if she refused to join the Old Order."

"I believe you're right," Nora said with a nod. "Just goes to show you how much more progressive— and forgiving—the folks in Willow Ridge are. Lord knows I set this town on its ear last year when I came back from living English!" she added with a chuckle. "My parents were disappointed when I joined the Mennonite church, but—like Miriam—my *mamm* was so glad to have me back in town, she praised God that I joined any church at all, and that I came back to be near my family."

Loretta sighed. How would it feel to be embraced

by forgiveness such as Nora and Rebecca had received, rather than enduring Dat's constant chastisement? She set aside her glum recollection of his latest lecture to concentrate on the way Nora wanted her to write out tags for several new place mats and pot holders they'd received from a River Brethren seamstress near Jamesport, as well as a big bagful of faceless, stuffed Amish dolls that Seth Brenneman's wife, Mary, had made.

The morning flew by. Loretta grew more confident as she waited on ladies who purchased four place settings of pottery dishes and some table linens to go with them. When Nora offered to fetch lunch from the mill store, Loretta was delighted. She'd told her sisters she wasn't sure she'd make it home over the noon hour to share the casseroles she'd made for them—and after Dat had spoken so harshly to her, Rosalyn and Edith would understand if she stayed at the store. Because Simple Gifts was air-conditioned, with big ceiling fans whirling slowly to create some air movement, Loretta enjoyed the cool, relaxing time she spent straightening the displays while Nora went next door to the mill. She planned to suggest to Rosalyn and Edith that they come to the store with their supplies for making wreaths and baskets, if only because humid August afternoons were a lot easier to bear here than at home.

When Nora returned, what a treat it was to spread Nazareth Hostetler's goat cheese on slices of the zucchini bread she'd also made to sell at the mill store. Bishop Tom's wife had been a godsend, providing goat milk for little Leroy and Louisa when powdered formula had upset their tummies, and she was a thoughtful, compassionate neighbor, too. Loretta couldn't stand to see the last piece of the nutty, sweet zucchini bread sitting on the plate, so she snatched it up and slathered more goat cheese on it.

"This was so delicious," Loretta said with a satisfied moan. "*Denki* for sharing your lunch with me, Nora."

"It's a pleasure to spend time with you, Loretta. I suspect your *dat* was none too happy about your coming here today."

"You got that right. But I'm determined to make it work." Loretta wiped her hands on a napkin and helped Nora clear the crumbs from the worktable where they'd eaten. "How about if I go to the Schrocks' quilting shop and buy some fabric for the rug class?" she suggested. "This afternoon I can start cutting the long strips our ladies will need—or I'll do that whenever you don't have something you want me to do," she added quickly. Far be it from her to tell Nora how she was going to spend her time.

"You've read my mind," Nora replied. "And if recent sales of our quilts and your rugs tells me anything, it's that restful shades of blue, yellow, and cream—pastels, in general—are selling really well. Then again, we also have customers who love bright, vibrant colors."

"I'll go for a variety," Loretta decided. "Who knows? Some gals might like to mix things up with splashy prints and plain-colored pastels. I'll ask Mary and Eva Schrock what's selling well in their store, too."

"Take your time, dear. I'm eager to see what you pick out—and to have you talk me through the way you make your rugs." Nora smiled at her as though no one was more dear or special. "Consider me your first student, Loretta. It'll be fun to sit for a bit and make fabric strips whenever we don't have customers."

Loretta beamed. Nora made her feel as though she

could do no wrong—as though she was actually an expert at making rugs and teaching, as well as working in the Simple Gifts store. She walked down the road past Zook's Market with a smile on her face and a song in her heart, grateful to God for giving her life a new sense of purpose.

Nora was writing out checks when Rebecca Oliveri entered the store and gazed around appreciatively. "*Gut* to see you, girl! It's been too long," she called out.

Rebecca came toward the worktable with a laptop tucked under one arm, carrying a camera in her other hand. "You won't believe how busy I've been designing websites for local folks. I just finished a simple one to advertise Adam Wagler's home-remodeling business, and this morning I updated the Detweiler Furniture Works site with new photos of some impressive pieces they've refurbished."

"I've gotten some new pieces in as well," Nora remarked. "And Loretta Riehl's going to be teaching classes on making her toothbrush rugs, so I'd like to put something about that on my site today."

"Toothbrush rugs? That's a new one."

"Here—let me show you her latest. All I know is that she uses a toothbrush handle sharpened to a point as her needle, and she makes rows by passing the needle through her previous stitches." Nora led Rebecca to the front of the store, where the Brennemans' sleigh bed anchored a large display. "See there? It's a rag rug of sorts. Loretta will be back with some new fabric soon—but meanwhile, we can update my site with whatever catches your fancy, Rebecca. You have a fine eye and *gut* instincts for what will bring folks into my store."

Rebecca had set her laptop on a nearby shelf and popped the lens cap from her camera. "Something tells me these rugs will be a big hit," she said as she squatted with her camera at her eye. "And maybe a shot or two of Cornelius Riehl's clocks? I think I've almost got him talked into a simple website—can you believe that?"

Nora's eyes widened. "I think you could sell ice packs to Eskimos, Rebecca. I hope Cornelius realizes that if he advertises online, he's going to have to keep up with his clock repairs and make his new ones faster," she remarked quietly. "I've heard a few local folks saying he's had their clocks for a long while."

Rebecca's camera clicked rapidly as she shot the rug alongside the sleigh bed, as well as the new pottery display. "He absolutely refused to let me take photos of his workshop," she said, "even though folks would be interested in that, I think. And if he can't accept the fact that even a basic website requires an investment of time and money on his part, he might decide not to have one."

"He doesn't want to pay you?" Nora frowned. "He certainly makes enough trips fetching parts—hiring a driver—that I wouldn't think he'd balk at paying for promotion."

Rebecca smiled wryly. "Don't repeat this, but I suspect he disapproves of my being born into the Amish faith yet not joining the church—not to mention the fact that I'm a working woman who wears jeans most of the time and who shows no inclination to marry."

Nora's laughter rang in the high-ceilinged store. With her tousled, collar-length brown hair and red striped blouse over denim capris, Rebecca Oliveri appeared anything but Amish—yet she always seemed upbeat and optimistic, as though her life fulfilled her perfectly. "You've hit the nail on the head, I think—and here's Loretta, his middle daughter," she added when the front door swung open. "But she's nothing like her *dat*, trust me!"

Nora approached her new employee with open arms. "Let me help you with all those sacks, girl," she said as she relieved Loretta of the two bulging plastic bags in her right hand. "Let's spread your fabric on the bed to see what you chose—and so Rebecca can take a picture for my website. Rebecca," she added as she returned to the furniture display, "this is Loretta Riehl, one of our new neighbors, and my employee as of this morning! Loretta, this is the Rebecca I was telling you about earlier. The gal who's designing websites for so many local folks."

Loretta appeared a bit shy, but she shook the hand Rebecca extended. "It's *gut* to meet you, Rebecca. From what Nora's told me, you're another young woman who made a big splash when she came back to Willow Ridge."

"I did," Rebecca said with a laugh. "I was also the talk of the town because I first showed up with spiked hair dyed black and black fingernails, wearing black clothing, chains, and metal jewelry," she added. "Once I got reacquainted with my mother, however, I no longer needed to lose myself in the Goth trend. Mamma's sunshine made me bloom as my real self."

Loretta's face reflected the glow on Rebecca's as she took folded fabric from her plastic sacks. "That's such a wonderful story. It makes me glad we Riehls came to Willow Ridge—and now I'll be teaching a rug-making class here in Nora's store! Never in my life could I have imagined that."

"Oh, and look at these colors," Nora put in, deftly arranging the squares of folded fabric on top of the bed. "I love these bright calico prints, and the pastels, plaids, and stripes. And all these fabrics feel nice and sturdy, for rugs that will last a long time. Will this make a good shot, Rebecca?"

"Fabulous," Rebecca replied as she put her camera to her eye. "I'll make a moving banner for your home page that will alternate between a shot of these fabrics and a notice about the classes Loretta will teach. After I get a few shots of those clocks and whatever else you want, we'll update your site."

Nora slipped an arm around Loretta's shoulders. "Come into the office and watch the way Rebecca works. She's amazing! I'm not sure how she does this website stuff so quickly, but it always looks pretty and fresh."

"Computer magic," Loretta said, and they all laughed.

Once Rebecca had set up her laptop in the office so she could import the photographs she'd just taken, Nora watched in awe as she tweaked the pictures. When she'd brought up the Simple Gifts website, Loretta leaned forward with a low "Wow."

"I love working on Nora's site," Rebecca remarked as her fingers flew across her computer keyboard. "She always has such pretty items to display—always something new to keep her customers coming back and to catch the eye of folks who decide to visit her store for the first time."

"She's welcoming without always trying to sell you stuff, too," Loretta said, smiling at Nora. "I suspect some of her customers come in just because she's so friendly. So upbeat and positive."

Nora reached over to grasp Loretta's arm. "*Denki* for saying that," she murmured. "My customers will enjoy meeting you, Loretta, because you're very helpful and kind."

About half an hour later, Rebecca was testing the new revolving banner she'd added. She asked Nora to check everything before the updates went live online. "That's perfect," Nora said, delighted with the way her customers would see Loretta's fabrics and the advertisement for her upcoming classes. "I'll write out your check—and I'll pay for those fabrics while I'm at it, Loretta."

Loretta handed her the receipt from the Schrocks' quilt shop and turned her head when the bell above the door rang. "I'll get that while you ladies finish up."

As her new employee strode out of the office, Nora smiled. "What do you think, Rebecca? Can you help me put in a *gut* word to Cornelius about his daughter working here? He's giving her a rough time about it."

"I have no trouble imagining that," Rebecca said as she closed her computer. "He reminds me of the stern, stoic—rather overbearing—Amish men I recall from very early in my life. I'm so glad the atmosphere in Willow Ridge has changed now that Tom Hostetler and Ben Hooley are the mainstays of the local church."

"Amen to that," Nora remarked. As she handed Rebecca her check, she looked up at Loretta in the doorway. "Already made a sale, sweetie?"

Loretta's smile teased at her lips. "There's a fellow here asking to see Rebecca," she said in a low voice. "He's English, and dressed in a suit and tie—and really *gut*-looking!"

"Tell him I'll be right out," Rebecca said, waving her off. "I don't know many men who fit that description."

Nora said her goodbyes and went into the main room of the store behind Rebecca. The man Loretta had mentioned was studying the display of tooled saddles and specialty tack Matthias Wagler had consigned. He *was* good-looking—maybe forty, and far more polished and sophisticated than most men who passed through Willow Ridge. Nora had a hunch, from his understated tweed jacket and conservative tie, that he was also rather wealthy.

"Hi there," Rebecca said as she set aside her equipment and offered him her hand. "If you're looking for Rebecca Oliveri, that would be me. How can I help you?"

The man looked up from the saddles, a suave smile spreading across his face. "You're the one who's designed the websites for so many Willow Ridge businesses?" he asked as he took her hand. "I'm Wyatt McKenzie. It was the online presence you've created for this town that convinced me to purchase the tract of land adjoining the mill property on the other side of the river. I just introduced myself to Luke over at the mill, and he thought you'd be here about now."

Nora's eyes widened as she went to join them. She'd had no idea the undeveloped land behind their property was for sale. "That's big news, Mr. McKenzie. Welcome to Willow Ridge," she said as she extended her hand. "I'm Luke's wife, Nora, owner of this gift shop. If you're looking for someone to give you an online presence, I can attest that Rebecca's top-notch."

McKenzie's grip was firm as he assessed Nora with blue-gray eyes. "Your husband said the same thing and attributes his marketing success to Ms. Oliveri's computer savvy. It's such a pleasure to meet you folks," he added with a nod toward Rebecca and Loretta. "Willow Ridge seems to be exactly the sort of place I've been searching for to raise my Thoroughbreds."

Their new English neighbor smiled at Rebecca. "Is this a convenient time to discuss some website business, or shall I make an appointment?" he asked. "I know your time's valuable, and I just showed up out of the blue."

"Shall we chat on the way back to my office?" Rebecca suggested as she picked up her equipment. "It's just a short walk—and I can give you the low-down on Zook's Market and the Grill N Skillet Café we'll be passing on the way there, if that works for you."

"Excellent. Let's do it."

As Wyatt preceded Rebecca so he could open the door for her, Nora had the feeling that he would bring a whole new energy to Willow Ridge—with Thoroughbred horses, no less. Amish farmers used draft horses, such as Belgians, for doing their field work, but when it came to horses for their buggies, they often indulged in showier horseflesh. No one for miles around bred or trained horses, so Wyatt might get a lot of local business—and Nora suspected he'd already researched that angle.

"Well, now," Loretta murmured after the door closed behind them. "I could be wrong, but Mr. McKenzie seemed to be giving Rebecca quite a looking-over. Not that it's any of my business," she added playfully.

Nora laughed. "In a town this size, our new neighbor and his high-dollar horses—and his love life—will soon be everybody's business," she said. "But for all we know, he's married, so we shouldn't be speculating about him and Rebecca."

An impish grin flitted across Loretta's face. "He wasn't wearing a ring," she pointed out. "And a fellow who's that well turned-out would probably be sporting a really fancy ring, maybe with a diamond."

Nora blinked. Old Order girls didn't usually pay attention to jewelry, because church members weren't allowed to wear it—and Nora hadn't noticed that detail about her new neighbor.

"You have a keen eye, Loretta," she said as they began to stack the fabric arranged on the sleigh bed. "Just be aware that when you work with the public, an ability to keep your observations to yourself—or between us—is an even more valuable asset."

Loretta chuckled. "I've spent most of my life keeping my opinions and observations to myself—or just whispering them to my sisters. Ain't so?"

Nora had to agree. With such a controlling father as Cornelius, the deacon of their church district, the Riehl girls knew how to tend their business with tightly sealed smiles.

Loretta was going to be an even better employee than Nora had anticipated.

Chapter Six

Rebecca wondered how her office had suddenly become so much smaller. Or was it that Wyatt McKenzie filled it with his elegance and understated manner as he sat in the chair on the other side of her desk chatting with her? During the walk from Simple Gifts, he'd shed his tweed sport coat, loosened his tie, and unbuttoned the top button of his pale blue shirt to allow for the August heat and humidity. He'd rolled his sleeves partway up his forearms, as well—and Rebecca caught herself staring at his well-defined body and beautiful skin. With his sun-streaked brown hair and summer tan, Wyatt reminded her of Robert Redford in his heyday. She warned herself not to behave like a clueless groupie.

"You've lived in Willow Ridge all your life?" Wyatt asked. He had the low, modulated voice of a PBS station announcer and a way of holding her gaze just a smidgen too long with his arresting blue-gray eyes.

Rebecca tried not to sound adolescent. "I was born here—born Amish—but when I was a toddler, I was washed away when the river rose during the flood of nineteen ninety-three. A couple in New Haven found me and adopted me," she recounted softly. "But when my mother—or at least the woman I'd believed was my mother—died, I found a tiny Amish-style dress in the bottom of one of her trunks."

Rebecca still got goose bumps when she recalled the moment she'd realized the Oliveris weren't her birth parents. "Instinct led me back to Willow Ridge, and when Miriam Lantz recognized me in her Sweet Seasons Bakery and Café, it was quite a reunion," she continued. "Even though I was in my Goth phase, dressed in black with spiky, dyed hair, I resembled my two sisters, Rhoda and Rachel. They were shocked to learn we'd been born as triplets instead of their being twins. But I'm rattling on about—"

"My God, what a shock it must've been for all of you," Wyatt murmured, leaning on the desk to study her features. "But I have to wonder why they didn't go searching for you after you'd washed away."

Rebecca considered this for a moment. "The men looked for me, but it's not the Amish way to involve the sheriff's department in searches," she explained. "My poor mother was told to let it go at that—that it was God's will I had vanished. She had a hard time facing the fact that I'd surely drowned—for what are the odds of a three-year-old surviving a log ride on a flood-swollen river?"

"Slim to none," he said.

Rebecca nodded. "So imagine her shock—and delight—when they discovered that the girl with the black fingernails and tattoo was her long-lost daughter. I was a bit of a celebrity for a while. I was a miracle."

Wyatt laughed. "I bet you were."

"But the biggest miracle was the way Mamma took me in without demanding that I shed my English ways to join the Amish church," she continued in a faraway voice. "I was just starting to do some graphic design and had no intention of giving up my computer skills to become an Amish *hausfrau*—"

"Thank goodness," her guest blurted out. "No offense, Rebecca, but you don't impress me as the sort of woman who could sacrifice herself to the restrictions the Amish impose upon their members. And please don't take that as a put-down of your family or the other people who live here," he added quickly. "Everyone I've met in Willow Ridge has amazed me with his or her openness and acceptance."

She smiled wryly. "If you've met Luke and Nora Hooley, you've been dealing with our Mennonite neighbors, who are a lot freer about technology and driving cars and such," she pointed out. "The local bishop, Tom Hostetler—he owns that herd of dairy cows down the road behind us—is accommodating of our English neighbors and visitors, but you'll get a bit more resistance from Preacher Henry Zook, who owns the market. Preacher Ben, who married my mamma last year, is more liberal, like Tom. All things considered, the Willow Ridge Amish community is a lot more progressive than most others are."

"Was I foolish to think I could establish Thoroughbred stables here, in an area where Amish practicality demands horses that aren't so pricey?"

Rebecca was so drawn in by Wyatt's steady gaze, it took her a moment to reply. "I don't know the answer to that," she murmured. "But you don't impress me as a fool who's soon parted from his money—unless he knows exactly why he's spending it and what he'll get in return."

The tiny lines around his eyes crinkled with his

smile. "And unless I miss my guess, you're not a woman to suffer fools, Rebecca."

She blinked. Was he flirting with her? "I, um, guess that makes us even, then."

"It makes us equals, the way I see it."

And what else did those penetrating blue-gray eyes see when they looked at her? Rebecca swallowed, not daring to say something girlish when her office felt supercharged with a tension that both delighted and terrified her.

"Am I out of line to invite you to dinner?" he asked in a voice so low she had to listen carefully to follow it. "If you're married—"

"Nope," she managed to say. "But if *you're* married, you're out of line. And if you lie about that and I find out the hard way, I guarantee you my family and friends will run you out of town, Mr. McKenzie."

Where did that come from? Rebecca gripped the arms of her desk chair, appalled at the veiled threat she'd made to this stranger—this potential client. But she couldn't unsay what had rushed from her mouth before her mind could stop it. Wyatt was so handsome and easy to be with, he surely had a wife—or an ex or two in his past.

For several long moments, Wyatt gazed at her. "I could easily find a website designer online," he said in a no-nonsense tone. "I've checked out several of them."

Rebecca's insides shriveled. He was right. *Open mouth, insert foot—and bite down hard.*

"And I could handle the details, updates, and payments online as well," he continued evenly. "Much simpler all around." The muscles in his face remained absolutely still . . . perhaps waiting for her to grovel, or at least apologize.

It took all the strength Rebecca possessed not to flinch. She *had* overstated her family and friends' reactions if Wyatt was keeping his marital status a secret—but otherwise she'd meant what she said. She wanted nothing to do with a man who was going to wine and dine her and then slip home to a wife.

After what seemed like forever, Wyatt murmured, "But if I'd hired an online web designer, I wouldn't have needed you, Rebecca. And I'd be kicking myself, now that I've met you face-to-face."

Her entire body tingled with joy and relief. *I wouldn't have needed you, Rebecca.* But she wasn't letting him off with pretty words. "So are you married?"

Wyatt's chuckle teased at her senses. "Nope. Came close a couple of times, but saw the writing on the wall and walked away—just as you're ready to do." He cleared his throat. "So once again, that makes us equals. I have other places to be for a couple of days, but what if we go to the Grill N Skillet Friday night, where everyone in town will see us together and gossip about it all weekend? Will that make you feel safer?"

Rebecca laughed harder than she had in a long while. "You've got that right, you know. These Amish are dyed-in-the-wool matchmakers—and when they learn you've bought the land that adjoins Luke and Nora's property, you'll be the talk of the town."

"But if they see me with you, Rebecca, they'll surely know me for a man of impeccable taste and sterling reputation, no?"

She sat straighter in her chair, aware that Wyatt was studying her closely as she took hold of the hands he'd stretched across her desk. "All right," she murmured, releasing him after a quick squeeze. "The Grill N Skillet may be the only café in town, but you'll find no place that serves better food."

"Agreed. My lunch there was excellent, and the owner and I had a nice chat."

"Josiah Witmer and his sister Savilla are relative newcomers," Rebecca remarked. "But they're lovely people. Passionate about down-to-earth comfort food."

"What would life be without passion?" he murmured as he stood up. "I'm old-fashioned, so I'd like to pick you up. Six thirty work for you?"

Rebecca nodded. "I live—"

"In that new brick house about a quarter mile down the road," Wyatt said with a nod. "Hope you don't mind that I did my homework—concerning your website expertise and your professional reputation, of course. I insist on being informed before I become involved."

She could only look at him. Her ability to breathe and form the simplest sentences seemed to have vanished, victims of Wyatt McKenzie's way with words . . . his unerring ability to take her by surprise. "Of course you do," she whispered. "I would expect no less."

"I'll see you at six thirty on Friday night, then. I'll show myself out." With a nod, he rose to leave—but at the door he turned, his expression utterly serious. "Just so you know, Rebecca, I plan to see that tattoo someday. Soon."

When he grinned mischievously and shut the door, Rebecca fell back against her chair. *What just happened here?*

A moment later she was online, Googling Wyatt

McKenzie to check out his holdings, his business connections, his presence on the web. If he had already done his homework, it behooved her to prepare herself for whatever he might spring on her at dinner.

Rebecca chuckled, at herself mostly. Wyatt probably knew exactly what she was doing right now, and knew everything she might find about him online.

And that keeps us equals, no?

Chapter Seven

Drew hammered the final decorative tack into the rocking chair he'd just reupholstered and laid aside his hammer. He liked the chair's sleek vintage lines, and he was pleased with the way his brother's stripping and staining had brought the wooden frame back to life. With its new cushion in earth-tone stripes, the farmhouse-style rocker should sell pretty quickly—even faster, if he could convince Nora to put it in her shop.

He wiped his face with a bandanna and glanced over at Asa, who was drilling screws into a drop leaf table he was refurbishing. When the whine of his air compressor died away, Drew asked, "Want something cold to drink? I think I've sweated out everything I've sipped since lunch."

Asa set down his drill. "*Jah*, it's a hot one. The ceiling fans are just moving muggy air."

"I'll mix up some more of that pink lemonade and be back in a few."

Drew took the stairs two at a time up to his apartment, which felt even hotter than the shop. He measured the pink lemonade powder into a plastic pitcher, mixed it with water, and took a tray of ice cubes from the freezer. When he glanced out the kitchen window, he noticed that Luke, Ira, and Will were setting posts in the large, flat parcel of plowed land Luke had designated as his future vineyard. They had to be inviting heat stroke out there in the blazing sun.

Drew emptied the tray of ice cubes into the pitcher and then opened the cabinet below the sink and found a half-gallon glass jar. He mixed another batch of lemonade in it, iced it down, and carried it to the shop. "I can't believe the Hooleys and Will are out there setting posts this afternoon, when it's so blazing hot," he said as he set the big jar on the worktable beside their drinking glasses. "I'm going to be a nice guy and take them a pitcher of this stuff."

Asa's eyebrows rose as he poured two glasses of lemonade. "Luke's used to an air-conditioned house," he remarked. "I'd think he'd really be feeling this heat—and maybe put up his vineyard lines in the early mornings, when it's a few degrees cooler."

Drew downed his glass of lemonade in a series of gulps and wiped his mouth on his short shirtsleeve. "His wife has an air-conditioned shop, too," he said, "and after I carry out my mission of mercy with his crew and take a shower, I'm going over there to see if we can consign a few of these pieces."

Asa let out a short laugh. "Just so happens Loretta's working today, too, ain't so?" he teased.

Drew shrugged good-naturedly. "You could go along," he said. "Doesn't cost anything to see what the Brennemans have put in Nora's shop lately—and the cool air would be a nice break for you."

"I want to get the new leaf made for this table before I quit for the day. But thanks for the offer." Asa walked over to the rocker, nodding as he walked around it. "This looks really *gut*—and the Brennemans only make wood pieces, without upholstery, so it would be something different from what Nora already carries. Could be that folks will like single pieces—like this chair—instead of having to invest in a whole dining room or bedroom set, too."

"That's what I'm thinking. We've picked up a lot of odds and ends lately that won't take long to fix up."

Drew went back upstairs to fetch the pitcher of lemonade, as well as a few plastic glasses. As he stepped out the shop's back door, the bright afternoon sun struck him, and he was glad he'd put on his sunglasses. The gray sky in the west suggested that rain was on the way, so he hoped a cool front would come with it. Once he'd crossed the yard of the house where Asa and Edith lived, he was walking on the ground Will had plowed earlier for the vineyard.

Ira, the shorter of the Hooley brothers, spotted Drew and waved. "Is that lemonade I see?" he called out hopefully. "You're a saint, Detweiler!"

Drew chuckled. Considering the way the folks of Willow Ridge had been talking about him when he'd ruined Asa's original wedding day, *saint* was a huge improvement. He suspected Luke's support had won him favor around town since then; he hoped carrying refreshments to the fledgling vineyard would continue the process.

"We're knocking off for the day," Luke said as Drew reached them. "But you're still a sight for sore eyes, Drew—not that I think you're *gut*-looking, understand."

Ira laughed as he accepted a plastic glass and Drew's pitcher. "Hah!" he teased as he poured. "To your way of thinking, brother, nobody else is nearly as *gut*-looking as you are."

"I'm glad you've noticed," Luke said as he, too, accepted an empty glass, "because now you realize your looks will never measure up. *Gut* thing Millie felt sorry for you and married you anyway."

When Drew offered the last glass to Will, he immediately sensed a drop in the emotional temperature. Gingerich was scowling, wiping his sweaty forehead on his sleeve—and pointedly refusing to accept the glass. Luke poured his lemonade and handed the pitcher to Will, but he refused that, too.

"I'll head on home now, *denki*," Gingerich muttered. "See you fellows tomorrow."

"Bright and early, *jah*—six, when it'll be cooler?" Luke asked.

"I'll be here." Will started across the plowed soil as though something invisible and unpleasant were nipping at his heels.

"Huh. Wonder what put a burr up his butt?" Ira said as he grabbed the pitcher for a second glassful. "He seemed fine until a minute ago."

"Sour grapes." Luke held Drew's gaze. "Will was as mad as a wet hen last Saturday when you lured Loretta away from him. Apparently, he'd been working up to courting her again—proposing to her—when she flat-out walked away to be with you."

Drew considered this. He didn't owe Luke and Ira any explanation, but it wasn't a good idea to voice the sarcastic remark that first came to his mind, either. "I asked Loretta if she wanted to go for a ride, and she joined me," he said. "The choice was hers."

Luke rubbed his forehead with his cold glass. "Will gave me quite an earful about how you would ruin her reputation—ruin *her*—and how she wouldn't be able to avoid that fate."

"Sounds like a train wreck waiting to happen," Ira said with a chuckle. "But from what little I know of Loretta, she'd be telling you where to get off if she didn't want your attention, Drew. None of the Riehl sisters impress me as the doormat type."

For a fleeting moment, Drew recalled his times alone with Loretta—the way she'd eagerly accepted his invitations, suggestions . . . and kisses. It might have been true that he'd kissed Loretta in his buggy partly to irritate Will, but her response had told him she'd liked it as much as he had. "Seems to me this is a matter for Will and Loretta to sort out between them."

Luke smiled. "That's the same advice I gave Will. But he's a fine farmer—every bit as hardworking and reliable as Asa promised when he asked me to hire Will a few months ago. I'm hoping this little bump in his road won't distract him."

Drew shrugged. "Wasn't my intention to upset him when I came out here with lemonade. If Will has a beef with me, he'd be better off confronting me with it rather than stewing over it."

"Nora and I have agreed to keep our noses out of it, so I see no point in wasting more time and talk on the matter." Luke drained his glass of lemonade and poured another one.

After Ira topped off his glass, the pitcher was empty, and he handed it back to Drew. "*Denki* for thinking of us. We'll drop the glasses off at your shop on our way home."

Drew nodded, starting back across the expanse of plowed earth, which was partially dotted with rows of fence posts. He showered quickly, spending the last full minute under cold water for the welcome relief it brought. After he'd shaved and combed his wet hair, he put on a deep blue short-sleeved shirt and fresh broadfall trousers. Then he went downstairs to load the rocker into a hand-pulled cart.

"Somebody's looking for some sugar," Asa teased. He placed the drop-leaf table's good leaf on an unfinished maple board so he could draw around it. "Is that fancy aftershave I smell?"

"Same aftershave that's in your bathroom cabinet, I suspect," Drew shot back. "And I'm not the only man in this shop who's hooked on sugar. From what I've seen, Edith keeps you mighty happy."

Asa's face lit up, and he laughed. "You've got that right. *Gut* luck talking Nora into taking that rocker. Give Loretta my best, too."

As Drew started down the road in the oppressive heat, pulling the cart behind him, he wondered if hitching up the horse would've been a better idea. A breeze was starting up, however, and the clouds he'd seen earlier were casting shadows over Willow Ridge. He'd heard folks say their gardens would welcome a slow, steady rain, because God's water always did more good than what came from a hose.

Annie Mae Wagler and her sister Nellie waved at him as they came out of Zook's Market with armloads of groceries and four younger siblings darting around them. Lydia Zook paused in taking laundry off her clothesline to wave to him as well. He felt good, knowing the folks around town were becoming his friends. As he pulled the cart up the lane toward the Simple Gifts shop in Nora's red barn, he felt the first raindrop splash his face.

Drew parked the cart on the side of the building and carried the rocking chair inside. A red SUV was parked in Nora's lot, so he reminded himself not to embarrass Loretta by flirting with her in front of customers.

What he saw as the door closed behind him made Drew smile proudly. Three middle-aged English ladies were standing near the high stool where Loretta sat demonstrating how she made her rag rug. The women appeared awestruck, hanging on every word she said—and one of them seemed honored when Loretta asked if she'd like to make a few stitches herself with the pointed plastic gadget that held the strip of purple fabric she was working with.

Nora, who was standing an aisle behind the ladies, waved when she noticed Drew. He set the rocker on the floor, pleased at the smile on her freckled face. As she approached him, she seemed as fresh as a springtime daisy in her yellow and white checked dress. "What have we here?" she whispered, placing her hand on the top of the rocker. "Please tell me you want to consign this with me."

Drew nodded, relieved that he didn't have to make a sales pitch. "That's what I was hoping you'd say," he said softly. Then he nodded toward Loretta. "Looks like she's in her element, showing those ladies how she works."

Nora's face lit up. "Loretta's got a real knack for demonstrating how she makes her rugs. On Monday we sent out a notice about the two classes she'll be teaching, and we already have a dozen ladies coming."

"Wow. That's fabulous."

"So's this rocking chair," Nora put in quickly, holding his gaze with her hazel eyes. "How much do you want for it? I predict it'll be gone by Saturday."

Drew blinked. He'd heard the Brenneman brothers talking about how quickly Nora sold most of their furniture, so he didn't question her remark. "Hundred and fifty? You might be a better judge of what your customers will pay."

"This little gem outshines anything you can find in a store selling new pieces," she said as she sat in the chair and rocked. "And it's the perfect size for a shorter person. You chose nice colors for the upholstery, too. Go for a hundred eighty. With my percentage added on, it'll be just under two hundred—and considering other things I've sold lately, that price won't make my customers blink."

Drew's eyebrows shot up. "Well, we can start that high and come down if we need to, I guess."

Nora waved him off. "Oh, ye of little faith," she teased. "I'll get my tags. We'll put this out right now."

Drew watched Nora make her way between the displays of linens and some baskets he recognized as Edith's. The ladies around Loretta were nodding and stepping away from her. "We're really looking forward to your class next week," one of them said.

"Now that I see how easy it is," another gal remarked, "I think I'll get the hang of it once you start me off, Loretta. It's a real treat to have an Amish girl teaching us, too!"

Nora spoke encouragingly about the class to her customers as she came back to tag Drew's rocker—and the three of them followed her.

"Oh, my aunt Dorothy had a chair similar to that one!" the first lady exclaimed.

"You know, my poor old sewing rocker is so loose in the joints I don't dare sit on it anymore," the short woman behind her remarked.

Nora's smiling face was thoughtful. "This is Drew Detweiler, who owns the furniture refurbishing place down the road," she said. "I bet he could make your rocker *gut* as new—"

"*Jah,* I could do that," Drew put in with a nod.

"It's a good thing you can get your chair repaired, Melba," the third lady said as she sat down in the rocker, "because this one would look just dandy beside my fireplace. And it fits my back like it was made for me—so don't even bother to tie on that tag, Nora. Let's just ring it up."

As the two women headed for the checkout counter, Drew's mouth dropped open. In all the years he and Asa had operated a shop, he'd never made a sale so quickly—without saying a word to the customer. "I just finished upholstering this piece this morning," he remarked to the lady, who was still sitting in it, rocking happily. "I'm really glad you like it. And here's my card," he said as he reached into his shirt pocket.

Melba, the woman with the weak chair, took a card, too. "Perfect. I live on the other side of Morning Star, so would you pick it up and deliver it?" she asked. "My husband can't lift anything anymore—"

"Let's jot down your address and phone number," Drew said. He was delighted that Loretta had anticipated his need and come over with a pen and a pad of paper. "When's a *gut* time for me to come for it?"

"Tomorrow morning? Around ten?" she asked eagerly.

"I'll be there. Thanks for bringing your business to our new shop." Drew wondered if his grin resembled a little kid's as he lifted the rocker. "Shall we put this in the car for your friend?"

About ten minutes later the English ladies had driven off and the rain was coming down in earnest.

When Drew ducked back into the store, Loretta was chuckling and Nora was holding out money.

"She paid cash, so here's your share, Drew," the redheaded storekeeper teased. "Was I right about how fast that chair would sell, or what?"

"I stand in awe," he said with a little bow.

"Maybe you should be standing in your shop, fixing up more pieces to consign," Loretta said lightly. "The same thing happened the day I brought my first rugs to Nora."

"I recall that," Nora remarked. "And I'm really glad that I suggested you come to teach some classes that day, too, because look how that idea's turned out. I hope Rosalyn's busy making fall wreaths. Come September, I'll sell everything she can bring me."

"She's been working on some," Loretta said with a nod. "Every minute we don't spend keeping up the house and garden, we're busy bees, crafting pieces for your store."

Nora smiled at the two of them. "This rain will probably make for a slow afternoon, so I'm going to catch up with some bookwork. And I'll add a page for you in my consignment account book, Drew," she added. "You and Asa are a wonderful addition to our little town, because you do quality work—and your refurbishing doesn't take any business away from the Brenneman brothers, who always build new pieces."

Drew had rarely felt so blessed. Nora wasn't one to slather on the compliments unless they were sincere, so her words gratified him. And was it his imagination, or was the shopkeeper wearing a mischievous expression as she left him and Loretta alone in the store?

Loretta's pretty upturned face left him no choice. Drew grabbed her hand, headed for a secluded corner, and led her behind a tall ornamental metal gate designed to resemble a patch of sunflowers. "Come here, sugar," he whispered. When he reached for her, Loretta was already on tiptoe, ready to return the kiss she apparently needed as badly as he did.

When they came up for air, she eased away from him. Her cheeks were pink, and her hazel eyes glowed like molten caramels. "Naughty boy, leading me astray behind the gate Preacher Ben made," she teased.

It was a good thing Loretta walked back into the main shop, or Drew might've kept her in hiding for several minutes longer. "I suspect Preacher Ben will admit to stealing a few kisses in his day," Drew said in a voice tight with longing. "Did somebody tell me that he and Miriam haven't been married all that long?"

"Well, Miriam was married several years ago, back when she had Rachel, Rhoda, and Rebecca," Loretta replied as she straightened a stack of quilted place mats. "But she'd been widowed when Ben breezed into town, and he apparently fell for her the moment she fed him one of her pastries. That was back when she ran the café—before Josiah Witmer rebuilt and expanded it this past winter."

"Most men follow their stomachs," Drew remarked. The sound of rain drilling the roof told him he wouldn't be walking home anytime soon, and with the fans in the high ceiling gently moving the cooled air, he was in no hurry to step back out into the heat and humidity, anyway. "There's some remarkable stuff in here. I'd like to look around, so if you've got work to do—"

"My number one job is to make folks feel at home—and feel like spending money—in Nora's store," Loretta interrupted sweetly. "But maybe, after our little disappearing act, I should sit here on my stool where Nora can see me working on my rug."

Her prim tone only tempted him to kiss the playful smile from her face. Loretta settled on her high stool and took up the rug she'd started, and Drew tried not to gawk as she tucked her shapely ankles behind one of the stool's legs. Her eyes were focused on the plastic needle as she slipped it under a strip of purple fabric, but her thoughts were playing with her eyebrows and lips as she concentrated on not looking at him.

Our little disappearing act makes the loft look awfully inviting, Drew thought as he gazed up at it. The unique banners hanging there would prevent any incoming customers from seeing them—but the last thing he wanted was to jeopardize Loretta's standing with Nora, who was obviously thrilled to have her for an employee.

"Nora makes those three-dimensional banners. Aren't they amazing?"

Drew's jaw dropped. "Am I seeing things, or is that little Amish girl on the swing wearing a real *kapp*?"

"You've got it right," Loretta replied. "And Nora attached half of a little boy's black straw hat to the one where he's sitting on a hay bale with his puppy— which is a stuffed toy she cut in half and attached to it."

"I've got to check this out." Drew passed a walnut bookshelf he recognized as the Brennemans' style, with one of Cornelius's clocks sitting on it, and then headed up the sturdy wooden staircase. The walls were hung with colorful pictures and planks of wood with Bible verses painted on them. When he reached the upper level, he saw twin-sized bed forms angled against the wall to display quilts, with more quilts hanging on poles that extended from the walls. Brightly colored shelves displayed handmade stuffed toys, hand-carved train sets, and other toys that enticed him to run his fingers over their glossy wood. He gazed for several moments at a shiny black rocking horse with a mane and tail of thick black yarn.

When he looked closely at three more of Nora's three-dimensional hangings, he was even more impressed with her imaginative work. The largest piece was a clothesline that had real, toddler-sized Amish clothes hanging on it, with real wooden clothespins. The background was a typical farm scene, with a red barn, horses, and cows sewn onto it. Another banner of a little Amish boy fishing—wearing real pants, a blue shirt, suspenders, and a straw hat—did unexpected things to his heartbeat. He and Asa had been avid fishermen as boys . . .

Fighting a grin, Drew descended the stairs. Loretta was still perched prettily on her stool, running her plastic needle around the loops of her rug, but it was Nora he needed to see. He stopped at the doorway to her office, peering in. "Got a minute?"

Nora looked up from a notebook of handwritten entries. "What can I do for you, Drew? As hard as the rain's pouring down, I don't blame you for sticking around with us."

"I want that banner you made of the little guy fishing," he blurted, pointing toward the loft level. "And the little girl in the swing to go with it—and I have to have that black rocking horse, too. Leroy and Louisa are growing up in a family devoted to their Percherons, you know."

Nora's smile warmed him. "The Mennonite man who made that rocking horse lives in New Haven. He was a little concerned that folks would prefer lighter-colored horses for their kids," she said as she stood up. "I'm happy you proved him wrong, Drew. And I'm sure you, as a man who's acquainted with items made of wood, will appreciate his craftsmanship more than most. Your kids and *their* kids will enjoy that horse—and between you and me, Edith has been eyeballing those banners for weeks. She'll be delighted that you chose them."

Drew felt almost light-headed as he followed Nora up to the loft. He'd never been particularly drawn to kids' things, yet as he took the banners she unclipped from their hanging line, he knew he was doing something special for Asa, Edith, and the twins. He wasn't much of a shopper, either, but he valued Plain quality, and it didn't even matter how much the banners and the rocking horse cost. He was grateful to God that Asa and Edith were raising the children he'd fathered in a less-than-honorable situation, so providing some wall hangings and a rocking horse felt *good*. His heart was thumping as he followed Nora back downstairs and to the checkout counter.

"I'd be happy to drive these over to the house, if you'd like," Nora said as she clipped the tags from the banners. "They'll stay dry—"

"And clean," Drew pointed out. "Even if it stops raining, that old cart I brought the rocker in has wood shavings and all manner of loose crud in it." He laughed, delighted with the plan that sprang to his mind. "When you take them over, don't tell Asa and Edith who sent them. I'll get a kick out of watching them try to guess."

"You're on!" Nora folded the banners into a large plastic bag. "But I suspect they'll figure you out pretty fast."

Drew shrugged. "*Jah*, Asa knew I was coming over

here with that rocker. It's still fun to make him happy, you know? He's a better *dat* for those kids than I would ever be."

"Don't sell yourself short, Drew. Your time will come."

Nora's words did funny things to his heart—especially when he realized Loretta had come to stand beside him. She was gazing at the rocking horse as she picked up on the conversation.

"What a wonderful-*gut* gift," she murmured. "Edith and Asa provide everything those babies need, but the horse and hangings will be special because they're from *you*, and they're things Edith wouldn't spend the money on."

Drew smiled at Loretta's assessment of her younger sister. He had a feeling none of the Riehl girls were very spendy, living with a *dat* like Cornelius—and he'd heard them bemoaning the way their tightwad father refused to replace their *mamm*'s worn-out rugs, curtains, and furniture.

Food for thought. He smiled at Loretta, noting the way she gazed at the items he'd purchased. When Nora slipped him the bill, Drew pulled the money she'd paid him for the rocking chair from his pocket and added fifty more from his wallet. The purchase all but cleaned him out, but it was worth it to see the wonder in Loretta's eyes as she observed the transaction.

"I'm glad you found some items you liked, Drew," Nora said as she placed the money in her cash drawer. "I'll drop them off this evening after the rain stops."

"*Denki*, Nora. As soon as Asa and I have more pieces finished, I'll bring them by." The sudden silence in the store made him look out the nearest window. "The rain's letting up, and here comes the sun. I should probably head back to the shop and let you ladies get back to what you were doing. Have a great day."

As Drew returned Loretta's smile, his gaze lingering on her lips, he was already searching for ways and reasons to see her again. Just being in her presence healed him; made him want to be a man worthy of her affections.

Chapter Eight

Will glared out his kitchen window, watching Detweiler grab the handle of his pull cart. How long had that bounder been in the Simple Gifts store—and why had he gone there in the first place?

Loretta. What other reason would he have for going to Nora's store? Certainly not shopping.

Will finished rubbing his wet hair and threw the towel down in disgust. His shower hadn't washed away the resentment he'd felt from the moment Detweiler had crossed the vineyard with that pitcher of lemonade. He'd pretended to be doing them a cold favor on a hot day, but Will knew better. Detweiler had seen a chance to rub Will's nose in the fact that he'd snatched Loretta away, and his do-gooder intentions were a ruse. Everyone else in Willow Ridge might have forgiven Asa's errant twin, but Will believed Drew's conversion was only skin-deep. Any man who'd so cruelly deceived Molly, Edith, and his own brother wouldn't change his evil ways so quickly, so effortlessly.

A few moments later, Nora pulled her black van up to the door of her store and left its engine idling.

Will's pulse accelerated. Did this mean Loretta would be minding the store while Nora made a delivery? As he watched to be sure Detweiler really was heading down the road, a plan filled him with anticipation. He dressed in fresh pants and the last clean shirt hanging in the closet. Maybe when Loretta saw how rumpled he looked, she would take pity and sew him some new shirts out of the no-iron fabric from which she and her sisters made their dresses.

His heart sang as he descended the stairs into the mill shop. The sign in the door was turned so *BACK SHORTLY* faced outward, and the little clock's hands were on the twelve and the three—which meant Luke and Ira were probably out picking up eggs from their suppliers in nearby towns. Will paused in front of the refrigerated case. He grabbed a little tub of Nazareth Hostetler's goat cheese—the kind she'd flavored with raspberry jam—and then spotted a bagged loaf of Miriam Hooley's banana bread on the counter. Lunch had been a long time ago, and sharing these treats with Loretta would surely sweeten her attitude.

Will waited at the back door until he saw Nora's van turning onto the road. As he strode across the mowed lot that ran behind the mill, Ira's place, and Luke and Nora's white house, he elevated his thoughts to the mission at hand. It wouldn't do to carry his resentment for Detweiler into the store, because the opportunities to see Loretta without her family around were as scarce as hens' teeth.

You have to get the words right the first time—have to convince her you're the man whose heart's in the right place.

Will's breath caught as he stood outside, peering through the glass in the shop's door. Loretta was seated on a glossy walnut bench facing him, as pretty as he'd ever seen her. Her light blue dress was fresh and summery, as though the July heat and humidity weren't affecting her. She was focused on the rug she was making as she waited for customers.

Waiting for you to sweep her off her feet. Will said a quick prayer and opened the door.

When the bell jangled, Loretta looked up with a smile that morphed into an expression of wary surprise. "W-Will," she stammered. "What can I help you find? Nora's store is full of—"

"Money can't buy what I'm looking for, Loretta." Will closed the door behind him, resisting the urge to lock it. "I brought us a snack, hoping we could talk."

Before she could protest, he sat on the other end of the short bench, only a few feet away from her— alone with her at last. Hoping to ease the doubt that furrowed Loretta's brow, he held out the tub of goat cheese and the banana bread.

"Go ahead and eat. I'm not hungry," she said.

Will frowned. This wasn't going according to his anticipated script. "I wanted us to have another chance to—"

"Will, it's not going to work," she said as she rose, clutching her rug. She was looking around the store, as though hoping she could conjure up customers— or hasten Nora's return. "I'm sorry I ran off the other day when you were talking about us courting again, but—"

"*Sorry?*" Will blurted. "You didn't look any too sorry when you were kissing Detweiler!"

Her desperate little squeal warned him that he'd lost control of the conversation—and of Loretta. "Please don't be angry, Will," she pleaded, backing away. "You and I are different people from when we lived in Roseville. You've gone through so much, and—and I've changed my mind about getting married."

Will felt the loaf of banana bread splitting in his grip. "You're going to marry Detweiler, is that it?" he cried out. "You hardly even know him, and already—"

"You're making some mighty wild assumptions, Will," Loretta fired back at him. "I've apologized for leaving you on the porch, and if you can't accept that, you'd better leave. I'm sorry it's come to this, but you're not hearing a thing I've said."

Will stood up, dropping the food on the bench. "Tell me again why you don't want to marry me. I'm listening."

Loretta's face crumpled. She stepped behind a chair at the Brennemans' dining room table as though she were afraid of him—as though she might throw the chair if he came closer. "All right, I'll be blunt," she said in a shaky voice. "I didn't want to come right out and say this, knowing how you're still hurting from Molly's death and—"

"Just spit it out. We've been down this road already." Will sensed he'd lost any chance to redeem himself now, but he wasn't leaving until he'd heard the truth.

Loretta pressed her hand to her mouth, staring at him as tears ran down her face. "My mind and my heart have changed, Will, and . . . I—I don't love you anymore. Please try to understand—"

"What? I can't hear you!" His voice echoed in the high-ceilinged room. Too late, Will realized he was sounding just like Cornelius.

Loretta picked up a pottery vase from the center of the table. Would she really throw it at him? Gentle, sweet Loretta?

"You're out of your head, Will," she stated sadly.

"The way you're acting only confirms my sense that you've changed dramatically—and that it would be a big mistake for me to marry you. Please, Will. *Please* try to understand," she pleaded.

Will's breath left him in a rush. He clenched his fists, and for a moment he wanted to rush over and grab her shoulders—to shake some sense into her.

That would prove she's right, wouldn't it? You're out of your head, man. You've scared her half to death, and now she never wants to see you again.

"Fine. Have it your way," he said in a raspy voice. "And if Detweiler does you dirty, I'll be the first one to say *I told you so.*"

Will pivoted, striding away so Loretta wouldn't see his face puckering. Once outside, he slammed the door so hard its glass rattled. As he jogged toward the mill, sun diamonds glistened on the gently flowing river, enticing him. If he got a couple of bungee cords from Luke's storage closet . . . lashed big rocks to his feet and jumped in, his troubles would all be over. Then maybe Loretta would be *sincerely* sorry about what she'd done to him, instead of just mouthing the words. He stood on the riverbank, sizing up the rocks until he'd spotted two that would be heavy enough to take him to the bottom of the river and hold him under.

The sound of a motor on the road made Will glance behind him. Nora's van was coming up the gravel lane toward her store. If she spotted him, his plan would be interrupted. Everyone in town would hear about how he'd tried to end it all, and he'd have to endure their sympathy, their well-intentioned attempts to counsel him.

Bad enough that Loretta's going to tell Nora about your visit, so everyone in town will soon know you've lost it.

Go home, Gingerich. You're such a failure you can't even get rid of yourself without messing it up.

Nora held Loretta close and let her sob against her shoulder. "Sweetie, what happened?" she asked softly. "Were you uncomfortable being here all by yourself, or—"

"Will was here," Loretta blurted. "He—he got really mad. Made me tell him why I didn't want to marry him anymore, and—and—"

Nora's eyes widened. Only a desperate man—a glutton for punishment—would ask such a question. "Loretta, did he hurt you?" She eased away to study Loretta's tear-streaked face, relieved to see no bruises or signs of a slap.

Loretta shook her head. "I had a vase ready to throw at him . . . which was probably a little extreme," she admitted ruefully. "But Will was so bitter about me going out with Drew, and he insinuated that I'd be sorry for getting involved with him."

Nora cleared her throat. "*Are* you involved with Drew?"

"Not that way!" Loretta replied quickly. She shook her head sadly. "Will has it in his head that he and I can be together again. It hurt like anything to tell him I don't love him anymore, but—but at least he left."

Nora hugged Loretta again before releasing her. The last thing she wanted was to upset Will even more, but she couldn't have him coming into the store and intimidating Loretta again, either. "Luke and I will talk with him. And until we're sure Will's got his act together, I won't be leaving you alone in the store, all right?"

Loretta nodded, wiping her face with her apron. "I'm sorry to cause you so much trouble."

"This is hardly your fault," Nora insisted. She smiled purposefully until Loretta managed a small smile of her own. "It's one thing to have a lovers' quarrel—or an ex-lovers' quarrel. It's another thing altogether when it happens in my store, with one of Luke's employees. You were right to tell Will the truth, Loretta, even if he wishes he could turn the clock back."

"*Denki* for seeing it that way," Loretta whispered.

"Happy to help. Someday we'll all look back and realize this was just another little bump on the road to your happiness, and Will's." Nora smiled brightly. "And by the way, Edith was ecstatic about the rocking horse and banners Drew picked out."

Loretta nodded and went back to the bench where she'd left her rug. With a sigh, Nora returned to her office. She suspected voices from the mill store could be heard in the upstairs apartment, so instead of calling Luke, she went to her computer and emailed him.

Once we're home tonight, we need to discuss Will. Keep this between you and me.

Chapter Nine

By six o'clock on Friday evening, Rebecca had changed her outfit three times. As she began to hang up the unsuitable clothing she'd tossed onto her bed, she shook her head. She'd been out on the occasional date while she'd attended graphic design classes, yet those guys had seemed adolescent and geeky compared to Wyatt McKenzie. She'd finally decided that a date at the Grill N Skillet didn't require anything fancy, thank goodness, because her wardrobe didn't measure up to the way Wyatt had been dressed when she'd met him. He would have to accept her in khaki capris, a denim vest, and a pale beige shirt—and if her appearance didn't suit him, well, it was best to find out he was a clothing snob before she got too interested in him.

Hah—too late, her thoughts mocked her. After her extensive online search, Rebecca was all too aware that Wyatt could have chosen a big design firm to launch a new website worthy of his enterprises. And despite the fact that she'd only spent an hour with him, she definitely found him interesting.

But why was a man who owned estates and horse

farms in Lexington, Kentucky, and Sarasota Springs, New York, establishing a Thoroughbred farm in Willow Ridge? From what she could find out about him, Wyatt ran with the top dogs of horse racing and breeding—and the major tracks where his horses raced were all far, far away from Missouri, in both geographical distance and the social status of the folks with whom he did business.

Why did he seek me out to design his website? I'm a mere novice compared to the metropolitan design firms his peers have hired. He could've worked with whomever designed the sites for his other two farms . . .

Rebecca looked out the window for the umpteenth time, despite the fact that it was only ten after six. She laughed at herself for feeling so tingly and apprehensive and giddy, because dinner tonight was probably just a business meeting—a place to discuss the website Wyatt wanted. Should she be wary of the fact that he hadn't said a word about his site on Tuesday?

Should you be alarmed about the fact that a forty-year-old man is hitting on you?

Rebecca sighed. When she'd found photos of Wyatt on the Internet, he'd either been standing beside a fabulous racehorse from one of his stables or he'd had a wealthy-looking blond socialite in a red evening gown on his arm. The sight of him smiling directly toward the camera, with his sun-streaked hair catching the light, decked out in a slate blue tuxedo, a black bow tie, and a white shirt had made her gaze so intently at her computer screen, she'd printed the picture—after cropping out the socialite, of course. As Rebecca held the page, Wyatt had such a presence—such a self-assured smile—that he might as well have been standing in her office talking with her.

But then, when had she ever beheld a real man in

a tuxedo? The high school boys at prom hardly counted compared with the virile maturity Wyatt McKenzie exuded.

When Rebecca realized she'd been gawking at the photo for way too long, she set it aside and went out to her front porch to wait. A big maple tree shaded the west side, blocking the intense sun. As she rocked in the swing, she wondered what to talk about—besides websites. She didn't know much about horses . . . had never attended a horse race. She'd grown up in a middle-class home in a small town. Her adoptive dad, Bob Oliveri, was a man of means who'd invested in a few Willow Ridge businesses to assist her Amish family—he'd bought her mother's Sweet Seasons Bakery building, and he'd financed the new Grill N Skillet that had risen from the bakery's ashes.

But Bob, bless him, was almost bald and a little too cushioned around the middle, and he easily disappeared in a crowd. Growing up with him had not prepared Rebecca in the least for dealing with Wyatt's magnetism.

She glanced at her watch. "Hmm. Fashionably late," she murmured. She couldn't recall the last time she'd felt so nervous, so ready to impress someone who already impressed her immensely. And maybe arriving at the Grill N Skillet after most of the supper crowd had left wasn't such a bad thing.

Ten minutes later, a white van with pictures of flowers on it pulled into her driveway. Rebecca stood, her eyes widening as the delivery kid strode toward her carrying the largest bouquet of red roses she'd ever seen.

"Um, let me find you a tip," she murmured, grabbing her purse.

"No need," the young man said with a grin. "The

guy who sent you these has already taken care of it. Big-time."

Rebecca gestured for him to set the large vase on her wicker porch table. Did these flowers mean Wyatt would be late? Or was this a kiss-off? Her home phone and cell hadn't rung—so was there a reason he didn't want to talk to her? Or text her?

As the delivery guy jogged back to his van, Rebecca stood before the bouquet in awe. Maybe it was tacky to count—but then, when had she ever received three dozen absolutely stunning roses? They were the lush color of Christmas-red velvet, and she marveled that every single flower was open slightly, flawlessly promising her several days of enjoyment.

Rebecca carried the bouquet inside so it wouldn't wilt in the evening heat. As she set it on her dining room table, she noticed that vase was made of exquisite faceted glass—not like the cheap, plain glass containers that often accompanied floral deliveries. She was almost afraid to open the little ivory envelope she plucked from the wide band of shimmery gold ribbon that was tied in an elaborate bow around the vase.

My dearest Rebecca, I'm so sorry I can't be with you this evening. Ever yours, Wyatt.

Rebecca frowned. That was it? No explanation? No mention of calling or coming another time? Even though she knew it hadn't rung, she pulled her cell phone from her pocket. She found no message or missed call from him.

As she dropped down onto her couch, she felt totally flummoxed. If she was Wyatt's dearest Rebecca and he was ever hers, didn't those sentiments—and such a sumptuous bouquet—imply a relationship?

A connection worth gracing with a few explanatory words about why he'd stood her up?

"You are such a fool, little girl," she muttered. For all she knew, Wyatt was escorting that socialite in the Internet picture to a fancy-dress ball at some billionaire's estate, via his private jet, and couldn't be bothered with showing up in Willow Ridge. Oh, he was a pretty package who said all the right things and knew precisely how to make her hang on his every perfect word, but what else was he? Why had he walked away from those two women he'd almost married—or had they shown him the door? Had Wyatt showered those women with gifts, too, until they'd seen through his broken promises?

Before her lower lip could tremble, Rebecca grabbed her purse and headed out the door. Dinner at the Grill N Skillet was still a wonderful option— much better than sulking at home—because she would see folks she knew, none of whom had any idea she'd been stood up. And she could stop at Mamma and Ben's house for a visit, too, because chatting with them while playing with six-month-old Bethlehem would be a surefire lift for her wilted spirits.

The image of Wyatt wincing because her tiny sister had spit up on his expensive silk shirt made Rebecca laugh out loud. It was clearly time to fill her head with images of someone besides the alluring man who'd so quickly captured her fancy.

What Wyatt says paints a pretty picture, she thought as she pulled her Ford Escape out of the garage. *It's what he doesn't say that sketches in the wrinkles and warts.*

Chapter Ten

Loretta quickly dried the plates Rosalyn was stacking in the dish drainer, feeling a little on edge. Nora had asked her to come to her house around seven thirty this evening, but she hadn't elaborated on the purpose of the visit. Maybe she wanted to talk about the two rug-making classes, which were attracting more interest than they'd anticipated— but wouldn't they know even more about how many ladies to expect by next Tuesday, when Loretta would be working in the shop again?

"You'd better scoot, missy," Rosalyn said as she glanced at the kitchen wall clock. "You don't want to keep Nora waiting."

"And what in tarnation does Nora want from you *now*?" Dat groused. He was sitting at the kitchen table behind them, catching up on the week's edition of *The Budget*. "You were with her all day yesterday in that fancy, fandangled shop of hers. If she wants you to work more days each week, the answer is *no*. It's not fair to leave your sister responsible for the house and the garden—"

"I don't intend to work any more days than I do now," Loretta insisted, more sharply than she intended. Dat had been irritable all day, and she was eager to escape for a little while. "I have no idea how long our visit will take, so please be patient."

She hung her damp tea towel over the back of her chair at the table. "See you later," she said, returning Rosalyn's wink. "Let's pick zucchini tonight, before they get as big as ball bats."

"And we'll dig up our poor sun-bleached lettuce and spinach," Rosalyn put in. "The heat has really gotten the best of them."

Loretta nodded her agreement and headed out the back door before Dat could think of any other reason to detain her. She jogged past the garden and the chicken yard, where the hens and rooster pecked at the dry dirt in one corner of the fence. The Grill N Skillet was having a typical busy Friday night, judging from its parking lot full of cars and buggies. The aroma of grilled beef filled the air, and Loretta wished they could eat at the café more often, as a break from having to cook and clean up every single evening. Now that she worked three days a week, she better appreciated the reason why so many people flocked to Josiah and Savilla's restaurant for their lunches and suppers.

Once she'd passed behind Zook's Market, she walked on the shoulder of the county highway, amazed at the cars that passed in either direction. Willow Ridge was a lot busier than Roseville had been, yet it was still very much a small, Plain community where a few Mennonites and English lived among the Old Order Amish. Up ahead, the big waterwheel of the mill was still, and the mill's parking lot—as well as the Simple Gifts lot—stood empty.

Loretta strode up the Hooleys' driveway, pausing to catch her breath when she'd reached the porch of the biggest white house in town. She'd only been inside Nora and Luke's home once, on the day Ira and Millie, Nora's daughter, had gotten married. It was no surprise that Nora had been watching for her.

"Come on in, sweetie!" she said as she stepped out the door. She was barefoot, wearing a loose seersucker dress. "On a day as hot as this one, I have to admit that having an air conditioner is a real advantage to being Mennonite."

"*Jah*, it's really warm at home," Loretta remarked as she entered the spacious front room. "Rosalyn and I baked cinnamon rolls and canned about twenty quarts of tomatoes today. I should've brought you some!"

"Nothing prettier than fresh tomatoes in a jar," Luke said as he came from the kitchen. "But then, I can say that because I'm not the one who has to do that hot canning work. *Gut* to see you, Loretta," he added, gesturing toward the overstuffed chairs and matching couch. "Help yourself to lemonade."

Loretta eagerly poured a glass of the pale yellow liquid, recognizing it as fresh-squeezed rather than made from powder. She caught the look Nora and Luke shared as they glanced at the rustic barn board clock that hung above the sofa.

"I might as well fill you in," Nora said as she came to sit in the chair nearest Loretta's. "After your run-in with Will the other day, Luke and I decided we needed to iron out this situation before it gets out of hand."

Loretta's eyes widened. She appreciated the Hooleys' efforts on her behalf, but what could they possibly say to change Will's attitude?

"I asked Will to come over this evening, too," Luke continued. His handsome face was set in a serious expression. "I hired him on Asa's recommendation—and Will's an excellent farmer—but we can't have him threatening you or causing any further trouble. It's one thing to be grieving the loss of his wife. It's another thing entirely for him to fly off the handle at you because your feelings toward him have changed."

When the doorbell rang, Loretta lost all taste for her refreshing lemonade. She had a pretty good idea that Will would feel he was walking into a trap when he saw her here. *But what can he do? Luke and Nora are in charge.*

Would Will resent the Hooleys' interference? Would he scowl every time he saw her from now on because he believed she'd asked Luke and Nora to take her side?

As the two men's voices drifted in from the porch, Nora smiled kindly at her. "It'll be all right, Loretta," she said quietly. "We're just setting some boundaries for—ah, hello, Will," she said as Luke and Will entered the front room. "*Denki* for coming over."

Will's expression said it all: when he spotted Loretta, his facial features tightened and his eyes frosted over. "So . . . what's going on here?" he demanded.

Loretta forced herself to hold Will's gaze instead of looking away. He appeared haggard in his rumpled shirt, with dark circles beneath his bloodshot eyes and hair that needed washing.

"Will, we need to address your recent confrontation with Loretta in Nora's shop," Luke said matter-of-factly. "Have a seat, and let's see what we can do to remedy this situation."

Will didn't move. "None of this would've happened if Loretta hadn't—"

"I said I was sorry!" Loretta blurted. "I was just trying to tell you the truth so we could both move on."

"By the looks of that squashed loaf of banana bread I found in my store," Nora said before Will could respond, "it's a *gut* thing you didn't have your hands around Loretta's neck. From here on out, Will, my shop is off-limits to you. I can't have you bursting in and venting your frustrations on Loretta while she's working." She gazed at Will until he looked up at her. "Do you understand, Will?"

Long moments of silence squeezed Loretta's conscience. She hadn't foreseen such repercussions after Will's visit, and she felt almost as bad now as she had when he'd gotten so angry in the store. She gazed self-consciously at her lap, wondering how this encounter could possibly get any more uncomfortable.

Will exhaled loudly. "So you two have become Loretta's guardians now, protecting her from me?" he asked, looking from Nora to Luke. "Was that your idea, or hers?"

Luke crossed his muscular arms. "Ours," he insisted. "You two are our employees, but more importantly, you're our friends. I'll confess that when Ira and I got home and saw the way you were contemplating the river and the big rocks on the bank—looking as desperate and defeated as I've ever seen a man—I knew you were in a bad mental state even before Nora told me you'd confronted Loretta in her store."

Loretta swallowed hard. Will's expression told her that he had indeed been standing on the riverbank with dangerous ideas running through his mind. Had she done this to him? Had she been so focused on her own feelings that she'd totally missed the anguish he'd been suffering?

"We would've immediately jumped in to rescue you, Will," Luke continued softly. "We're relieved that something changed your mind, because we *like* you. We want to help you out of your depression."

When Will finally dropped onto the couch, he appeared embarrassed . . . and maybe bitter about the fact that Luke and Ira had been watching him. "Okay, so I was upset," he said in an accusatory tone. "Can you honestly say *you* wouldn't have been irrational after the woman you loved turned you away—raced off to be with another man—and then acted as though you were going to hurt her?"

"Will, we're sorry—we feel bad for you," Nora said, gently placing her hand on his arm. "That's why Luke and I are concerned about your emotional state. But we're also aware that you put Loretta in a very sticky spot."

Will crossed his arms, looking away. "It all started out as a chance to just visit with Loretta—bring her some goodies and chat in the store," he said in an unsteady voice. "But right off the bat, she shut me down."

"I—I didn't know what to say!" Loretta protested. She took a deep breath to settle her ragged nerves. "I admit I wasn't very considerate when I left you sitting on the porch swing and went off with Drew . . . but then—and Thursday in the store—I was trying to be honest about my feelings, and you were having none of it. Didn't hear a thing I said."

Tears dribbled down Loretta's cheeks.

"I'm so sorry, Will—for all you've been through, and for the pain I've caused you," she whispered. "But that doesn't mean I can marry you. Please try to understand."

Nora brought over the box of tissues from an end

table and offered them to Loretta. Luke sat down on the couch beside Will, his expression somber. For a moment, the only sound in the room was the sound of Loretta blowing her nose—and letting out a little sob, despite her efforts to control her emotions.

Will propped his elbows on his knees and buried his face in his hands. His shoulders shook with silent sobs until he inhaled deeply to settle himself. "I am so tired of crying," he said.

Luke placed a hand on Will's shoulder, while Nora walked over to put her arm around him. "We can't imagine your pain, Will," she murmured. "We don't want you to hurt yourself, and if you'll agree to some counseling—or whatever Andy Leitner, our local nurse, recommends—we'll be happy to pay for it. We want you to be well."

"We want you to be happy again," Luke put in softly. "Everyone in Willow Ridge is glad you've come and wants you to find a new life here, too. A new purpose."

"*Jah*, that's right," Loretta said, dabbing her eyes. "It's not easy, moving to a new place and having to get settled in with new neighbors, but I think you—and our family—have come to the right place."

"And when you can think about such things again," Luke began with a careful smile, "I've seen the way some of our single gals have been checking you out."

"Yeah, right," Will said glumly.

"Just a couple hours ago Savilla Witmer was chatting about you while we were eating supper at the café," Nora said quickly. "And don't forget about Hannah Brenneman and Katie Zook—and Nellie Knepp," she added after a moment's thought.

Will scowled. "They're just girls. Not even twenty—"

"Savilla's twenty-five," Luke interrupted with a

knowing smile. "I asked how old she was tonight, thinking of you, Will. She's a looker, ain't so?"

When Will laughed and rolled his eyes, Loretta had a sense that he might be turning a small emotional corner. With her coal black hair and brown eyes like strong coffee—and her ability to cook and help run the Grill N Skillet—Savilla Witmer was definitely the most attractive single woman in Willow Ridge. And she was only a couple years younger than Will.

"It's not like we're trying to get you matched up before you're ready," Nora insisted. "But Savilla sounded very interested in the work you're doing—planting the vineyard and helping Luke and Ira raise their grains." She shrugged, her smile brightening. "I bet living with Josiah and Lena and baby Isaiah might make her feel like a fifth wheel sometimes, even though they all get along so well. She'd probably welcome the chance to get out now and again."

"But everything in its own *gut* time," Luke said with a purposeful glance at his wife. "How about if I give Andy a call? See if he can chat with you tomorrow and get you some help?"

"He's an awfully nice man," Loretta remarked softly. "He's been such a help with Leroy and Louisa—made time to see them on really short notice, too, one night when Edith couldn't get them to stop vomiting."

When Will looked at her, Loretta felt more sorry for him than frightened. The blatant desperation had left his eyes, and he no longer appeared to be accusing her of starting this troublesome situation. Because she held no grudge against him—wanted him to be well and happy—it seemed only right to take the next step.

"Will, I'm sorry about the pain I've caused you," Loretta repeated softly. "I hope you can forgive me for behaving so rudely, the day I left you on the porch swing to go with Drew."

His eyes widened, and he bit back a retort. Then his shoulders relaxed as he let out a long sigh. "I crossed the line in the shop yesterday," he admitted. "I was so focused on my own wishes I couldn't hear what you were trying to tell me. Guess I'd better get over that."

The room around them seemed to sigh as the tension dissipated. Nora poured a glass of lemonade and offered it to Will. "Glad to hear it," she said encouragingly. "Life's too short to let negativity and hurt feelings come between friends."

Will gratefully gulped the lemonade, pausing only once before he drained the glass. "Go ahead and call that Leitner fellow. Probably time I made his acquaintance anyway."

"I'm on it," Luke said as he rose from the couch. "His number's in the kitchen."

Within minutes Will joined Luke to speak with Andy Leitner, and Loretta relaxed. "This session turned out better than I thought it might," she admitted. "*Denki* for stepping in, Nora. Now that I've heard about Will almost jumping into the river, I'm really glad you and Luke have insisted that he get some help."

"And he said, of his own free will, that he was out of line to be so angry with you," Nora said with a nod. "That's huge. But *jah*, for a while I was wondering if we'd get Will to come around. Without Luke's influence, we girls might've just aggravated the situation more."

Loretta nodded. She had even more respect for

Luke and Nora now . . . and it made her wonder. In a difficult situation, would Drew take the high road— as Luke had—rather than getting defensive or making Will out to be less than masculine because he couldn't handle his emotions?

Loretta made a mental note to take her time getting to know Drew better, to wait for incidents that called for spiritual strength and see how he reacted to them. Now that she wouldn't be running to Drew to escape Will's hopeful overtures, she needed to allow her relationship with him to unfold at its own pace.

No need to tell Drew what happened here with Will, either. What happens at Nora's house should stay at Nora's house.

After Will left for his apartment, Loretta walked home at a leisurely pace. The sky was the shade of pale, translucent blue that followed the sunset and preceded nightfall. The *clip-clop, clip-clop* of a buggy made her look up and wave. Was that really Aaron Brenneman with Katie Zook in his courting buggy?

Loretta smiled. After she crossed behind the market and the café's parking lot, she gathered the chickens into the chicken house for the evening. Then she grabbed a couple of big baskets, slipped out of her shoes, and entered the garden at the end where the squash plants and melon vines formed loose circles around the hills where they were planted. The warm soil soothed her feet as she lifted floppy green leaves to reveal zucchini and yellow squash that were ready to be picked.

As she filled her baskets, Loretta gave thanks for the fertile soil of the garden, and for the open hearts and true friends they'd made in Willow Ridge. *And be with Will in his time of adjustment, Lord,* she added fervently. *He needs more care than we humans can give him.*

The creak of the back door made her look up. Rosalyn was approaching with a hoe and a smile.

"I *thought* I heard somebody sneaking around in our garden," she teased. "But this time it's not Drew helping himself to our salad greens."

"*Jah*, he won't be doing any more of that," Loretta remarked as her sister began to dig up the wilted row of lettuce. "But we might need to find a hundred and one ways to use all this zucchini! Especially since Dat doesn't like it."

"Dat's snoozing in his recliner," Rosalyn put in quickly. "So it's just you and me enjoying the peace and quiet."

Loretta smiled as the sky darkened around them. Peace and quiet was a bigger blessing than Rosalyn knew, after the tension of her confrontation with Will. "I say we get some ice cream at the café when we're finished here. My treat," she suggested. "I get paid tomorrow, so I'm feeling flush."

And I'm feeling like a big load's been lifted from my shoulders, too, Lord, she added silently. *Denki for Your grace and providence.*

Chapter Eleven

The week passed quickly for Nora. She was pleased that during the three days Loretta had worked so far, whenever she wasn't helping with customers, charming them with her helpfulness and pretty smile, she was busy cutting long, two-inch-wide strips of fabric to prepare for her first rug-making class. Nora suspected the intense August heat was keeping customers at home, but the eight ladies who'd signed up for the first class on the twenty-fifth would fill the shop with chatter. She'd ordered a large cookie tray from Lena Witmer and would offer lemonade and coffee as well. Loretta's students wouldn't be able to eat while they were working on their rugs, but they would welcome refreshments during a break—and it would be nice publicity for Lena when they oohed and aahed over her decorated sugar cookies.

"Are we ready, Loretta?" Nora asked when she came to work on Thursday. "It's your big day, and you're going to be a huge success!"

Loretta appeared a little nervous as she set a basket on the checkout counter. "*Jah*, it'll go well—now that I've got the toothbrushes all filed down with holes in them so each gal gets a needle," she remarked. "I couldn't believe it when Dat fussed over all the toothbrushes I bought. Said it was such a waste to cut new ones down," she added, shaking her head. "I assured him—twice—that I bought them with money from my paycheck. So what could he say?"

Nora had a feeling Cornelius was finding plenty of things to say about his daughter and her new job, but she didn't want to pry. "The ladies in your class will be very grateful that they don't have to make their needles," she said as she took one from Loretta's basket. "Some of them would have trouble cutting off the toothbrush head and filing the end to a point— not to mention cutting the slot in the handle so you can thread the fabric through."

Loretta smiled. "Truth be told, I showed Drew my needle and asked him to make these new ones just like it," she said. "My needle was Mamm's, and I have no idea how she made it, but I figured Drew would have tools in his shop. He made twenty-five needles in about an hour."

"They're filed off nicely, too," Nora said as she ran her finger along the needle's blunt point. "We should keep him in mind when we need small tables and shelves for our displays. The lady who had him fix her old rocking chair called me and went on and on about what a wonderful job he did and how polite he was."

Loretta's cheeks turned pink. "He has a way of pleasing the ladies," she said with a giggle.

The bell above the door jangled before Nora could tease Loretta about her statement. The two English women who came in—a mother and a daughter, by the looks of them—said they'd seen her website and knew Simple Gifts was a store they needed to visit, so Nora gave them a quick tour before letting them browse. By the time she was ringing up the tea towel sets and other table linens they'd selected, Loretta's students were arriving. Nora had set up chairs and a long worktable in the large back room she used for storage, and Loretta had assembled all of her needles and fabric strips there.

"Welcome, ladies!" Nora called out as she folded the linens into a plastic sack. "Go right on into the back room so you can put on a name tag and choose your fabric colors! Loretta's ready, and it's going to be a wonderful afternoon."

"You've got a class today?" the older woman at the counter asked. "What sort of craft?"

"My employee Loretta's going to show our students how to make a rag rug—like that one beside the sleigh bed," Nora added, pointing.

The younger woman gazed through the door where the ladies were choosing their fabric strips. "That looks really cool! Can we watch for a while?"

With a patient smile, Nora handed each of them a flyer about Loretta's classes. She saw no reason to let these two walk-ins receive the same information their paying students would receive. "This class is full, but we have another one on Saturday," she said diplomatically. "Loretta needs to know in advance that you're coming so she can have enough materials ready, you see."

"Great! I'll look this over when I get home and maybe give you a call," the younger woman said as she stuffed the flyer in her sack.

After they left, Nora compared the names on her list to the stick-on tags the attendees wore and introduced Loretta. She decided to return to the main room of the store so Loretta wouldn't feel she was hovering. Once everyone had taken a seat, they got quiet in anticipation. Loretta spoke in a clear voice, standing at the far end of the long table, telling about the toothbrush needles and showing how to fold a fabric strip and guide it through the slot in the end. The women were hanging on her every word, watching and then imitating what Loretta was showing them.

You go, girlie, Nora thought proudly.

As the class continued, Loretta made her way around the table to help her students make the first few stitches that formed the center of the rug—assuring them that this was the trickiest part of the project. "And always remember," Loretta pointed out with a smile, "that if your stitches look uneven or loose, you can pull them out and rework them. Nobody gets it perfect the first time."

Nora sat back on her stool, pleased that her hunch had been correct: Loretta was a natural teacher, patient and confident. Some Amish girls were extremely shy around English people, mostly because their parents and church leaders taught them not to trust outsiders, but Loretta had risen above the fears her autocratic father had instilled in her. Loretta was one of a kind.

After about an hour, the ladies took a break. They exclaimed over the platter of cookies Nora placed on the table and welcomed the coffee and lemonade she'd prepared for them. "How's it going with your rugs?" she asked.

One of the older ladies—Margaret, who frequented the shop—shook her head. "I suspect it'd be a lot easier if my fingers worked the way they did twenty years ago," she said jovially. "But it's a fine thing to try new crafts and learn something that doesn't come easy. Keeps your brain sharp."

"You've already got the sharpest brain I know," Margaret's friend Lucy put in with a laugh. She held up a small circle made of the rounds she'd woven with her toothbrush needle. "The center of my rug would probably be twice this size if I hadn't taken out so many stitches. But Loretta keeps telling us to be patient, so I'm gonna keep at it."

"Loretta's such a nice girl," Sara, a regular customer, chimed in as she joined them with coffee and a cookie. "Offering these classes is a really good idea, Nora. I suspect some of us will have a whole new appreciation of what goes into making the handcrafted items in your store—"

"And we'll buy them instead of trying to make them ourselves!" Sara's friend Jenn said with a laugh. She held up the lumpy center of her rug with a sigh. "I can see that making rag rugs isn't my best talent— but it's not because Loretta isn't giving me excellent help with it."

As Nora circulated among the other women in the class, she heard many similar compliments. A couple of ladies asked for Lena's name and number because they wanted cookies made for anniversary parties, and a few were ready to shop rather than focus on their rugs any longer—which Nora could understand. Making her three-dimensional banners took time and patience, but they went together quickly because she'd been making them for so long. She wasn't sure she'd be any good at making rugs.

Once the class resumed, Nora sat at the checkout counter cutting boy-size straw hats and little *kapp*s in half to use on four new banners she was making. She was pleased with how many of her unique pieces customers had bought, and when she worked on them she entered a pleasant zone of immersion that shut out the rest of the world. When she'd begun making the three-dimensional banners to support herself, working so intently on them had eased the pain of her unexpected divorce.

Nora smiled as she applied liquid glue to the edges she'd cut so they wouldn't fray. Her life with Luke, being his wife and running the store of her dreams, more than made up for the rejection she'd suffered because her first husband had found another woman. It was such a blessing to live near her family again, to have their love and acceptance. Living Plain suited her on a soul-deep level that far surpassed the pleasure of driving the red BMW convertible she'd owned at this time last year.

A burst of conversation in the storage room told Nora the class was letting out. The first few ladies who entered the store's main room appeared happy to be up and moving—and eager to see the items she had in her shop. As Loretta's other students ambled out, they carried their rugs and some extra strips of fabric in plastic bags Nora had provided for them.

"This was really fun, Nora!" Lucy said as she and Margaret passed the checkout counter. "Well worth our time and money. I think I've got the technique down well enough to finish the whole thing this week."

"Loretta's a sweetheart for putting up with us," Margaret said with a chuckle. "I might finish my rug—or I could use what I've woven so far as a nice mat to set under a potted plant."

Nora nodded. "The best thing about most crafts is that you can repurpose whatever doesn't turn out exactly as you'd imagined it," she remarked. "We're so glad you came. Come see us again sometime."

After all the ladies had left the storage area, Loretta joined Nora at the counter. She was smiling, happy to remove tags from the many items her students were buying from the store. When they'd bagged the last set of pot holders and carefully boxed one of the clocks Cornelius had consigned, the store became quiet again.

Nora slipped her arm around Loretta's shoulders. "So how was it? From my vantage point, you looked totally comfortable and capable, and your students adored you—even the ones who discovered that rug making isn't their cup of tea."

Loretta laughed. "*Jah*, a few of them were ready to give up when they couldn't get the beginning knots and the first round to work out," she said. "But they were good-natured about it. And right now I feel totally drained."

"I bet you do," Nora said. "It's amazing how much energy you expend when you're keeping up with so many students who need your help all at the same time. You handled them like a pro, Loretta. I'm really proud of you."

Loretta's pink cheeks glowed. "It was a lot of work, but really gratifying to see the way some of those ladies got the hang of it. One of the younger ones—Vera—had a twelve-inch circle finished and chose enough fabric strips to complete most of her rug."

"Do we need to be making more strips? Or buying more fabric before your Saturday class?" Nora asked. "I'm giving you the rest of the afternoon off—with pay—so if you need to visit the Schrocks' shop, feel free."

Loretta's hazel eyes widened. "But I still have three more hours—"

"And the business you brought into the store today more than paid your wage for that time, sweetie," Nora insisted with a smile. "But then, if you want to work on your fabric strips and stay here where it's cooler, that's fine, too."

Loretta laughed. "*Jah*, there's that. After I drink some lemonade, I'll go buy fabric and come back. Two of my students ordered rugs this morning and specified the colors they wanted."

"See there?" Nora crowed, hugging her. "All that prep work and teaching your class for a couple of hours has really paid off—for both of us."

Loretta poured the last of the lemonade into a glass and drank it down. When she smiled at Nora, her face shone with happiness. "*Denki* for believing in me, Nora," she murmured. "Working in your shop this past week has been a wonderful-*gut* way for me to see a world beyond housework and gardening and canning."

Nora felt a rush of love—a real sense of accomplishment. It wasn't her intention to lure Loretta away from her Old Order faith, but what did it hurt to give the girl a glimpse of other life options from the haven of her store? The Simple Gifts shop was providing income and a craft outlet for many area Plain women, so why shouldn't the Riehl sisters benefit, too?

"Luckily, Rosalyn understands why I love coming here," Loretta said softly, "even if it means she has to do more of the cooking and redding up on the days I work."

Nora nodded. "Tell Rosalyn she's welcome to work

on her wreaths here in the store. Customers would enjoy watching her, and they'll snap them up."

"We'll see about that. I can already tell you that Dat won't go along with it." Loretta set her glass on the counter, recovering her smile. "I'll be back after I buy my fabric. Hope you sell a bunch of stuff while I'm gone!"

When the jingle of the bell above the door had died away, Nora sat in the quiet coolness of her store. She'd known all along that both Riehl girls would catch static from their *dat* if they spent long blocks of time away from home—but Loretta seemed better able to handle it than Rosalyn was.

Nora picked up her phone to leave a message for the head of their household. "Hey there, Cornelius, it's Nora," she began, choosing her words carefully. "I sold another of your clocks today, so I only have one left. I hope you can bring in a few more soon—and I hope you know Loretta did a beautiful job of teaching her class today. She's a fine young woman."

Nora paused, figuring it was best not to elaborate on Loretta's attributes. "Hope you're doing well, Cornelius. Thanks for consigning your clocks in my shop—I'll send your check home with Loretta today. Bye now."

She hung up, wondering what Cornelius's response would be. It didn't bother her one bit that he didn't approve of her Mennonite lifestyle or the way she'd convinced his middle daughter to work away from home three days a week. She didn't want to make trouble for Loretta or Rosalyn, though. Where Cornelius was concerned, it was best to concentrate on selling his clocks at a profit and to stay out of his personal life . . . even if she still wondered why he made so many trips to the city to buy parts.

Some folks are just a mystery, Nora reminded herself. *And some mysteries are best left alone.*

When Loretta arrived for work on Saturday, Rosalyn came along as well. She was pulling a cart with tall sides through the door, and when Nora saw its contents, she was amazed. "How many wreaths have you made?" she asked excitedly. "You picked a great day to bring them, because the twenty ladies taking your sister's rug-making class will be delighted to see them."

Loretta chuckled. "That's what I told her, Nora," she said as she carefully lifted out a grapevine wreath decorated with silk brown-eyed susans and sunflowers.

"Dat went to Kansas City for clock parts early this morning, so I thought it would be a *gut* day to come over," Rosalyn remarked. She breathed deeply, gazing about the store. "Truth be told, it's nice to come into your pretty, air-conditioned store, Nora. Running the canner really heats up the house."

"I hated canning vegetables as a kid, but the past couple of evenings I've been helping my *mamm* put up her tomatoes. It's a lot of hot work," Nora agreed. She held up a wreath Rosalyn had decorated with a calico bow, fresh pine sprigs, cinnamon sticks, and baby's breath, inhaling deeply. "Oh my, this smells *gut*. What a wonderful kitchen wreath!"

Rosalyn smiled shyly, unaccustomed to praise. "Once our garden's more established, I'll have some thyme and bay leaves and other herbs to dry for my wreaths," she remarked as she placed the last one on the countertop. "I hope customers won't mind that I made several with silk flowers this year. Come winter, though, I'll be making fresh pine wreaths."

"They'll all be quick sellers," Nora assured her. "Silk flowers stay pretty a long time, and there's a wide variety of colors, so they'll sell well, too. And what have we here?"

Rosalyn leaned over the side of the cart and removed the towel wrapped around a box-shaped object. "Dat's restored a couple more clocks," she replied. "This one sits on a shelf, and the other one hangs on the wall."

"He's been finding clocks at flea markets and estate sales," Loretta put in as she picked up an oval wall clock. "He was hoping to find a few more today while he's in Kansas City. Here's his price list."

Nora glanced at the invoice with *Riehl Clocks—Riehl Service, Riehl Timely* printed across the top. It sounded as though Cornelius was now finding clocks he could clean up quickly and consign with her—for higher prices than he'd previously charged, she noted immediately—rather than spending as much time making new clocks.

"Let's get these tagged now, before customers come in," she suggested. "And don't undercut what you paid for your materials or how much time it takes you to make a wreath, Rosalyn," she added firmly. "Shoppers gladly pay top dollar, knowing our items are locally made by folks who sell them for an income."

As Nora went into her office for tags and string, her thoughts were buzzing like bees. Why did Cornelius always send his clocks with his daughters instead of dealing directly with her? And why was he consigning these two pieces that appeared cheaply made instead of providing her with the same quality of merchandise he'd had when he first moved to Willow Ridge? If he continued sending clocks that weren't handmade, she would have to remind him of the standards she'd set for her merchandise . . . and perhaps refuse to accept the mass-produced ones.

Nora glanced out at Loretta and Rosalyn, who were such sweet, decent young women and were delighted to be making money from their beautiful rugs and wreaths. She would keep her niggling doubts to herself rather than upset them with her questions, but once again she had to wonder what was going on with Cornelius.

Maybe she was too suspicious . . . but she could recall two earlier visits he'd made to Kansas City this month. How many clock parts could he possibly need? It was a wonder Cornelius got any work done on his clocks when he seemed to spend so much time out of his shop.

Chapter Twelve

As Wyatt pulled his Lexus out of his new acreage and onto the county blacktop, he fought deep, relentless cravings. He felt like a sugar junkie going to visit a bakery knowing he couldn't indulge in doughnuts once he arrived. He'd been telling himself for three endless weeks that he should leave Rebecca alone—should cut his losses and hire another person to design his new website. It was Sunday, September 4. Wyatt hoped Rebecca would be in church so he could avoid the temptation of gazing into her beautiful blue eyes and succumbing to the timbre of her voice, the richness of her laughter, while he cut his ties and left her.

As he drove through the first intersection, he saw a long line of black buggies parked along a lane down the hill from Nora Hooley's gift store. All of the shops were closed, of course, and Willow Ridge seemed to be taking its Sunday afternoon nap. A rainstorm the previous evening had ushered in a cool front, so riding with his top down was a pleasure—except there'd be no way to hide if Rebecca caught sight of him.

Wyatt drove slowly past Zook's Market and the Grill N Skillet, where the windows were dark. Across the road, a couple of hybrid tea rose bushes on either side of the gravel lane burst with large, perfect flowers in a shade of dusky pink he instinctively knew Rebecca would love. On impulse he pulled into the lane and took his Swiss army knife from his pocket. Wyatt helped himself to three of the most perfect blooms, cutting the stems long and carefully avoiding the thorns. The bushes were so loaded with fragrant roses, their owner would never know he'd taken any.

At least I'll have a peace offering, he thought as he slipped back into his car. *Maybe she'll give me points for choosing blooms as flawless as her face.*

At the next intersection, the road off to his right ran past the Brenneman cabinetry shop and the newer Detweiler Furniture Works. Rebecca's house was only a quarter of a mile away. His insides twitched with the adolescent need to chicken out of this challenge, to turn around and return to the new trailer he'd parked on his property, but he convinced himself to keep on driving past the small clinic on the corner.

A forty-year-old man shouldn't have to play mind games with himself.

Wyatt let out a humorless laugh. He should be able to face a woman who was young enough to be his daughter—if he'd sired her in high school, anyway—without fearing that she'd consider him unworthy at best and worthless at worst. He'd dealt with all sorts of women all his life, and people said he had a way with them.

Yet Rebecca spooked him. After spending only a couple of hours with her, he'd fallen under the spell of her unassuming presence—*No, you fell in love with her,* the voice in his head taunted him. His mind told him that a relationship with her was an emotional train wreck waiting to happen—for both of them—but his body and soul weren't listening.

Here's one for you: you've bought property in a very small town where everyone will know your business. Do you really think you can avoid seeing Rebecca, even if you're not her client? For all you know, she's already told everyone you stood her up . . .

Despite his warring thoughts, the rural landscape soothed him. The tidy patchwork of Amish farms seemed a world away from the old-money establishment and social climbing that pervaded the world of horse breeding and racing in Lexington and Saratoga Springs. In Willow Ridge, the locals were simple and sincere. The air smelled fresh, and only the calling of crows broke the stillness around him. A deer grazing near a small creek lifted its head to gaze at him. Willow Ridge felt like a pristine paradise, and when he'd purchased his tract of land here, he'd known immediately that he wanted to relocate.

But he had to deal with his feelings for Rebecca. It wasn't right to put her off so unfairly. Remaining cool and detached when he told her he'd found another website designer was the key. It was a lie—but so was telling himself he could stop wanting her.

When her cozy red brick home came into view, Wyatt slowed the car. Rebecca was leaning over in her front flower bed, wearing a pink tank top and matching knit shorts that left nothing to his imagination.

She's not dressed this way to tantalize you, idiot. If she'd known you were coming, she'd be fully covered—and probably baring her claws.

Wyatt swallowed hard. He had a feeling Rebecca wouldn't appreciate his showing up out of the blue, catching her in her grubbies, when he'd tucked a white silk shirt into designer jeans. He pulled into her driveway, though, figuring it was best to settle this situation. Rebecca's glare and scathing remarks would keep him in his place, and he'd say what he had to before making the most dignified exit she would allow him.

He deserved her rancor. He deserved to flinch and grimace after Rebecca told him exactly how disappointed she was with him because he'd stood her up.

At the sound of his car's approach, Rebecca straightened to her full height. The moment she recognized him, her eyes widened with surprise and she tossed her gardening claw down to cross her arms. The set of her jaw told him he would have to speak first, and choose his words well.

Wyatt smiled, feigning confidence. He'd been handling high-maintenance mares most of his life, so why should this delightfully disheveled filly present any problems he couldn't handle? Rebecca's brown hair appeared uncombed and she wore no makeup . . . as though she'd just gotten out of bed. The thought made his pulse pound, and he was so focused on her that when he grabbed the roses on the seat, a thorn punctured the pad of his thumb.

"Ah, *crap!*" Wyatt saw the blood seeping around the embedded thorn and kissed his businesslike intentions goodbye. He opened his car door and carefully held his injured hand and the roses away from himself to avoid staining his white shirt. He was at Rebecca's mercy now. And the way she was glaring at him was anything but merciful.

Wyatt shook his head, imploring her compassion. "This wasn't how I'd planned to make my entrance,

Rebecca," he said sheepishly. "It seems I'm going to need a Band-Aid—"

"That's what you get for cutting Mamma's roses," she blurted out. With one eyebrow raised, she looked dispassionately at his bleeding thumb. "If this is your way of worming yourself into my home—begging for my pity—you'd better go back to wherever you came from. You can do better than this after three weeks of avoiding me, Mr. McKenzie."

Wyatt was ready to defend himself, but Rebecca spoke before he could. "Okay, so it's only been twenty days, but who's counting?" she protested sarcastically. "Every day of your rude, inconsiderate silence has been piling up like manure. You deserve to be shoveled out, got it?"

A large drop of blood dripped from his thumb, yet she showed no inclination to take the roses he was holding toward her. Wyatt eased out the thorn, wincing as he pressed the wound hard against his fingertip to stanch the bleeding. "All right, I deserved that," he murmured.

"And what do *I* deserve?" Rebecca demanded in a voice that wavered slightly. "I think I'll go inside now and act as though you didn't stand me up and then send that ridiculously extravagant bouquet of roses as your unacceptable excuse for disappearing."

When she started up the porch steps, Wyatt was close on her heels. "I can explain! I'll show you why I was tied up at my Lexington farm—" He barely caught the door before she slammed it on him.

Rebecca turned on Wyatt before he had both feet in her living room. "And this explanation is something you couldn't have shared with me earlier?" she demanded. "In this age of technology, you surely could've called or emailed or texted me, Mr. McKenzie.

Get your hand under the faucet before you bleed all over my carpet."

When she pointed toward the kitchen, Wyatt knew better than to wheedle. As he passed her dining room table, the huge arrangement of shriveled, dead roses in its center told him precisely what Rebecca thought of him. He set the pink roses on the counter beside the kitchen sink and ran water over his bleeding thumb. The thorn had come completely out, so the wound was clean, but his situation with Rebecca felt like it might seep raw emotions for a long while.

Several minutes passed. Wyatt was beginning to wonder if Rebecca had abandoned him—maybe left the house through a back way—when she entered the kitchen. Her hair was combed, she'd powdered her freckled nose, and she wore denim cut-offs with an old black T-shirt that was baggy enough to camouflage her attractive figure. Not that it kept his desire at bay.

But this was no time to flirt or slather on the sweet talk. When she tossed a tube of ointment and a box of Band-Aids onto the counter beside him, Wyatt knew he was on his own as far as dressing his wound. He tore off a section from a paper towel roll, reminding himself that he'd tended far more serious cuts without assistance . . . Yet he was more humbled by his deep craving for Rebecca's touch than by her earlier scathing words or her current chilly silence.

"Rebecca, I've been a horse's ass, telling myself to stay away from you," he muttered, pressing the crumpled paper towel against his wound. "Fact is, you scare the—the living *heck* out of me."

Her abrupt laughter echoed in the kitchen. Wyatt chided himself for allowing his confession to come out unchecked, even if this was the first time he'd accurately framed his feelings. It made no sense that a man of his experience and means should cower before this young woman, but there it was: *fear.* He was afraid of feelings he couldn't corral or control, because he knew that Rebecca, in her unassuming way, held the reins of this relationship in her small yet capable hands.

"Wyatt, you can cuss in front of me—but cuss like you mean it." Rebecca sounded exasperated with him. "I'd rather hear you state your true intentions—the way you really feel—than suspect you're pussyfooting around behind pretty words and false promises. With me, honesty counts."

Wyatt sighed. Her cornflower eyes challenged him to man up, to keep her in the loop of his thoughts and emotions—not that he'd ever allowed a woman that sort of access to him. "All right," he began softly, "what I really want is for you to help me with this puncture wound. Then I'll show you why I couldn't be in Willow Ridge to have dinner with you. And then I hope we can discuss my website. Strictly business."

Liar, liar, pants on fire, his thoughts taunted. *Accent on the* fire *part.*

Rebecca tried not to fall for the little-boy plea in his voice, yet she hoped the *strictly business* part was only a facade Wyatt was hiding behind to protect his pride. A man in his position didn't knuckle under to a simple prick from a thorn, nor did he allow a small-town graphic designer to buffalo him. Why was he afraid of her?

Rebecca reminded herself not to fall prey to his masculine appeal, his resonant voice, or his perfectly cut hair and chiseled chin, either—not after the way he'd left her hanging. The longer she stood trapped in his blue-gray gaze, however, the easier it would be to pretend he hadn't hurt her deeply. She reached for the tube of ointment.

"Just so you know," Rebecca said as she unscrewed the cap, "those specialty rosebushes you robbed were a gift to my mother from her husband, Ben Hooley, the local farrier. He's a fellow whose favor you might want to cultivate—unless you plan to bring your own staff to tend your horses' needs."

Wyatt extended his hand, palm up, as though inviting her to place her hand in his. Rebecca reminded herself that this was strictly first-aid business and focused on the small red slit in the pad of his thumb. She slipped her hand under his to support it, also reminding herself to ignore the little shimmer of awareness that made her arm tingle.

"I've met Ben. He's one of the reasons I bought land here for my new horse farm," Wyatt murmured. "Thanks for the heads-up on your family connection, though. And thanks for your medical assistance. I'm right-handed, so when it comes to getting a Band-Aid secured correctly with my left hand, I'm, uh, all thumbs."

Rebecca smiled. He seemed to be coming off his high horse. "I suspect I won't often see you in a dependent, submissive frame of mind," she teased, "so I should milk this moment for all it's worth."

"Don't bet on it. I'm putty in your hands, Rebecca."

His words did funny things to her stomach. When she looked up, Wyatt was gazing at her as though his life depended on her. "You say that to all the girls," she shot back.

"There aren't any others. Which is why I should

treat you with a lot more respect and consideration than I've shown lately." Wyatt's hand relaxed in hers as she squeezed a small dab of the ointment on the wound. "I'm really sorry I didn't call you, Rebecca. Is there any way we can start over?"

Her eyebrow rose. She released his hand to cap the ointment and take a Band-Aid from the box. "Is this how you'll always handle relationship mistakes, Wyatt? You'll ask for a do-over, as though you can simply erase the rough spots from my memory?" Rebecca asked in a purposeful tone. "I'm not feeling the love here."

As she turned to tear away the bandage's wrapper, Wyatt gently caught her face in his left hand. He kissed her ever so softly before moving in to explore her mouth with tender thoroughness.

Rebecca's thoughts blared like sirens, warning of impending disaster, but her body was following the most basic of instincts that Wyatt had called up with his kiss. When he eased away, his blue-gray eyes suggested that he was as surprised as she was that he'd taken hold of her—but he wasted no time before kissing her again. He pulled her close, cradling her in his left arm, making her aware of how perfectly they fit together and how long it had been since a guy had kissed her.

Not that Wyatt could be considered a mere guy. He was a man, fully conscious of what he was doing to her—and leaving no doubt about where this kiss was leading them.

Despite her best businesslike intentions, Rebecca realized she was now the dependent, submissive one. She stepped away from him with a sigh that sounded far too needy. "So—about this Band-Aid. Let me just unwrap—"

"Rebecca." Wyatt's voice enveloped her like a gossamer web.

When she looked at him, his eyes reflected the same desire that her flushed face was no doubt broadcasting. "Yeah?"

He smiled furtively. "Will you come to my farm—to take pictures for the new website?" he added quickly.

She rolled her eyes as she peeled the protective strips from the bandage. "Why does this sound like an updated version of *Wanna come upstairs and see my etchings?*"

Wyatt laughed. "You're too young to know about that old come-on—"

"I'm old enough to know what you're doing—and what you're after," Rebecca stated firmly. "Quit wiggling."

Wyatt held very still as Rebecca deftly secured the Band-Aid over his injury. "Thank you for being my nurse," he whispered. He framed her face with his hands. "I *am* after you, Rebecca. I want you—as a site designer and a whole lot more," he added quickly. "Is that all right with you?"

His husky baritone voice sent all rational thought out the window. When Wyatt held her gaze with his mesmerizing eyes, Rebecca feared—yet yearned for—everything this man seemed to be promising her.

Was she reading too much into Wyatt's innuendo? Maybe he was only making a bid for sex rather than implying an emotional commitment. Despite her doubts, however, she nodded. Rebecca sensed that although she could fire back snappy one-liners to keep him at arm's length, deep down she was fascinated by Wyatt . . . and a lifestyle that was so completely different from her upbringing.

"Oh, thank God," he murmured as he hugged her hard. "For a moment there, I thought I'd really stepped in it. No fool like an *old* fool."

Rebecca leaned back against his arm to study his handsome face, daring to trace the laugh lines around his beguiling eyes with her fingertip. "Okay, so you're older than I am," she murmured. "But—"

"By eighteen years, if my math's correct," Wyatt interrupted softly.

"—what I really want to know is why *me?*" she continued before she lost her nerve. "I'm just a small-town, small-time designer who surely won't fit into your sophisticated world—your upper-crust lifestyle—"

He gently placed a finger across her lips to silence her. "A change of attitude can change a person's world, sweetheart. When I set foot in Willow Ridge, so steeped in its Amish simplicity, I realized my life was due for a major renovation," he explained. "Meeting you was all the more reason to risk going in a whole new direction. At an age when most men are satisfied to settle in, I suddenly feel compelled to start fresh—with you."

"It's too soon to be saying that, Wyatt," Rebecca protested, even though she wanted to believe him.

He shrugged. "You asked me to be honest," he reminded her. "Does this conversation scare me? Damn straight, it does. I came here with the intention of breaking away from you, Rebecca, but in less than an hour you've convinced me that I'll regret it if I don't try to win you over."

Rebecca could only stare. Wyatt was holding her gaze, sounding totally sincere yet appearing as vulnerable as she felt. He had a boyish sense of adventure about him that appealed to her, and she suddenly wanted to experience life from a different perspective than any she'd ever been offered. "All right, let's give it a shot," she murmured. "But if either of us reaches a point where we want to put on the brakes—or it's not feeling comfortable—we're going to say so. Right?"

He let out the breath he'd been holding. "I can live with that. I don't see it happening, though."

Rebecca fought a grin. "There's a lot we don't know about each other, Wyatt. Give me enough time, and I'll make you feel mortified and appalled and exasperated—maybe all at once."

"That could work both ways." Wyatt's smile lit up the kitchen as he pulled his cell phone from his hip pocket. "Here they are—Rachel and Rhoda, the twins that were being born the Friday night I couldn't get here," he said as he held the phone so she could see it. "They came early, and their mother's built small, so I needed to be there with the vet to be sure my mare and her foals made it through the birth all right."

Rebecca blinked. The knobby-kneed bay fillies that filled his screen took her breath away, but their names bore no resemblance to the high-class monikers of the other McKenzie horses she'd seen online. "Why on earth did you name them after my sisters?" she asked. "I mean, I'm assuming you did."

Wyatt scrolled down to another photo, and another, obviously delighted with the beautiful young creatures. "For one thing, they're twins," he replied lightly. "But mostly, I wanted names that sounded appealing and down-to-earth—something different from the high-falutin names you hear at the racetrack."

Rebecca busied herself with throwing away the

loose bandage papers on her countertop. "I guarantee you those fillies will be a lot higher-maintenance than my Plain sisters," she said with a laugh.

"They symbolize a major change—a decision to move in a different direction with my horses . . . with my life," Wyatt said softly. "While I was acquiring my other two farms over the years, I was in it for the status—the thrill of breeding and racing fine horses only an elite clientele can afford."

Rebecca remained silent, waiting for the other conversational shoe to drop. Even though he'd clearly stated his interest in her, gazing at online pictures of Wyatt with his trophies, ribbons, and well-heeled cohorts—some of them female—had given her the idea that he was deeply ensconced in the high society of high-dollar horses. The wistfulness of his admission puzzled her.

Wyatt gazed at the photos on his phone. "But it's time to step away from that upward spiral of pressure," he said. "I'm tired of trying to outdo myself, and tired of being in constant competition for higher prizes. I just want to breed and sell reliable horses."

Rebecca's eyes widened. "You want to get out of racing?"

"Yup." The pupils of his eyes were large and dark as he looked at her. "I can ease my way out at the end of this season—or just sell those horses outright."

His "easy come, easy go" attitude surprised her. "What'll you do with your farms in Kentucky and New York?" she asked cautiously. "If you've spent your life building up your reputation with Thoroughbreds—"

"There's something to be said for horses that pull their weight," he put in with a dreamlike sigh. "Last time I was here, I watched a young man driving a hitch of the tallest, darkest mules I've ever seen, and I was struck by their beauty. Their purpose."

She smiled. "Those are Percheron mules, and Luke Hooley got them from a fellow over in Bloomingdale. Most of the other farmers hereabouts favor Belgians."

"From what I've heard and researched, nobody's raising draft horses in this area," Wyatt said. "Now that I own a farm in a Plain area, why shouldn't I provide the animals these folks need?"

"They often buy retired racehorses and train them to pull their buggies," Rebecca pointed out. "Pride is a sin among the Amish, but the men hereabouts indulge themselves in some fine-looking horseflesh. You probably know that, though," she added quickly.

"I value your insight. I know you're giving me pertinent information instead of trying to impress me or sell me something." Wyatt slipped his phone back into his pocket. "I have someone who can take over my other two places—or I can sell them. And I have some horses that are ready to retire from racing, so you've just given me an opportunity to provide them a useful life."

He inhaled deeply, refusing to lower his gaze. "Meanwhile, I'd really like to show you my acreage— ask your opinion about where to put the corrals and barns. And the house."

Rebecca stood absolutely still, afraid that if she breathed, the threads of this fairy tale Wyatt was weaving her into would drift apart like dandelion silk in the breeze. She sensed he sincerely wanted her thoughts—that he wasn't just sweet-talking her.

Red flags were waving wildly in her mind, however, reminding her that she'd only spent a few hours in this man's company. *And don't forget how he vanished without a trace of contact for three weeks.*

Rebecca proceeded cautiously. At this point, she didn't know what else to do. "I—I don't know the first thing about horses," she admitted.

"And I don't understand enough about the Amish culture to be able to contribute to the neighborhood," Wyatt said as he took her hand. "Once again we're equals. Partners. I won't have it any other way, Rebecca."

When he kissed her again, she knew there would be no resisting Wyatt McKenzie. She might get burned, and she might find out she didn't fit into his world—but she wouldn't know that—or discover a life such as she'd only dreamed of before—unless she went along for the ride.

Chapter Thirteen

Drew walked Loretta home after church and the common meal at the Wagler place had ended, feeling particularly gratified as he held her hand. It was September 4, nearly five months after he'd first set foot in Willow Ridge, and folks around town were accepting him as a neighbor—and beginning to consider him and Loretta a couple. Will was acting friendlier and more relaxed, too. He'd even come over to talk with them before they'd left, which was a notable improvement over the way he'd stalked off the day Drew had carried lemonade to him.

"Do you suppose Will's got a girlfriend?" Drew asked as the vineyard came into view. New metal fence posts and wires caught the afternoon sunlight, forming shiny silver pinstripes across the plowed brown earth.

Loretta shrugged. "I have no idea. Why do you ask?"

Drew smiled to himself. Loretta appeared demure, holding the empty basket in which she'd taken muffins for the noon meal, but the quick flash in her hazel eyes said she knew more than she was going to tell him. "Will seems happier now. More at peace," he suggested.

"Luke might've had a heart-to-heart with him," Loretta hedged. "And maybe he's gotten some counseling to help him deal with Molly's passing."

Drew nodded. He still suspected Loretta wasn't giving him the whole story, but he didn't quiz her, because she seemed much more relaxed in Will's presence. He certainly understood why the circumstances of Molly's passing would eat at Will, and he hoped Gingerich was on the mend emotionally. It would be a relief—for him and Loretta both—when her former fiancé finally moved beyond his abrasive behavior.

The breeze whispered in the evergreen windbreak, giving Drew a tempting idea. "How about cutting around behind these trees?" he asked, gesturing toward the tall, dense spruces. "I'd like to get a *gut* look at the Hooleys' new vineyard now that the stakes and wires are all in place."

Loretta's knowing expression told him she saw through his excuse. "You probably have an excellent view of the vineyard from your upstairs apartment— but what could it hurt to stand in the shade for a bit?" she teased. "It's a pretty day, and I'm in no hurry to go home. Dat left the common meal early, which probably means he's in a sour mood—or secretly working in his clock shop on Sunday."

"Let's go," Drew whispered, his heart racing as Loretta jogged beside him. Once they were behind the windbreak, hidden from the view of anyone on the road or at the Riehl house, he turned and pulled her into his arms. "Kissing you was on my mind all during church, Loretta," he murmured. "I have no idea what Preacher Ben's sermon was about."

"God was listening to your wicked thoughts, you know." Giggling, Loretta let go of her basket. She stood on tiptoe to wrap her arms around his neck.

Drew reveled in the sensation of holding her warm, shapely body against his as he pressed his lips to hers. She responded eagerly, playfully, making him moan with desire. Loretta seemed as needy as he was—and more responsive than usual—and after all the torture he could handle, Drew eased her away. "Whoa," he said breathlessly. "Let's come up for some air, sugar. A man can only stand so much."

Loretta stepped out of his embrace, a question furrowing her brow as she turned away. Drew immediately regretted the disappointment he'd caused her, but she was unaware of the physical effect she had on him—naive about the ways of men and women.

"Was Molly really pretty?" she asked wistfully. "If—if you loved her, maybe I'm a poor substitute for—"

"It's not that way!" Drew insisted. He stood behind her, loosely holding her shoulders. "She was nothing like you, Loretta. Molly was attractive, *jah*, but she was also a tease and a heartbreaker. She played me false."

"But you . . . knew her, in the biblical sense."

Drew closed his eyes against an onslaught of memories. He'd loved Molly with all his being and had given himself to her with every intention of marrying her—only to be rejected and then left in the dark about her pregnancy. "*Jah*, that's how Leroy and Louisa came about," he said softly. "And before you say any more, my answer is *no*. I'm not going to bed you, and bundling isn't an accepted practice in Willow Ridge, so—"

"How do you know that?" Loretta protested, turning to face him. "I have these—these *feelings* for you, and I want to find out where they lead. Edith looks so happy now that she's married . . ."

Drew swallowed hard. Was Loretta asking him to make love to her? "Think about it," he began hesitantly. "It's September, and your room upstairs is too hot for one of us to lie under the covers on your bed while we cuddle. And you've told me your *dat* has a way of showing up before you know he's there. If he found us together that way, he'd put me out—and forbid me to see you anymore."

Loretta sighed. "*Jah*, there's that. I'm just curious about such things, and Mamm's not around to answer my questions."

Drew considered his options. He doubted that most Amish mothers imparted explicit details about sex, even on the eve of a daughter's marriage. More likely, if Loretta's *mamm* were still alive, she would sketch things out using vague terminology and allow nature to take its course—*after* the wedding. A daughter's dabbling in premarital pleasure was a sin, after all.

"You're a beautiful young woman, Loretta," he whispered. "I want you, too, but we've got to be responsible. I'm not going to have folks whispering about you—the women, especially—because they think I've taken advantage of your innocence."

"Innocence is highly overrated!" she blurted out.

Drew bit back a laugh, because in some ways she was right. Loretta's cheeks blazed, and her full lips beckoned him. It would be so easy, so satisfying to lie down in the shady seclusion of the evergreens and gently teach her what she wanted to know . . .

"It's a matter of honor," he said in the steadiest voice he could manage. "Everyone knows I was with Molly, but I don't want you to suffer the same fate—the same dubious reputation she got when they realized—"

"There are ways to be careful," Loretta stated uncertainly. "Right?"

Drew exhaled hard. He'd never expected to be explaining the intimacies a man shared with a woman, much less delving into matters of birth control. "*Jah*, but you have to anticipate—to be prepared beforehand. I'm *not*, and we're not starting down that path, either, Loretta," he said in the strongest voice he could muster. "Folks—especially your *dat*—will notice the change in your behavior, the same way you've seen a difference in Edith since she and Asa got married."

"*Jah*, I'll look radiantly happy," Loretta said with a sigh. "Is that such a bad thing?"

"It is when we're not married," Drew replied in a terser tone than he'd intended. He inhaled deeply, but he needed more than fresh air to settle him. "I'm sorry to be such a killjoy, sweetheart. But I've been down that road, and I'm not taking you down it with me. Please try to understand," he pleaded. "I'm doing this for you."

Loretta appeared unconvinced, and his heart went out to her.

"After we're married—if we get married—wild horses won't be able to keep me away from you," Drew said. He died a little when his choice of words made her turn away from him again.

"Maybe I should go home now," Loretta whispered. "If there's a question about whether you'll marry me, I'll only embarrass both of us if I stay, ain't so?"

Drew watched sadly as she strode away. How had their enticing flirtation ended on such a sour note? Loretta was on the other side of the evergreens before he realized she'd forgotten her basket, but he thought better of following her to give it back. She was upset, stewing over more questions than he'd been willing to answer, and it seemed best to let her cool down.

IF we get married? What possessed you to plant such a doubt in her mind?

Sighing, Drew started for home. He'd been seeing Loretta for nearly a month, and he was pretty sure she was the woman he wanted for a wife. After the way he'd fallen too quickly for fickle, flirtatious Molly, however, he was wary of committing to marriage so soon—he saw the advantage of a long courtship, even though he'd desired Loretta ever since they'd met. Drew hadn't popped the question, but Loretta had always seemed hopeful, assuming he wanted to marry her, ever since the afternoon he'd lured her off the front porch away from Will.

Drew paused across the road from the Riehl house. Rather than return the basket and discover he was unwelcome, he decided to check the answering machine in the phone shanty he and Asa shared with the Riehls. Sometimes customers left messages about pieces of furniture they were having restored—and English folks often called on Sunday afternoon.

The little white building by the roadside was only large enough for one person to be seated in front of the small phone table, on a hard wooden chair that didn't inspire folks to chat for very long. If the original owner hadn't built a window into its back wall, it would be a stiflingly hot place to hold summertime conversations. As Drew approached the shanty, he heard a man talking.

"Be here by six tomorrow morning, and don't honk your horn," he was saying. "I'll be waiting for you—and *jah*, we'll be out all day, as usual."

Drew's eyes widened. The covert tone of Cornelius's voice made him step to the side of the little white building, where he wouldn't be visible through the glass of the door.

"If tomorrow won't work, then come on Tuesday," Cornelius continued impatiently. "There are plenty of other drivers I can call if you can't—won't—accommodate me."

Drew held his breath, sensing he'd better be on his way before Loretta's *dat* discovered him eavesdropping. Why did he suspect Cornelius had left the noon meal at the Wagler place so no one would hear him placing this call?

"Fine. Six o'clock Tuesday morning. There'll be a nice tip in it for you."

When Drew heard the receiver being slammed into its cradle, he dropped the basket beside the shanty and sprinted behind the tall, old lilac bush that grew beside the Riehls' front porch. He peered through its leafy green branches, waiting for Loretta's burly *dat* to come out. Cornelius would demand an explanation if he suspected Drew had overheard his conversation, so before the other man left the shanty, Drew hurried along the side of the Riehl house.

The basement windows were open so air could circulate through the screens, and on an impulse he stooped to peer inside. Recalling that Loretta had told him Cornelius's clock shop was on the front side of the house, Drew located the workshop's closed door. He also noticed the shelves of jarred vegetables along one wall and the large open area that could accommodate the district's pew benches when the Riehls hosted a church service.

He felt sneaky and dishonest, yet something about Cornelius's terse phone conversation—and the fact that his workshop door was closed in such hot weather—raised red flags in his mind. As Drew quickly made his way across the Riehls' backyard, heading toward the row of trees at their property line, he wavered about what to do next. Was it really any of his business, how Loretta's *dat* operated—how often he left town? Surely Bishop Tom, along with Preachers Ben and Henry, felt confident about Cornelius's ability to manage the responsibilities he'd assumed when he'd moved here last spring and replaced Reuben Riehl as the district's deacon. And yet . . .

If you don't say something, who will? Loretta and her sisters might not know what he's up to—and wouldn't dare speak up, even if they suspected something was amiss.

Drew jogged across the parking lot behind the Grill N Skillet. Down the road a ways, buggies still lined the Waglers' lane. Men sat in lawn chairs in the shade while kids laughed and played in the yard. He should probably confer with the bishop or Ben, yet Drew sensed that the other men would see his concerned expression and want to be in on his conversation with the church's leaders.

What if your assumptions are all wrong? What if you stir up a hornet's nest of suspicion when Cornelius is just going about his clock business?

Drew paused behind Zook's Market to catch his breath and consider his options. When he saw Nora's black van parked behind the big white house on the hill, he knew what he should do. A few minutes later he was knocking on the Hooleys' front door, hoping Luke and Nora could lend some perspective to his doubts about Loretta's *dat.*

* * *

When Nora heard someone pounding on the door, she lowered the recliner's footrest and went to answer it. Luke was indulging in a Sunday afternoon nap, stretched out on the couch with his head on a cushion and his bare feet dangling over the other end, so he hadn't heard the knock. As she padded across the cool hardwood floor, she checked the position of the small, circular *kapp* that covered her bun, in case someone from the Mennonite church was stopping by for an unexpected visit. It seemed that while she'd been reading the paper, she might've nodded off for a bit, too.

The sight of Drew brought her fully awake. Nora smiled, opening the door. "What's on *your* mind, young man?" she teased. "I thought you'd be keeping Loretta company on this fine afternoon."

Was that a hint of regret flickering across his lips? As Drew stepped inside, he cleared his throat. "I was with Loretta earlier, *jah*," he replied. "But I've heard something that bothers me, and I hope you and Luke can help me make sense of it."

Nora's eyes widened. Had Will been giving Loretta a hard time again, even after he'd talked with Luke and visited the counselor Andy Leitner had recommended? "Let me give Luke a nudge," she said as she preceded Drew into the front room, picking up loose newspapers as she went. "We get a little lazy after we come home from church."

With a folded section of the paper, Nora tickled her snoozing husband's nose. "We've got company," she announced loudly. "I'll go pour us some iced tea while you finish waking up."

Luke's eyes flew open, and when he saw Drew

standing behind her, he swung his feet down and sat up.

Nora went to the kitchen and quickly arranged some store-bought cookies on a plate before setting glasses and a pitcher of tea on a tray. It seemed awfully soon for Drew to be asking their advice about taking his courtship of Loretta a step further—and Drew's expression hadn't suggested that he was on such a happy, hopeful mission, anyway. When she returned to the front room, the men were discussing the work Luke and Will had been doing to prepare for planting the vineyard next spring.

"Ira and I have decided to raise table grapes," Luke was saying. He flashed her a smile, completely unaware that his hair was standing on end in the back. "Lots of small, private vineyards and wine labels have sprung up in central Missouri over the past fifteen years, and small-time guys like us can't compete with them—so we'll offer a couple of varieties folks can either eat or use to make juice and jelly."

"*Jah*, we wouldn't want our neighbors to start making wine," Nora said lightly. "That would be leading them into temptation." She set her tray on the coffee table and poured a glass of tea for Drew.

When he accepted the glass, his expression waxed pensive. "I'm really intrigued about your new venture, Luke. You seem to succeed with every project you undertake." He took a long drink of his tea. "I, um, heard something a few minutes ago that makes me wonder what Cornelius is up to, however, and I'd like you to keep this to yourselves. I may be way off base, and I don't want folks getting the wrong idea."

Nora's eyes widened. "What did you hear?" she asked as she handed Luke his tea. "I have a few suspicions about him myself. He seems to make a lot of trips to

Kansas City to buy clock parts. And frankly, the two clocks he sent over with the girls yesterday aren't nearly as nice as the ones he was consigning at first. They're obviously mass-produced and cheap."

Drew nodded. "After I walked Loretta home, I was going to check my phone messages," he began. "The shanty window was open, and Cornelius was talking to a driver, pretty much demanding that he show up at six tomorrow morning—and not honk his horn. When all was said and done, he agreed to go on Tuesday morning instead, but—well, it just seemed odd."

"How was it odd?" Luke asked. He stirred sugar into his tea, noisily clinking the sides of his glass with his spoon. "I may have a few details to add as we go along."

Drew shook his head slowly. "He sounded extremely pushy with the guy he was talking to—not that his tone was any different from the way he talks to Loretta and Rosalyn," he added with a sigh. "I don't know. I can recall seeing him from my apartment really early in the morning at least a couple of times over the past month. He's been waiting in front of the house with a big case of some sort. An English guy in an old green van picks him up, and he's gone all day."

"We could assume that the case is where he puts the clock parts he buys," Luke said, but he didn't sound convinced.

"Or we can assume that Cornelius is doing something totally unrelated to his clock business," Nora put in, thinking back. "A few months ago I found an old invoice in a clock he consigned. When I called the elderly lady whose name was on it, she told me that after Cornelius had seen her husband's obituary, he'd tried the pass the clock off as a surprise gift her husband had ordered right before he'd died. And of course he'd expected the lady to pay for it—but she'd realized it was a scam and sent him packing."

Drew frowned. "Why would a clockmaker take advantage of a widow that way? He's the only fellow for miles around who works on clocks, so he's surely making a *gut* income without cheating people."

"Just between you, us, and the coffee table," Luke said as he knocked on the wood, "I once overheard a conversation between Bishop Tom and Ben about the way Cornelius has placed his workbench against the doorway where . . . well, it's where the district's emergency funds are kept," he added cautiously. "They were concerned about how to access that money if Cornelius was out of town when they needed some of it. But they were giving him the benefit of the doubt, as far as his being the district's deacon— the keeper of their funds."

Nora's thoughts spun faster. The more she heard, the more she suspected an unsavory situation. "I grew up as a preacher's kid here—my *dat*, Gabe Glick, was a church leader before he retired," she added for Drew's benefit. "I didn't know where the church money was kept—very few folks do, because it's considered a secret bank. Over the years, catching bits of conversation when Bishop Hiram Knepp and Preacher Jesse Lantz and my *dat* were in charge, I came to the conclusion that the collected offerings and special contributions had added up to a *phenomenal* amount of money."

"I grew up in Lancaster County," Luke remarked, nodding at Drew, "and now that I'm a businessman, I remain amazed—*appalled*—that so many Amish folks still have a distrust of English banks. When somebody's house burns down or a family has sky-high medical bills, the district's emergency fund covers it—like an unwritten insurance policy for folks who don't believe in English insurance. And all that money is kept at a church member's home."

"*Jah*, that's the way it works where we Detweilers come from, too," Drew said. "We grew up with the understanding that the district's money was kept someplace secret that only the church leaders knew about, so the other members wouldn't be tempted—or able—to dip into it."

Luke drained his glass and set it on the table with an emphatic *clunk*. "I have reason to believe that some districts have hundreds of thousands of dollars—or more—squirreled away to cover unexpected needs. Why would Willow Ridge be any different?"

Nora bit her lip, uncomfortable with the ideas that were forming in her mind. "So if we believe this district's money is in the basement of the Riehl home, where Cornelius has his shop—and he's put his workbench in front of the door where it's stored—"

"Then we might have *gut* reason to be suspicious about all these trips he's making to Kansas City," Luke finished her sentence. "I'm not a member of the Amish church, but I don't like the sound of this. Truth be told, I don't trust Cornelius any farther than I could throw him. He talks loud, and intimidates his daughters, and I've always wondered if he's hiding something. Now I believe he is."

Nora sighed. "On the one hand, we didn't join the Old Order, so this matter is none of our business—"

"But I can assure you that my brother Ben would want to know about these goings-on," Luke interrupted her. "I feel it's our responsibility to share our suspicions with him. If Cornelius has been playing fast and loose with the district's money—"

"We don't know that," Drew chimed in. "I just had a funny feeling when I overheard his phone conversation. Maybe we should verify our suspicions somehow before we take them to Bishop Tom and Preacher Ben."

Draining her glass, Nora considered Drew's remark. "What if . . . what if you and I followed Cornelius and his driver in my van?" she murmured. "Loretta works on Tuesdays, so if I ask her to run the store because I have an out-of-town errand, she won't suspect why I'm gone. And if the girls know their *dat*'s going to Kansas City for clock parts, I'm betting Rosalyn will join Loretta in the store. They'll be fine."

"I can look in on them, too," Luke said in a thoughtful tone. "But what if the driver realizes you're tailing him? It's not like a lot of folks drive a black van without any chrome."

Nora arched an eyebrow at him. "I used to drive a red BMW, remember? And I managed to avoid all the cops who were out looking to ticket fast red cars," she added as the idea grew on her. "The van Cornelius rides in will go right past the mill, heading north to the city, so we can be waiting—ready to pull out after he gets past our intersection."

Luke considered this. "Actually, from our hill you'll be able to see that green van when it pulls away from the Riehl place," he mused aloud. "But what'll happen if you lose him in city traffic?"

Nora shrugged. "With Drew helping me keep that van in sight, we'll have two sets of eyes on it," she said. "And it's not like I'm a total stranger to Kansas City. My ex and his family lived on the Kansas side, in Shawnee Mission, but I learned to drive on some of the nearby highways that went near the Plaza and in the downtown area. I've got it covered."

"And that green van's easy to spot," Drew said, sounding more enthusiastic as they fleshed out their plan. "The back bumper's been hit on one side, and, as I recall, the back license plate is missing a bolt and hanging loose."

Luke smiled. "It's a sure bet you'd be better at tailing this driver than I would," he admitted. "As long as you keep your cell phone handy and call me if you get into a sticky situation, I suppose I'm all right with your mission. But let's not forget that if Cornelius figures out you and Drew are spying on him, he'll retaliate."

Nora nodded. *The best way to avoid his retaliation is to remain invisible . . . off his radar screen. I can do that.*

She looked from Drew to her husband, tingling with the excitement of their upcoming adventure. "Once we see Cornelius go into a clock shop, it's not as though we have to tail him all day," she said with a little shrug. "We can put our suspicions to rest, knowing we were watching out for the Willow Ridge church district—our friends and family. That would be well worth my time and gas."

Drew appeared pleased and relieved as he stood up. "*Denki* so much for your help with this—and for the tea. I hope he really is shopping for clock parts— or secondhand clocks—and that our concerns have all been idle speculation."

Nora saw Drew out, pausing in the doorway to watch his long-legged stride. When Luke came up behind her, she relaxed against his firm, fit body. "Care to wager any money—or a nice restaurant meal—that Drew and I catch Cornelius at something other than clock shopping?"

"Nope," Luke murmured, nuzzling her temple. "I think our instincts and Drew's are spot-on. I just hope we figure out what Riehl's up to before he does something drastic and detrimental with the church's funds."

"Me, too," Nora said. "Let's pray that we don't learn things we never wanted to find out about him."

Chapter Fourteen

Wyatt inhaled the fresh air, reveling in the feel of Rebecca's small, sturdy hand in his. It was a beautiful Sunday afternoon and a perfect day to walk around his new property. Its rugged contours and uncut prairie grasses were a far cry from the manicured grounds of his two other farms, and he had visions of preserving some of the land's natural aspects rather than civilizing them.

Rebecca, wearing a ball cap and dark sunglasses, was shading her face with her hand, gazing appreciatively in every direction. He wasn't sure if she was trembling slightly because she was apprehensive, or because she was excited about seeing his property, but she wasn't pulling away—and she wasn't making any sharp remarks or asking candid questions he couldn't avoid answering.

He smiled. Rebecca's way of nailing him with one-liners was one of the things he adored about her.

"Once some of these trees come out," he said, gesturing toward a wooded area in the center of the grassy plain, "I've got an Amish builder named Amos

Coblentz lined up to build the barns this fall," he said. "Heard anything about him?"

Rebecca slipped her hand from his to remove the lens cap of the camera hanging around her neck. "You've hired the premier Plain builder in this area—despite his reputation for usually having more job offers than he and his son Owen can accept," she replied.

As she held the camera to her eye, Wyatt watched in quiet awe as she snapped rapid-fire shots of the lush trees. "There's a pond over that way," he said. "Would a shot of that look good as the header for my site, perhaps?"

"I was thinking we could get you started with shots of the land in its natural state, adding more photos as your barns and fences are constructed," she said. "Until all of your structures are in place and you have horses here, we can launch your site in anticipation of the working farm—and if we link this site to the ones featuring your established properties, the folks who already follow you will get a look at the new venture you're taking on."

"Good idea. Once we post my contact information, it'll be interesting to see how many calls and emails I get asking me what on God's earth I'm doing," he said with a laugh.

Rebecca lowered her camera to smile at him. "I think that's an angle you should consider," she said pensively. "This *is* God's earth, and without getting preachy or religious, you could emphasize any land conservation efforts you're making. You'll gain a lot of respect from your new Amish neighbors that way, too."

When Rebecca started walking, Wyatt kept pace. "I've always believed it's important to be a good

steward of the land, as well as of the animals I raise,"
he said. "When I talked with the county extension
agent a couple weeks ago, he gave me the name of a
timber cruiser who can mark the walnut trees—so I
can sell them for good lumber instead of just knocking them down and whacking them up."

"The Brenneman brothers might want to talk to
you about that," Rebecca suggested. She knelt quickly
to snap a shot of a red-winged blackbird on a cattail
at the edge of the pond. "Aaron, Seth, and Micah
make a lot of walnut furniture in that big metal building you can see from the county highway, and they
would know of a sawmill where the trees could be cut
into planks and boards. It would add intrinsic value
if their customers knew a piece—or a roomful—of
furniture had been made from locally harvested
walnut."

Wyatt smiled as they reached the thicket of weeds
and cattails that edged the pond. "Brilliant idea," he
murmured. "I knew you'd be an invaluable source of
information. As you can see," he added, gesturing at
the low, scummy surface of the water, "my pond
needs a lot of attention. But it's fed by springs, which
suggests I'll have some groundwater to tap into. The
extension agent's going to test it, to see if it's good for
wells I can use for irrigation, or perhaps even for the
water in my house."

Rebecca was nodding, snapping more shots of
vegetation he just thought of as weeds, which she
would probably use in an artsy way on his new site. "If
you expand the pond, or stock it with fish—anything
of interest to folks in this rural area," she added, "we
could post videos of those activities on your site. And
come time for your barn raising, we might want to
advertise it so folks around this area can come," she

continued excitedly. "When Amish builders work, it's poetry in motion to watch the way they raise the walls and trusses and handle their tools."

The light in her eyes intrigued Wyatt as much as her words. Her way of moving and shooting, with her camera as an extension of her hands and creative vision, fascinated him.

Rebecca shrugged, smiling. "But then, maybe you want no part of all these suggestions," she said. "I'm sure you already have a plan of action in mind, and you don't need me rattling off—"

"I do need you," he said quickly. He walked over in front of her and placed his hands lightly on her shoulders. "You know this area. And then there's this thing I have about wanting to spend time with you. Close to you."

A slow smile overtook her face as she raised her camera to her eye again. "Don't you dare move," she whispered. "Keep gazing at me . . . just like that—" She snapped two or three shots in succession.

"You surely won't use those shots on my website—"

"Why not?" She lowered the camera, studying his face until he wondered if he'd missed a spot while he was shaving. "A great face like yours will draw a lot of traffic to your new site," she said matter-of-factly. "And it's a different look from the suit-and-tie photos on your other two sites. Women will love it that your collar's open—"

"What about you, Rebecca?" He wasn't a man who sought compliments, but her opinion of him mattered. A lot.

Her eyes narrowed in thought. "You bring to mind Robert Redford in his role as the Sundance Kid," she murmured. "It's a rugged, manly, all-American look that sells a lot of clothing for high-end menswear catalogs. You're hot, Wyatt."

Heat rushed up from beneath his collar as Rebecca's remarks, her husky voice, told him even more than he'd hoped to hear. This wasn't a high-dollar horse client casting a line, trying to catch his eye and curry his favor. Rebecca, in her cutoffs and baggy T-shirt, was as genuine and sincere a woman as he'd ever met—sure to cut him down to size if he got too big for his designer britches.

"And you, Rebecca, have a face that launches a thousand fantasies," Wyatt murmured, gently caressing her cheek with his fingertips. He nodded toward his new double-wide trailer, a well-appointed temporary home that was parked in the shade, a short distance from the other side of the pond. "If you want . . . we could go inside and make a few of those fantasies come true."

One eyebrow arched, Rebecca turned to look at his temporary home. "If you want," she shot back, "we could go to my computer and start designing your new home page. You have a lot of photos to sort through."

Wyatt laughed. He needed to work on his technique, it seemed. "All work and no play makes Wyatt a dull boy," he quipped, sensing the sentiment would get her no closer to going inside with him.

"Plan your work and work your plan," Rebecca countered as she started back toward his Lexus. "If you work smart, it leaves plenty of time for play."

Wyatt caught up to her and slung his arm around her shoulders. It felt good to walk beside her, to match his stride to hers and inhale the wholesome, uncomplicated scent that was Rebecca's. She wasn't shrugging him off or shutting him down, so he decided it was best to work her plan . . . and see if he could eventually work it his way.

When Nora arrived at the Riehl place on Monday morning, Loretta and Rosalyn were hanging wet dresses on the clothesline, which ran parallel to the side of the house. She got out of the van and waved, hoping her request would come across as simple and sincere rather than as a cover-up for what she planned to do with Drew on Tuesday.

"Hello, girls! It's a beautiful day for hanging out laundry." Nora loved the sight of sheets, trousers, and shirts all hanging in organized rows visible from the road—concealing the undergarments that hung behind them. She had also come to love her automatic washer and dryer, however, so she didn't envy the sisters their morning of using a windup agitator washer and rolling the clean clothes through a ringer.

"We like to get our heavy work done before the sun's too high," Rosalyn said as she shook a pair of dark blue tri-blend trousers so hard they snapped.

"I bet you knew we'd be picking and snapping green beans today, so you decided you'd rather work in our garden than in your shop," Loretta teased from the porch. After she arranged a purple polyester-blend dress on a plastic hanger, she hung it on a short rope that was suspended between the two side pillars of the porch.

Nora laughed. "Millie and I helped my *mamm* pick her beans last night," she replied. "Mamm and Dat will snap them today, and I'll go over to help them pressure can them this evening."

"Millie told me at church that she's spending a lot

of time during the day with your parents," Rosalyn said as she hung the trousers with wooden clothespins. "I bet she's a real help—*gut* company—for them."

Nora nodded. Her daughter, Millie, recently married to Luke's brother Ira, had become a mainstay for her grandparents, Gabe and Wilma Glick. "*Jah*, and because she's with them, I'm able to run Simple Gifts without worrying about them. And on that subject," she continued, "I've been called away on some business Tuesday morning, and I'm hoping you'll feel comfortable running the store for a while, Loretta. Luke will unlock the door around nine o'clock and he'll check in on you now and again—unless you don't want him to."

Loretta's eyes widened. "You want me to mind the store? Wow," she murmured.

Rosalyn chuckled. "Just so happens that at breakfast, Dat said he was heading to Kansas City on Tuesday, checking some secondhand stores for more clocks," she remarked. "If you want, Loretta, I could bring along the materials for the two wreaths I'm making. We could have our own little crafting frolic and wait on customers together!"

Loretta brightened as she looked at Nora. "Will that be all right, the two of us being there?"

"Of course it will," Nora replied. "You'll probably sell all manner of items—along with some of your rugs and wreaths—while I'm away. You've seen how the ladies enjoy watching you work on your projects, and I've already sold three of the wreaths you consigned last week, Rosalyn," she added quickly. "I'll have your check waiting for you tomorrow when you get there."

Delight brightened Rosalyn's face. "That's amazing! *Denki*, Nora."

"You're welcome—and thank you both for helping me out. I'll be on the road early, so if you have any questions, let me know by tonight." She smiled at Loretta. "You know how to ring up sales and record them in the consigner's notebook, so you'll be just fine, sweetie."

As she got into the van and pulled onto the road, Nora thought about the secondhand clock story Cornelius had told his daughters—maybe it was the truth. Maybe she was just too suspicious. She had to admit that her spying mission with Drew intrigued her, though, even as she reminded herself that they might learn something they didn't want to know about the deacon of Willow Ridge.

She refused to think about what would happen if Cornelius caught them following his driver's van.

Chapter Fifteen

Drew leaned forward in the passenger seat of Nora's black van, where they waited on Tuesday morning in her customary parking spot alongside the Simple Gifts shop. From the hill where the Hooleys lived, he could survey most of Willow Ridge, and they had already seen the old green van pull up across the road from the Riehl house.

"There goes Cornelius with his case—and a brief-case," Nora murmured, leaning into the steering wheel as she watched. "Hmm. That looks more like a wheeled suitcase than a repairman's case. But what do I know?"

"It's the same case he's rolled out to the van before, when I've seen him from my apartment," Drew confirmed. "Okay, here they come . . . just turned onto the county highway, headed our way."

Nora started her engine. "We'll let them get a little way past the mill before we pull out," she said. "It's not like they can turn onto any side roads for a while—and they wouldn't do that, anyway, if they want to get to Kansas City in the shortest amount of time."

"What if that's not where he's really going?" Drew asked. He and Nora followed the green van's progress past the mill, and a few moments later, she pulled away from the shop.

"We might find all sorts of loopholes in his story," she replied. "I hope, for the girls' sake, he isn't up to his eyeballs in some sort of monkey business—or illegal transactions."

Drew sighed. "I wish I could trust him," he said softly. "If Loretta and I keep seeing each other, it'll be difficult to deal with discrepancies in his stories and business dealings. We might have to confront him—and that won't be easy."

"We'll keep the faith and cross that bridge when we come to it," Nora said, turning onto the county road. "And meanwhile, look at the big equipment at our new neighbor's place. Looks like Wyatt's making some major improvements on the landscape before he has his barns and stables built."

"Did I hear he raises fancy Thoroughbreds?" Drew asked. He stared out the van's window, noting huge dozers and the expanse of earth they'd already cleared. "Beats me why anybody would bring such an endeavor to Willow Ridge."

Nora smiled, settling into her seat. "Wyatt McKenzie impresses me as a man who does his homework and knows exactly what he's doing," she remarked, focusing on the road and the van a little way ahead of them. "I'm eager to see the website Rebecca's designing for him. Something tells me they're starting up a romance that'll give their Amish neighbors something to gossip about, too."

Drew laughed. "What would we Amish have to entertain ourselves if it weren't for speculating about newcomers and their intentions?"

Nora chuckled. "Pour us some coffee from the Thermos, will you? And open the tin of blueberry muffins. It was way too early for breakfast when I got up this morning, and my mind is crying out for caffeine."

After he'd prepared their simple refreshments, Drew watched the miles go by and chatted with Nora. It had been a long time since he'd had the occasion to ride with a driver, and he was enjoying the break from upholstering chairs in the shop. He was impressed with the way Nora eased back now and then so they wouldn't get too close to the green van—although Cornelius's driver was clipping along about ten miles per hour above the posted speed limit.

"He must figure he won't run across any sheriffs or highway patrol cruisers out here in the country," Drew remarked.

Nora turned on her blinker, slowing down a bit. "The road they're turning onto leads to the interstate, so he might have to be more careful about cops as we approach Kansas City," she said. "Even this early in the morning, we'll run into rush hour traffic, so you might have to help me keep track of that van."

They'd traveled about another half an hour when the green van pulled into a rest area. "Hmm," Nora put in as she followed it off the road. "I'll park several spaces away from them, on this other side of the building, and we'll wait until Cornelius goes inside before I make a dash for the ladies' room. If he spots me in my Plain dress and *kapp*, we're sunk."

Drew assessed the placement of shrubs and trees around the rest area's building. "I sure can't go into the men's room, but I see a big evergreen—and if he comes out before you do, I can keep track of him from there."

"And there he goes, along with his short, chubby driver," Nora murmured. "Why would he be taking that suitcase inside with him?"

"I guess we'll find out." Drew released his seat belt. "Leave your van unlocked so I won't be stuck standing outside it."

As Nora hurried up the walkway toward the low building that housed the restrooms, Drew walked quickly to the stand of evergreens behind the picnic area. A few moments later he returned to the car, hoping Nora wouldn't come out at the same time as Cornelius—or just ahead of him. She was wearing a pink and orange plaid dress that came down to the middle of her calves, with a small round *kapp* covering her auburn bun, so Cornelius would recognize her in an instant.

Luckily, Nora ducked back into the van before they saw any sign of him. A few moments later the green van's driver emerged and lit a cigarette. Other people came and went, and when a fellow in a pinstriped suit came outside, the driver tossed his cigarette to the sidewalk and smashed it under his shoe. The two men were exchanging words while Drew and Nora both stared through the windshield in disbelief.

"That's Cornelius in a double-breasted suit and striped necktie," Nora whispered. "He's combed his hair back . . . must've put his Amish clothes in the suitcase."

"And now I *really* want to know what he's up to," Drew put in, shaking his head. "He looks like anything but an Amish clockmaker."

When Cornelius stopped on the sidewalk and looked right at them, Drew swallowed hard. "Uh-oh. Do you suppose he recognizes your van—and sees us?"

Nora was holding her breath, staring at Cornelius with wide eyes. "Oh Lord, I hope not," she replied in a voice tight with anxiety. "But if he comes over here and asks us what we're doing, we'll have to tell him—"

Cornelius turned his attention to his driver again, and the two men got into the green van. Once they pulled out of their parking slot, Drew could breathe again. "Must've been looking at something else," he murmured. "You know, we could probably find easier ways to delve into Cornelius's secret than tailing him, if you'd rather not follow—"

"And miss out on such a mystery?" Nora teased as she started the van. "In for a dime, in for a dollar. We've come too far to chicken out now."

Drew laughed. After he fastened his seat belt, he reached for the container of muffins. "We'd better fuel up for the rest of our adventure," he said as he put a muffin on a napkin and laid it on the console for Nora. "Does Luke really approve of you doing this? He sounded okay with it on Sunday, but a lot of husbands would absolutely forbid their wives to chase after a man who'd get nasty if he was caught at something dubious."

Nora's eyebrows rose. "Luke isn't like a lot of husbands. If he were a more experienced driver, he'd be on this mission himself."

"Wow." Drew wondered if he could ever allow Loretta to engage in such a covert activity—and then he laughed. "I guess it was really never a matter of Luke approving or allowing you to do this. You were going to do it anyway—and Loretta would have the same idea about pursuing somebody's secret, if it didn't involve her *dat*."

"When I asked her to run the store today, I gave

her no clue about what sort of errand I was on," Nora
said pensively. "I know she and her sister aren't very
close to their *dat*, but they really won't want to know
if he's up to something that might involve the church
district's money."

"It would be tough to endure their neighbors' criticism and whatever punishment Bishop Tom would
decide upon. Most likely Cornelius would be shunned
and removed from his position as deacon." Drew took
a bite of his blueberry muffin, hoping this situation
with Loretta's *dat* didn't go that far. "What's next,
after we find out what he's doing?"

"We'll deal with that when the time comes. For all
we know, I'll lose him in this traffic."

Drew poured two more cups of coffee and settled
back. Soon he was helping Nora keep track of the
lane changes and location of the green van while
she maneuvered her vehicle in a way he truly admired.
After another half hour, he sat up straighter. "They're
getting off on the next ramp," he said, pointing to the
exit sign.

"Nice of him to use his turn signal," Nora muttered.
"Hang on."

She sped up, quickly pulled in front of a car, and
then got into the exit lane just as the pavement
veered away from the interstate. Nora slowed down,
pulling over to the shoulder so they wouldn't be right
behind the green van as it continued down the hill.

"He's turning left," Drew said. Nora was well aware
that the green van's turn signal was blinking this
time, but she knew he wanted to do something to aid
the chase.

"Yep, and we will, too, as soon as they're a short way
up the road," Nora said with a shake of her head.
"From what I recall about this area, it's mostly industrial

parks, and even a few warehouses that are built in huge natural caves. I can't think he'd find too many places that deal with secondhand clocks or parts for them."

Drew saw the strange expression on her face as they slowly made their way down the exit ramp and turned. "Have you noticed the billboards for all the casinos along this road?" he asked softly. "I've counted at least five—and they're all listed on the exit sign, too."

"Uh-huh," she replied. "But we won't believe that assumption until we see it."

A few minutes later, after they'd passed three huge casino complexes that included motels and restaurants, the green van turned in at a neon sign that flashed *DIAMOND JANE'S* in lights that alternated in red, white, and blue. When Nora made the same turn a few moments later, she drove past a couple aisles of parked cars beyond where the green van had gone to remain out of the van driver's sight.

The parking lot was packed with vehicles of all descriptions, and Drew could only stare. "You can't tell me that so many people at all these casinos have nothing else to do but gamble at eight thirty on a Tuesday morning," he whispered in disbelief. "Doesn't anybody in this area have a job?"

"Makes you wonder, doesn't it?" she murmured as she slowed the van at the end of the aisle nearest the large casino building. "I've always had a funny feeling about Cornelius, but I never in a hundred years would've guessed he was a gambler. It's interesting that he's chosen the smallest, least flashy casino we've seen so far—no motels near this one." Nora leaned forward, gripping the steering wheel. "There he goes, right through the main door, with his briefcase."

"Do you suppose it's full of money from the church district's fund?" Drew swallowed hard, thinking back on all the times Cornelius had gone to the city this summer. "*Maybe* he's here to repair this place's clocks, but I'm not going in there to find out."

Nora let out a humorless laugh. "No way! You and I would stick out like aliens from another planet. I've seen all I need to—we're heading home."

As Nora turned at the end of the line of cars to head for the parking lot exit, Drew had a sick feeling in his stomach. "How will we ever tell Loretta and her sisters about this? They won't know what to—"

"Don't breathe a word to them, Drew," Nora put in sadly. "We need to go much higher up the ladder with this information. Bishop Tom's the one to decide how to handle his district's affairs, not us."

Chapter Sixteen

When Loretta answered the door on Wednesday morning, she was startled to see Bishop Tom and Preacher Ben on the porch wearing very serious expressions. "*Gut* morning," she said as she opened the door. "Is everything all right? Is someone ill and needing our help?"

Rosalyn came from the kitchen, still holding her dish towel, as the two men stepped inside. "You're just in time to try some chocolate zucchini muffins," she said cheerfully. "It's a new recipe—a different way to use up all the zucchini in the garden. I think they grow several inches each night, and we have so many!"

Preacher Ben smiled, following Rosalyn to the kitchen. "I can't tell you how many different ways we've eaten zucchini this week, and today Miriam's grinding some and freezing it in quart bags."

"Maybe we'll have a minute to sample those muffins after we speak with your *dat*," Bishop Tom said as he and Ben hung their black straw hats on wall pegs. "Is he down in his shop?"

"*Jah*, he's been working on his clocks since breakfast," Loretta replied. "Go on downstairs and knock on his shop door."

Bishop Tom nodded, his expression a mixture of regret and purpose. "Nazareth has started a rag rug, and I'd like you girls to go help her with it for a while," he said. "Our business involves a church matter not intended for your ears."

Loretta's stomach tightened as the bishop headed for the basement stairway with Preacher Ben behind him. Not daring to speak while the two men could hear her, she shot a questioning glance at Rosalyn. Rosalyn shrugged, appearing more nervous now that she'd assessed the men's somber moods—and because they'd been asked to leave.

The tattoo of their guests' boots echoed in the stairwell. Loretta listened silently as Preacher Ben and Bishop Tom crossed the large open area of the basement's concrete floor.

The footfalls stopped. After a moment, Loretta and Rosalyn heard a loud knock.

"Cornelius, you'll need to unlock your door," Bishop Tom said loudly.

Loretta's eyes widened. She was aware that Dat always worked with his shop door closed, but why would he lock it? As young girls, she and Edith and Rosalyn had been instructed not to enter his workroom— not even to clean—unless he gave them permission. The sisters had rarely seen his workshop in the Roseville house, and they'd never set foot in this one.

"Ah, *gut* morning, gentlemen!" their father called out. "What brings you here on this fine September day? A problem amongst our members?"

Once again Loretta and her sister exchanged worried looks. Dat sounded startled—loudly cheerful—

as he greeted his visitors, which prompted Loretta to slip out of her shoes and walk quietly across the front room to the grate in the floor that allowed heat to circulate. Rosalyn followed her silently—but the *clank* from below them signaled that Dat had anticipated their eavesdropping and shut the grate.

Returning to the kitchen, the sisters stood beside the sink. "What's going on?" Loretta whispered. "This seems very strange."

"I have no idea, but I have a bad feeling about it," Rosalyn replied softly. "Usually when the church leaders meet, they go to Preacher Ben's or the bishop's."

Loretta considered this. "Do you suppose they learned we were both working at Nora's store yesterday, and they're telling Dat we need to stay home?" She sighed sadly. "I hope that's not the case. I really like being there."

Rosalyn absently took a dish from the drainer and ran her towel over it. "Seems to me that if they didn't want us working, they would've talked to us rather than to Dat."

"But Dat's the one responsible for our behavior— our comings and goings," Loretta pointed out. "I think they would speak to him about it first and let him break the news to us."

"*Jah*, but when Ben was chatting with me about zucchini, he seemed as pleasant as he always is," Rosalyn countered. "I didn't sense any disapproval about what you and I have been doing. It was Dat they were intent on seeing."

"Guess we'll have to wait and see." Loretta put half a dozen muffins on a plate. "We'd better be on our way. We don't want the bishop to think we've been snooping."

Rosalyn chuckled as they headed out the front door. "Why, we would never do such a thing!" she teased in a tight voice.

Loretta smiled, but her sister's attempt at humor didn't relieve the tension in her stomach.

Drew was loading a refurbished bedroom set into the big wagon when he caught sight of Bishop Tom and Preacher Ben walking up the lane to the Riehl house. They'd come from the direction of the Hostetler place together, which suggested that they'd been talking before they'd left to visit Cornelius.

Get over there. Maybe the basement windows are open.

Drew poked his head through the front door of the shop to holler at Asa, who was sanding a table with a sander that was plugged into a solar panel outlet. "Hey! I'll be back in a bit!"

The sander's whine stopped as Asa turned toward him. "Thought you were delivering that bedroom set to the gal in New Haven," he teased. "Has something put a burr up your butt? A sudden urge for Loretta to go along, maybe?"

Drew smiled. He hadn't told his twin the details of the trip to Kansas City—but he had a feeling that Tom and Ben were about to act upon the information he and Nora had shared with them after they'd returned. "I'm going to the Riehls', *jah*, but it's not what you think. All will be revealed in its own *gut* time, Asa."

Before his brother could quiz him further, Drew stepped outside and paused to contemplate the logistics of his mission.

As he jogged across the road, he was glad that Will

and Luke weren't working in the nearby fields or in their vineyard. He saw nobody else in the immediate vicinity, either. Bishop Tom and Preacher Ben had just stepped inside with Loretta, and they would eventually go through the kitchen to reach the stairway to the basement. He quickly crossed the front yard to the side of the house where the clock shop was.

Drew's heart was pounding more from his covert mission than from his sprint to the Riehl place. When he went around the lilac bush at the corner, he was glad to see that the two basement windows in the foundation were open. Deep down he knew he shouldn't be listening in, hoping to hear what the two church leaders discussed with Cornelius, but he sat flat against the house anyway.

You're doing this for Loretta. If you know how Cornelius responds during this meeting, you'll be better able to defend her from her dat*'s wrath,* he reminded himself. *He's going to blame the bishop's visit on somebody. Better you than his daughters.*

Drew heard boots on the concrete floor inside, crossing the large open area of the basement. When the footsteps stopped, they were directly beneath the open windows he sat between.

He heard a loud knock. "Cornelius, you'll need to unlock your door," Bishop Tom said loudly.

Drew's eyebrows shot up. Again he wondered why Cornelius would work behind a closed door—and why would he lock it? On a hot day, an enclosed workshop, even though it had windows, would be unbearably stuffy—and whom did he think was going to barge in on him? Several seconds passed with only the sounds of his breathing and his pulse pounding in his ears.

"Ah, *gut* morning, gentlemen! What brings you

here on this fine September day?" Cornelius asked a little too loudly and cheerfully. "A problem amongst our members?"

Drew nearly choked. He reminded himself that it was wrong to want Cornelius to squirm as he answered Bishop Tom's questions—but if Loretta's *dat* was gambling away the district's money, he should be held responsible. Drew heard a sharp *clank*, but couldn't identify the sound.

"Cornelius, when I agreed to let you put a solar panel on your roof to run your clock repair tools, I did *not* condone the use of an air conditioner," Bishop Tom said sternly. "Seems to me that if you left your shop door open and ran the gas ceiling fan that's in the main room, you'd get adequate ventilation."

"Although," Preacher Ben put in, "if you moved your workbench and clocks out into the main room, along the wall where they'd be out of the way come time for a Sunday service, you'd be even more comfortable while you work."

Drew let out the breath he'd been holding. He now understood why Loretta's *dat* spent so much time in his workshop. He couldn't believe Cornelius had the nerve to own an air conditioner—and he wondered why the unit wasn't visible, positioned in a window. From what little he knew about air conditioners, however, he realized that a window unit wouldn't work, because the Riehls' basement windows swung open from the bottom, into window wells.

"Truth be told," Bishop Tom continued without letting Cornelius respond, "Ben and I have come to discuss a much more serious matter than your comfort. As you'll recall, last spring when we saw that you'd placed your workbench in front of the doorway where we keep the church's vault, we asked you to move it. I'm highly disappointed that you've not complied with our wishes."

The bishop sounded more than merely disappointed. Drew had never imagined that kindly, patient Tom Hostetler could speak in such a vehement tone. Cornelius mumbled something Drew couldn't discern—probably hoping his daughters couldn't hear what was being said if they were upstairs.

"We objected to the placement of your workbench because we feared that, in your absence, we might not be able to access the funds," Preacher Ben said earnestly. "I'm awfully glad you're here today, Cornelius, because we've come for money to assist the Brenneman family."

"Oh? What's happened?" Cornelius demanded. "When I saw everyone at church on Sunday, Ezra seemed in fine spirits, and so did Naomi and their sons."

"Ezra's getting some physical therapy," Bishop Tom said.

After a moment, Cornelius said, "How much do you need? I'll get it out for you and—"

"No, we'll need to get the money ourselves, and to take a quick inventory of the funds," Preacher Ben interrupted. "We need to reassure ourselves that a rumor about you going to a casino in Kansas City can't possibly be true."

Drew listened very carefully for Cornelius's response, trying to imagine whether he appeared shocked or angry—or sorry. He didn't dare peek through the nearest window, however.

As he sat back against the house's foundation, lighter voices drifted on the breeze. Drew sucked in his breath. He wasn't surprised that Loretta and Rosalyn were walking down the road, because the bishop had probably sent them away—but what if they'd come out through the back door and caught him eavesdropping? He thanked God that he'd avoided raising Loretta's suspicions or alerting the men inside to his presence.

"In all my years as a deacon of the Old Order Amish church," Cornelius blustered, "I have *never* been accused of mishandling funds or—or *gambling*? Who started this outrageous rumor, anyway?"

"It came as a confidence from someone who's very concerned about the state of your soul—and the state of the funds our members have entrusted to our care," Bishop Tom replied.

"All you need to do is move your workbench," Preacher Ben continued, "and we'll compare the ledger in the vault with the one Tom keeps—and with the bundled bills we've accumulated over the years. Then we'll take the money Ezra needs and you can get back to work."

"If the rumor's not true, you have nothing to worry about, Cornelius," Bishop Tom pointed out. "With the three of us moving your workbench, it won't take any time at all—and we can put it against the opposite wall in here, or out in the main room, as Ben suggested. Let's do it. Now."

"Wait! We can't possibly shift this bench until I've moved these dismantled clocks and their loose parts," Cornelius blurted out.

"You pick up the clocks and we'll follow you with their pieces," Ben said. "The more you protest and stall, Deacon, the more I wonder if you really have gambled away some of our funds."

"Did you buy that fancy wall air conditioner with church money as well, Cornelius?" Bishop Tom demanded. "I've never seen the likes of it, and something tells me it cost a pretty penny—and that you chose it because no one walking past your house would see that you had one. If you're devious about the purchase of an air conditioner, why should your neighbors and I trust you with the church's money?"

Drew held his breath. When a bishop asked such a direct question, who would dare to lie—or refuse to answer? Either way, Tom and Ben would count the money in the vault, and they would know the truth.

After a long silence, Cornelius let out a sob. "All right, I confess!" he cried in a desperate voice. "My wife's passing has left me so lonely and confused, I—I turned to gambling as a way to soothe my soul. *Please* don't let on to anyone—especially the girls—and I promise I'll stop going to the casino. I'll pay back every penny."

"Confession is *gut* for the soul," Preacher Ben intoned, "and we'll hold you to your word about repaying what you've gambled away. Right now, however, we're going to move this bench and count the money, Cornelius. We need to know exactly how much your habit has cost us, and how much you'll be repaying."

"It behooves us to appoint another deacon, too," Bishop Tom put in. "And we'll move the vault so its temptation will no longer be in your basement."

"But—but then folks will assume I've done something wrong!" Cornelius protested.

"You *have*," the bishop countered sternly. "You've stolen from the neighbors who trust you. Answering their difficult questions about your dismissal will be part of your penance."

"We'll be expecting you to confess before the congregation at our next church meeting," Preacher Ben continued. "You must answer to God and to our members even if you're our deacon—*especially* because you're our deacon. If the members vote that you should be shunned, you'll face the consequences, as any of them would. Your position doesn't put you above our rules or exempt you from following them."

"Please! I swear to you," Cornelius pleaded in a shaky voice. "As God is my witness, I will renounce Satan's hold on me and I'll never darken the door of a casino again. I'll repay my debt in monthly installments— weekly, if you prefer," he added plaintively. "I beseech you to forgive me and allow me a second chance. We— we can move my workbench out into the main room right now, as you've requested."

Drew heard some shuffling and shifting in the basement and decided he'd listened long enough. Although he was itching to know how much money Cornelius had stolen, he sensed Tom and Ben might keep that information to themselves.

As he headed back the way he'd come, past the lilac bush and across the Riehls' front yard, Drew suspected that this episode with Cornelius was like the dirt that rose up around a mole's hole: what could be seen on the surface was small compared to the length of the mole's long underground tunnels.

After the bishop returned home and chatted with them for a bit, Loretta and Rosalyn walked back to the house in haste to prepare the noon meal. Dat was a stickler about having his dinner on time. But when they entered the kitchen, the house was so hushed they wondered if he was home.

What had the three men discussed in their absence? Loretta and Rosalyn knew better than to venture downstairs, just in case their father was working more quietly than usual. They peeled fresh carrots from the garden, as well as some onions, and placed them in a roasting pan with a little water and the meatloaf they'd made earlier that morning. They stirred together a salad of canned pineapple chunks and mandarin oranges, too, because Dat really liked it. A loud squeal, as though a heavy object was being dragged across the basement floor, alerted them to their father's presence.

"Why do you suppose Dat's still downstairs?" Loretta asked in a low voice.

"I'm not sure I want to find out." Rosalyn sighed. "Sooner or later, though, I'm sure we will. Let's go dig some beets and potatoes before dinner, rather than hanging around in the kitchen on pins and needles."

Nearly an hour later they carried two large bins of vegetables into the mudroom. As Rosalyn checked the roaster, Loretta glanced at the clock. It was a quarter past twelve, and Dat insisted on eating at noon. Why hadn't he come upstairs?

She opened the door to the basement. "Dinner's ready, Dat!" she called out.

"I can't be interrupted right now," he said in a voice that sounded strangely nervous. "You girls go ahead and eat—just leave me a plate in the oven. Then go ask Nora how many more clocks she has room for in her shop. Take your time and enjoy the store."

Loretta gazed at Rosalyn, who appeared equally dumbstruck by their father's response. Something very strange was going on. Loretta knew better than to ask Dat about it, so she closed the basement door. "I'm not hungry after the odd things that have happened this morning, but we'd better do as he says," she whispered.

Rosalyn nodded, pulling the roaster from the oven. "Who's to argue when Dat sends us to Nora's store? Still, I have a feeling something drastic has happened."

"*Jah*, Bishop Tom seemed even more unsettled when he got home than he was when he arrived at our house," Loretta mused aloud. "Something tells me that when the other shoe drops, we'll not be ready for it."

Chapter Seventeen

As Drew entered the Riehls' kitchen Thursday evening behind Edith and Asa, who were carrying Leroy and Louisa in their baskets, he tried to gauge the level of tension on Loretta and Rosalyn's faces. Rosalyn had appeared nervous this morning when she'd come over to announce that Cornelius was calling a family meeting at their house for supper, and she still wore a stressed expression. Loretta was bustling around the table to pour water in the glasses, her hands trembling slightly as she tipped the pitcher.

Drew tried to catch Loretta's eye to reassure her with a smile, but she was focused on getting everything completed correctly. It seemed such a shame that she and her sisters had prepared innumerable family dinners since their *mamm* had died, yet this evening they were behaving as though one little spill or an over-browned piecrust would set off their father's temper.

"I hope it's all right that I brought Mamm's recipe for zucchini casserole," Edith said as she set her foil-covered glass pan on the table. She glanced around and lowered her voice. "Where's Dat?"

Loretta pointed at the basement door. "He's been in a foul mood all day," she warned in a whisper.

"No, he's been wound as tight as a top ever since Bishop Tom and Preacher Ben came over yesterday," Rosalyn corrected. "We have no idea what happened, because the bishop asked us to—"

Heavy footfalls on the basement stairs made the three sisters scatter like mice escaping a cat. As Drew set the gelatin salad he'd made on the table, he spotted a beautiful cherry pie on the counter, for which he suspected no one would have an appetite by the time Cornelius had said his piece.

"Do I smell grilled chicken?" he asked with a hopeful smile. "A mouthwatering aroma met us as we came up the lane."

Loretta nodded. "At noon, Dat complained about how hot it was in the kitchen, so we baked some potatoes on the coals and cooked the chicken on the grill," she said.

Drew sighed to himself. He wondered if Bishop Tom had confiscated the air conditioner in Cornelius's shop—which would mean the deacon was getting a taste of the discomfort his daughters dealt with every day. When bishops discovered offensive items like televisions, cell phones, and computers, they usually asked members to put them away, trusting those folks to obey. Cornelius, however, had committed far more grievous offenses, so perhaps Bishop Tom had sensed he should remove the temptation of the air conditioner altogether.

Cornelius stepped into the kitchen and shut the basement door with more force than was necessary. His face was flushed and his forehead was damp with sweat. He eyed Asa and Drew suspiciously. "Where's Gingerich?"

Asa exchanged a glance with Drew, shrugging. "We haven't seen Will for a couple of days," he said. "I think Luke has him working over in—"

"Confound it, Loretta, you *did* tell him to come, didn't you?" Cornelius demanded. He stood behind his chair at the head of the table, glowering at her.

"I did, right after breakfast," Loretta murmured. Her hazel eyes burned with indignation. "Why are you lashing out at us, Dat? I told Will to be here at six o'clock—eight minutes from now."

"We've done everything you've asked of us," Rosalyn said in a pleading tone.

"*Someone* has done a whole lot more," Cornelius countered dourly. "And as the minutes tick by, I'm becoming convinced that Gingerich is involved. Still has an ax to grind because I told him he couldn't marry—"

"Knock, knock!" Will said as he let himself in. After entering the kitchen, he handed Loretta a loaf of banana bread and a tub of goat cheese. "I'm not much of a cook, so I figured Nazareth's bread and cheese spread would be a more welcome contribution."

"*Denki*, Will," Rosalyn said as she took a plate from the cabinet. "It's *gut* to see you."

"We're all here now," Cornelius stated brusquely, gesturing toward the table. "Take your seats. As we pray over this meal, we must ask for God's wisdom and guidance in dealing with a vexing situation."

Rather than taking his usual seat across from Loretta, Drew chose the place next to her, on the end opposite from Cornelius. She and Rosalyn had left their mother's customary chair at their father's left vacant. Across from them, Edith sat between Will and Asa, who took the seat to Cornelius's right.

As they bowed their heads in silence, Drew's pulse thrummed. *Help me deal with whatever venom Cornelius spews at us, Lord,* he prayed. *Help me to be a solution rather than a part of the problem—and bless Loretta and her sisters with Your healing, comforting grace.*

Cornelius cleared his throat loudly to end the prayer. Loretta quickly reached for the zucchini casserole as Rosalyn handed the bowl of baked potatoes to her *dat.* He stabbed a large potato with his fork and held it up, shaking it at them as he scowled. "We've got a hot potato on our hands, a situation that burns like the coals in the bottom of the grill—or the fires of hell," he said, glaring at each person around the table in turn. "Who among you is the Judas, betraying me to the bishop?"

The girls' eyes widened fearfully. Edith sucked in her breath. "What are you talking about, Dat?" she asked. "I have no idea what's happened to upset you."

"We don't know, either," Loretta whispered, setting the zucchini casserole on the table so she could fold her hands in her lap. "Bishop Tom sent Rosalyn and me to visit with Nazareth after he and Preacher Ben came over yesterday."

"W-we've been very worried," Rosalyn added softly. "We're guessing the bishop said or did some serious things, but we—how were we to know why he came to see you?"

"*Jah,* and after we returned home, you sent us away, too, Dat," Loretta put in. "I can't remember the last time you didn't eat your dinner with us."

In the tense silence that followed, Drew gathered his thoughts carefully. It was despicable, the way Cornelius was making his daughters fret as they tried to guess the situation that Bishop Tom had discussed with him.

Asa picked up the platter of chicken in front of him and took two pieces with his fork. "I'm at a loss as well," he said, shaking his head. "The work at the shop's been steady lately, so—"

"Someone at this table knows too much for his own *gut*," Cornelius interrupted bluntly. "Did you do this to spite me, Gingerich?"

Will leveled his gaze at Loretta's *dat*, speaking so low that Drew had to strain to hear him. "I have no idea what you're talking about. Why do you expect answers when you're not asking questions that make any sense?"

Cornelius let the potato drop onto his plate with his fork in it. "I do expect answers, because someone at this table dares to eat my food even as he sits tight on his grievous betrayal. And as I think back," he added tersely, "I believe Nora's involved, as well."

Drew sensed Cornelius would never admit the extent of his wrongdoing—and he wouldn't stop interrogating them until someone provided the answer he wanted. "All right, Cornelius, I'll confess—and then it's your turn," he said calmly. "After hearing some rumors and becoming curious about the number of times you've gone to Kansas City lately, Nora and I followed you Tuesday morning. As a member of the church, I was concerned about you—and now that I know where you've been going, I fear for your soul—and for the welfare of our district."

"You *what*?" Cornelius's voice rang angrily in the kitchen as he slapped the tabletop. "I should've known better than to trust that nosy woman who's too independent for her own *gut*! That *was* her van at the rest area, wasn't it? And you put her up to this!"

Drew winced when the babies began to whimper, startled by Cornelius's loud voice. He recalled the sight of Cornelius in an English suit and striped tie but he didn't think it wise to quiz the man at the other end of the table about such details. "*Jah*, that was her van. We saw where you went—"

"And I have confessed all that to Bishop Tom," Cornelius interrupted before Drew could get more specific. "I have acknowledged my mistake, and the slate has been wiped clean, so this matter is settled— and all talk of it is to go no farther than these kitchen walls."

Drew wasn't surprised that Loretta's *dat* was keeping the pertinent details of his confession to himself. Apparently he'd convinced Bishop Tom and Preacher Ben to keep silent as well, rather than bringing this matter before a meeting of the members at their next church service.

Or maybe he's fudging about that. And he'll keep hiding the truth—keep his family from knowing the details—unless you spell them out. Drew's thoughts spun faster as he saw the curiosity and concern tightening everyone else's faces.

"What you did was absolutely wrong, Detweiler," Cornelius continued in an agitated voice. "It's nobody's business where I choose to go. You are no longer welcome in this house, and I forbid you to see Loretta—"

"Dat, what on earth's going on here?" Edith demanded as she gazed from her father to Drew. "If you're swearing us to silence, you should at least tell us what—"

"I don't have to tell you a thing, Edith," Cornelius retorted. "'Honor thy father and thy mother—'"

"You and I need to talk, Cornelius. Let's step out

to the porch—or I can reveal everything I've seen and heard since Tuesday, so your family knows exactly what you've been doing," Drew said as he rose from the table. The twins were crying loudly now, so it was best to get their grandfather out of the kitchen, anyway.

His heart pounded as he passed through the front room with Cornelius close behind him. When he stepped through the door, Cornelius grabbed his arm.

"We can't talk here! Everyone in the kitchen will be able to hear—"

Drew spun around to hold Cornelius's gaze. "They'll only hear what you're angry enough to spout off about," he countered softly. "Why do you think you deserve to keep your secret? If you've truly confessed, the members of our church need to know what you've done—why you're pleading for their forgiveness. I really don't think Bishop Tom's going to keep silent about this matter."

"He said he would," Cornelius countered in a terse whisper. "He's giving me time to repay my debt—"

"How much?" Drew demanded.

Cornelius glowered. "That's none of your concern. And don't you go telling my girls anything about—"

"I intend to court Loretta and marry her when she's ready—if she'll have me," Drew insisted. His face was mere inches from Cornelius's, and he could smell the man's fear. "We'll be living here in your house, where I can keep an eye on your comings and goings, to be sure you're honoring your promise to the bishop."

"You have no right to—"

"I know about the air conditioner in your shop," Drew countered calmly. "I know you've been going to a casino, wearing English clothes, with a briefcase full of money. Do we have an understanding?"

Cornelius glared at him. "What do you mean, *an understanding*? I understand that you've been sticking your nose where it doesn't belong—you, who deceived my Edith on her wedding day, as well as that other woman Gingerich married," he muttered. "Why should I trust you?"

"Because I've confessed to those sins and I've been forgiven," Drew replied. "And because I know too much."

Cornelius spun on his heel, fighting for control of his emotions. "What you and Nora did is unforgivable! It was none of your business—"

"It will become everyone's business if you continue intimidating your daughters and don't stop your gambling." Drew waited until Cornelius faced him again. "If I suspect you're reneging on your promise to repay or that you're finding ways to go to a casino, your theft from the church's fund will become public knowledge."

Although Drew had often envisioned telling Cornelius just how he felt—telling him how despicable he was, treating his daughters so harshly—he didn't feel particularly triumphant now that he'd threatened to reveal Cornelius's secrets. The fact that he could hold this issue over Cornelius's head did nothing to improve his rocky relationship with Loretta's *dat*—and now he'd have to keep the truth from Loretta as he courted her, too.

"I should go to Nora's shop right now and take all my clocks back," Cornelius muttered. "I should never have consigned—"

"You'd be shooting yourself in the foot, considering

how many clocks she's sold for you—and how much money you need to repay," Drew pointed out.

Cornelius glowered at him. "What gives *you* the right to tell me how to conduct my business?" he demanded. "You and Nora are dirty birds of a feather—"

"Again, we know about your gambling habit," Drew repeated firmly. "We watched you enter a casino wearing an English suit, which you'd changed into at the rest area, and you carried a briefcase inside with you. Where's the money coming from that you're gambling away, Cornelius?"

Cornelius clenched his fists at his sides as his face paled. "You just had to go and blab to the bishop—"

"How many thousands of dollars have you lost?" Drew continued tersely, crossing his arms. "The folks in Willow Ridge have entrusted their funds to you and you've betrayed them. Do you really think you'll get away with this—with your secret intact?"

"Tom and Ben believe I'm a man of my word," Cornelius retorted. "In return for my timely repayment, they're allowing me to continue in my role as the district's deacon. It's a matter of *trust.*"

Drew let out a humorless laugh. "They're better men than I am," he said, shaking his head. "My lips remain sealed only if I see you express some appreciation and affection for your daughters—and if you stay away from Kansas City. Seems to me you'd save a lot of money by ordering your parts by mail or over the phone anyway."

"Again, it's not your place to tell me how to manage my business," Cornelius said haughtily. "Let's get back to the table. This nonsense has gone on long enough, and there's a *gut* chance that some curious ears have overheard anyway, now that those kids of yours have stopped bawling."

As Drew went back inside, he envisioned Cornelius eavesdropping on his daughters from the kitchen entryway—or his shop, or any number of other places in the house. He was a man who insisted on total control, and the knowledge he gained by listening in secret gave him more power to manipulate those in his household.

But the manipulation and the mind games are coming to a halt, Drew vowed to himself as he took his seat in the kitchen.

He reached for Loretta's hand under the table, gently squeezing it to reassure her. Somehow he had to gain her love and confidence while keeping his knowledge of her father's heinous behavior to himself—because if the Riehl girls learned the extent of their *dat*'s deception and thievery, their hearts would be broken and their belief in him would shatter like fragile china.

"Sorry we took so long and this nice meal has gotten cold," Drew said, nodding at the folks around the table. "I believe Cornelius and I have reached an understanding."

The man at the opposite end of the table clamped his mouth shut as he jerked his fork from the baked potato on his plate.

"Glad to hear it," Will remarked as he spooned some gelatin salad onto his plate. "Care to fill us in on the details? If Bishop Tom and Preacher Ben came by, and asked Loretta and Rosalyn to leave, that tells me they were delving into a problem of some magnitude."

Drew smiled, catching Cornelius's eye. "That's

between Cornelius and the bishop—and God. I've agreed to keep silent."

"Silence is golden," Asa remarked as he helped himself to the zucchini casserole.

Drew shook his head. *Silence is the color of money. A whole lot of money.*

Chapter Eighteen

Near the end of her shift at Simple Gifts on Saturday, Loretta buzzed with curiosity and excitement. Ever since she'd heard that Nora and Drew had gone to Kansas City on Tuesday, she'd hoped that Nora would reveal more about the mysterious errand she'd been running while Loretta had taken charge of the shop.

But Nora hadn't spoken of it, and Loretta didn't feel it was her place to ask questions.

When the bell above the door jangled, her heartbeat accelerated. Drew had invited her to supper, and he looked as eager to be with her as she was to be going out with him. His black hair was damp from showering, and he smelled intoxicatingly fresh.

"Hey there, Loretta," he said with a wide smile. "If you'll hold the door, I'll pull my cart inside. I've got some new pieces to consign."

"*Gut* afternoon, Drew!" Nora called out as she joined them. "I'm always happy to see you show up with your pull cart. What've you got for me today?"

Loretta inhaled Drew's fresh male scent as she

accompanied him to the door and held it open. "Another rocking chair—and look at that pair of pretty nightstands!" she said. "You've been busy this week."

"*Jah*, we have," Drew replied, pulling his cart into the store. "Moving to Willow Ridge was the best thing Asa and I could possibly have done to improve our business."

Loretta shrugged, feeling giddy. "I'm glad you came here, too—but my feelings have nothing to do with furniture," she added with a soft laugh.

When Drew focused his indigo eyes on her, she drifted into a private paradise—the dreams she sensed would come true with this handsome man, if she believed in him. "Hold that thought," he whispered, winking at her.

He pulled a sheet of paper from his back pocket and handed it to Nora, who was already fingering the pieces in his cart. "Here's the inventory sheet and my prices," he said. "Let me know if you think I'm shooting too high."

Nora skimmed the neatly written figures, shaking her head. "I think you're right on the money, Drew. Those retro nightstands won't be here long, and the platform rocker is absolutely gorgeous."

Slipping the price list into her apron pocket, Nora smiled. "I'm going to have you reupholster the two wing chairs in my front room, because you do such a meticulous job," she said. "Let me know when you'll have time to work on them. Your color sense is so *gut*, I'll even leave the fabric selection up to you."

Drew laughed. "That's a high compliment, Nora. Gee, I see this as an opportunity to use up a couple of big fabric remnants—stripes and plaids in teal and pink," he teased.

Nora laughed. "If anyone could make two uncoordinated prints look *gut* together, you could," she said. She turned, gazing around the shop. "Let's put the rocker in the corner by that bookcase, and the nightstands will look nice on either side of the new queen-sized bed Aaron Brenneman brought in earlier this week. Then you and Miss Loretta are excused to go have your Saturday night fun."

"You're very generous, letting me off an hour early," Loretta said. She lifted one of the nightstands from the cart and placed it at one side of the glossy wooden headboard. "Drew arrived before the time I told him—"

"And I'll be happy to kill some time," Drew chimed in. He placed the second nightstand on the other side of the bed. "*Gut* things come to those who wait."

Nora laughed, waving them off. "It's such a pleasure to work with both of you, because you give your best efforts and pay attention to the way I prefer to have things done," she said. "I'd be hard-pressed to find better help than you, Loretta. I know your *dat*'s still not crazy about your working for me."

Loretta smoothed the quilted coverlet on the bed, and for a fleeting moment she imagined such a fine piece of furniture in her own home someday . . . the home she would share with her husband. "I don't know what you found out about Dat in Kansas City. And I'm not sure what you said to him at supper Thursday night," she added, gazing at Drew. "But Dat seems . . . quieter. He spends more time in his shop and less time finding fault with Rosalyn and me."

Nora's smile held secrets. "That's *gut* news, Loretta.

I can't imagine that you and your sister do anything that deserves criticism. He's very fortunate to have you."

Loretta warmed with appreciation for Nora's kind words. She'd come to realize that the Simple Gifts store meant more than a chance to earn some money in the comfort of air conditioning. The time she spent with Nora enriched her soul and opened her eyes to a world where people were considerate and cared about one another's feelings.

"*Denki* so much for saying that," Loretta murmured. "I'm very fortunate to have you as well."

Nora beamed and came over to hug her. "We're all family, in God's eyes. When we bless one another with kindness, it's a gift that keeps on giving." She smiled at Drew. "What do you two plan to do this evening? Something fun, I hope!"

When Drew shrugged and smiled at Loretta, he seemed boyish and maybe a little shy. "I've heard there's a place in Morning Star that serves really *gut* pizza—"

"Oh, I love pizza!" Loretta blurted out. "Dat's not wild about it—doesn't consider it a real meal—so I haven't had pizza for a long time."

Drew held out his hand to her. "I won't admit how many pizzas I keep in my freezer for quick suppers, so having a fresh one sounds *almost* as *gut* as spending time with you while we enjoy it."

Loretta suddenly knew she was in love with the handsome man who stood before her. It was probably too soon to call it love, but the rush of joy she felt when she placed her hand in Drew's outshone the sun—and far surpassed the way she'd been craving his kiss, his embrace.

"I'm ready," she said softly.

* * *

Drew's emotions raced and swerved and whirled as though he were riding a roller coaster at breakneck speed, when in reality he was driving his open buggy down the road. Loretta was sitting at his left, so close that their thighs rubbed with the rocking of the rig. He couldn't help himself. He slipped his arm around her and kissed her for as long as he dared while he was driving.

"Wow, but I needed that," he murmured when they came up for air.

Loretta's cheeks were pink as her soft laughter teased at him. "They say kissing and driving don't mix. Too much of a distraction, and too much time with your eyes off the road."

"*You* are a distraction, Loretta," Drew shot back at her. "But *jah*, we'll have no more kissing until we're off the road and parked."

When she reached for his hand, Drew's heart swelled. For the past couple of days, he'd wondered if his chat with Cornelius concerning courting and marrying Loretta had been misleading. He certainly didn't want Cornelius to think he was only romancing Loretta to keep an eye on him.

Riding along with her, hand in hand, felt so right, however. And it wasn't as though Loretta hadn't been expressing her interest in him this past month. Her smiles, kisses, and long, hazel-eyed gazes told him she was interested in him—eager to leave behind her broken engagement to Will and to start a fresh relationship that had a future.

Don't rush in where angels fear to tread, he reminded himself. *You thought Molly hung the moon, too.*

But Loretta was different. She didn't have a deceptive

bone in her body. She wore her heart on her sleeve . . . and Drew felt certain she would entrust her gentle heart to him without a second's hesitation, if he asked her to.

"Oh, my. Morning Star must be quite a town," Loretta said as they came within sight of a car dealership. "Rosalyn and I have shopped a bit in New Haven, but we've never driven in this direction. Dat says we can find everything we need at Zook's Market."

Drew bit back a remark about how her father seemed to do everything in his power to keep his daughters under his thumb. "Henry and Lydia Zook stock a lot of groceries and bulk items," he agreed, "but for hardware and gardening supplies—anything that's not related to food—you have to go to the mercantile in Cedar Creek or visit the shops in Morning Star or New Haven. See?" he added, gesturing ahead of them. "This town has an Amish carriage shop, owned by a fellow named Saul Hartzler, as well as Matthias Wagler's harness shop, just down the way."

"Matthias is Adam's older brother, *jah*?" Loretta asked. "I've seen him a time or two at church, but Annie Mae has mentioned that he's married now and living in Morning Star. Nora carries some very pretty tooled leather saddles he's made."

"He does excellent leather work." Drew drove past a pool hall, a Laundromat, and a few other businesses before making a turn at the corner, where they could see kids in swimsuits running and playing among streams of water that shot up out of the concrete.

"What a nice park—and what fun those kids are having!" Loretta said with a laugh. "I've never seen the likes of that. It's like an upside-down shower."

Drew chuckled. "This is the first splash pad I've ever seen, too, but folks have told me they're all the rage in small-town parks. The city council of Clifford, where Asa and I moved from, installed one earlier this summer, too."

As he steered his black Percheron across the street to a large parking area, Loretta leaned forward eagerly. "A Plain bulk store! You always find such interesting things in those."

"Would you like to shop there before or after we have our pizza?" he asked. "I'm parking here because they have a hitching rail on the side of the building."

Loretta considered his question. "Let's eat first. They say you shouldn't shop on an empty stomach."

Drew chuckled. "Whoa, Raven," he said. When he'd set the brake, he kissed Loretta's temple. "All right, we'll start with pizza. If there's anyplace else you'd like to shop or walk around, we've got all evening—and there's a place that sells ice cream about a block away, too."

Loretta's delighted smile showed him how pretty she'd been as a little girl. "The sooner we eat pizza, the sooner we'll get to enjoy the rest of the temptations in this town."

Temptations.

Drew helped her down from the buggy, all too aware of her slender waist and womanly curves. Although all Old Order women wore the same modest style of cape dress and pleated *kapp* so that no one stood out or called attention to herself, Loretta transcended the crowd's uniformity. Her voice thrummed with emotion—and when she sang in church, Drew could pick her voice from among the other women's in the room. She smiled with a hint of mischief, and her hazel eyes glimmered with an underlying passion that kept him on edge whenever she was near.

Drew enjoyed every moment of sharing a sausage pizza with extra cheese. He chuckled as Loretta exclaimed over the little containers of sanding sugar, bags of soup mix, and kitchen gadgets she found in the bulk store. After he paid for the items she'd selected, walking around town to the other stores made him ridiculously happy. As daylight shimmered into dusk, they bought triple-scoop ice-cream cones and sat on the swings in the park to eat them.

"I hate for this day to end, Drew," she said dreamily as they were heading back to Willow Ridge in the rig. "I have such a *gut* time when I'm with you."

He closed his eyes for a moment. Did he dare ask her the question that had been on the tip of his tongue all day? The substantial *clip-clop, clip-clop* of Raven's hooves seemed to urge him on, yet he wanted to say the words just right—and with headlights coming toward them and cars sometimes passing them, he didn't want to get caught up in romantic yearnings while he was driving.

By the time they reached Willow Ridge, the stars were tiny diamonds in a canopy of blue velvet. Loretta was leaning against him, cradled beneath his arm, and Drew couldn't recall ever feeling so ecstatic, yet so settled. About a block away from the Riehl place, he pulled onto the shoulder and set the brake.

Kiss me, he was about to say, but Loretta was already seeking out his mouth with her soft, lovely lips. Drew let the kiss linger for several moments, wishing for more, yet knowing better than to suggest it.

"*Gut* night, sweet Loretta," he murmured as he held her close. "There's no church tomorrow, so you and Rosalyn and your *dat* are having dinner at Asa's, *jah?*"

"That's the plan. What can I bring for the meal?" she asked. "What are you hungry for?"

Drew yearned to answer honestly, but he merely smiled. "Whatever you can easily put together tonight, as I've kept you out late. Anything you bring will be my favorite."

Loretta smiled. "I'll bake a batch of cookies, and we have a fresh gallon of cherry chip ice cream in the freezer."

"Doesn't get any better than that."

Life doesn't get any better than this, Drew thought as he pulled up to the house and helped Loretta from the rig. *May it always be so, Lord.*

Chapter Nineteen

From her lawn chair on the deck of Wyatt's deluxe double-wide trailer, Rebecca had a fabulous view of the barn raising that was just getting underway. It was early Friday morning, September 16. Amos and Owen Coblentz had arrived, along with several Amish workmen and wagonloads of lumber and building supplies. Several men from Willow Ridge were showing up to assist them as well.

"This will be an amazing day," Rebecca said, shading her eyes with her hand. "By sundown, you'll have a barn where there's only a concrete foundation now."

Wyatt smiled, grasping her hand. "I hope you're not disappointed that I didn't publicize this event," he said. "I thought the carpenters should have a day of working without spectators who might get in their way."

"You're probably right," she admitted. "I've heard of farmers who brought in a lunch wagon and sold concessions to the crowd—made quite an event of it. But this way it's a work in progress that won't turn into a circus."

"And instead of lunch wagon food, we'll all be going to the Grill N Skillet for our lunch break," Wyatt said with a nod. "Your mother has also organized some of the ladies in town to bring in refreshments around nine thirty and again at three this afternoon. The congeniality—the sense of community purpose in Willow Ridge—astounds me."

Rebecca smiled proudly. Wyatt had always been a gracious man, appreciative of good craftsmanship, and he'd come a long way in understanding the Amish mind-set over the past month as well.

"For these folks, the only thing more important than family and friends is a sincere love of God," she said softly. "While the English world spins faster and faster, tethered to technology and microscopic computer chips, the Amish have maintained their people-oriented priorities."

"The two cultures are worlds apart, yet they coexist pretty well." Wyatt rose from his lawn chair, waving his hand high above his head. "Amos wants to go over some blueprint details with me and the carpenters before they begin. Come along, if you want."

Rebecca smiled. It felt good to be included in his grand plans. "You go ahead, and I'll catch up. Amos and Owen prefer to deal with men—and once the structure begins to take shape, I'll snap some photos from a respectful distance."

Wyatt's smile lit up his alluring eyes. "You've got a thing for muscular men wearing tool belts, don't you?" he teased. "I suspect I'll see several shots of Amish masculinity among the photos you take today."

Rebecca laughed out loud. "Maybe you should buckle on a tool belt and find out," she shot back. "Believe me, all these guys will remain fully clothed, even in the heat of the afternoon."

The sound of heavy hoofbeats made her look toward the road that ran in front of Nora's shop. "Here comes the wagon with the big watercoolers. Those black Percherons pulling it belong to the Detweiler brothers."

"Fine-looking horses, too," Wyatt remarked. He watched more closely as the wagon turned to cross the mill's parking lot, approaching them. "Looks like Savilla Witmer's riding along—most likely delivering our first round of refreshments a bit early. We certainly won't go hungry today."

He gazed at Rebecca, making her insides quiver. "But then, some hunger goes far beyond food, dear heart. I'll catch up with you later."

Wyatt turned with the graceful ease of a man accustomed to handling high-dollar horses in a show ring while dressed in a suit and tie. His Western-cut shirt hugged his broad shoulders and tapered into the trim waist of jeans that accentuated his long legs.

Rebecca smiled. She hadn't yet seen an angle of him that didn't appeal to her.

As though Wyatt sensed she was watching, he turned and blew her a kiss—right in front of all the men gathering to build one of his barns. She'd learned over these past few weeks that spending time with an older man had a lot of advantages, one of them being that he treated her like a queen. As Wyatt approached the bearded Amish men in their straw hats, short-sleeved plain-colored shirts, and broadfall trousers, he was welcomed with hearty voices and wide smiles.

Wyatt shook hands all around, looking each man in the eye and taking the time to greet him and call him by name. Rebecca watched with a deep pleasure as the Detweiler brothers, the Hooley brothers, the Brenneman brothers, the Wagler brothers, Will Gingerich, and Bishop Tom gathered around Wyatt, Amos Coblentz, and his crew for a few words about their building strategy.

Rebecca raised her camera to her eye, steadied the large lens with her left hand, and found the shutter button with her finger. She stood absolutely still, poised to shoot a series of images, a study of male faces intent on their purpose. Wyatt's deep blond hair and pale blue shirt stood out in contrast to the black straw hats and darker Amish clothing around him—and in truth, he didn't need a tool belt to appear manly. Swinging a hammer wasn't his forté, and he was comfortable admitting it.

Rebecca took a few shots of the water wagon, as well as one of Savilla sitting on the back edge of it, dangling her sneakered feet. In her goldenrod dress with a white apron and a pleated white *kapp* covering her black hair, she looked as fresh and pretty as a daisy—and apparently Will thought so, too, because he sauntered over to see what was in her covered containers.

They make a handsome couple, Rebecca thought as she focused on them. Or maybe she had romance on her mind—because when she instinctively shifted her camera back to the crowd of men, she found Wyatt gazing at her. Her knees turned to jelly as she shot a rapid succession of photos that were more for her to gaze at than for his website.

When she zoomed in on his face, the intensity of his eyes told her things he hadn't said with words. Rebecca found herself yearning for his touch, his kiss, and as she lowered her camera, she sensed it would be a day to record images that would touch her heart forever.

* * *

By the time the construction crew was walking down the hill to the Grill N Skillet for their noon meal, Wyatt was amazed at the progress the men had made. The lumber skeleton of a barn, complete with roof trusses and ceiling beams, rose into the sky as a testament to their teamwork—their ability to follow Amos Coblentz's plan without anyone second-guessing him or insisting that he had better ideas.

Wyatt was tickled that Amos had put him to work—unskilled laborer that he was—and he'd gladly fetched boxes of heavy screws and replaced batteries in the men's drills. Wyatt stood in awe of the way they charged their batteries using a car battery and an adapter and the way they put together an entire wall of studs and trusses on the ground before raising it into place with a pair of horses and a pulley system. Rebecca had been right: an Amish barn raising was poetry in motion, as efficient and graceful as a choreographed dance.

Wyatt found Rebecca waiting for him in front of his temporary house, her ball cap and jean shorts setting her apart from the crowd—yet at midmorning, she'd served cold water, lemonade, and cinnamon rolls alongside Savilla and Nora with the same comfortable ease with which she handled her camera.

"What a morning!" Wyatt crowed as he slipped his arm around her shoulders. "Can you believe how much those men accomplished?"

"Told you so," Rebecca teased as they walked between the mill and the Simple Gifts shop. "Turn around and look at it from here."

When Wyatt pivoted, a shimmer of awe coursed through him. "Wow," he murmured. "This will be a barn to outshine all the barns I've had built before. Even before the walls and roof are finished, I can see it's going to be magnificent."

"Just like the man who owns it," Rebecca said softly. "Got some great shots for your website—and for my own gratification."

Wyatt chuckled as heat rose from under his shirt collar. In many ways Rebecca was still as skittish as a filly around him, yet her words resonated in his soul—and there was no arguing about the quality of her photography or her design expertise. As he grasped her small hand and they continued toward the Grill N Skillet, he sensed that she'd never given herself physically or emotionally to a man. He believed patience and persistence would pay off as he tried to win her.

"After smelling Josiah's grills all morning, I'm ready to chow down on a lot of fine eats," Luke remarked as he reached the café's door and held it open.

"First thing I plan to do is drink a pitcher of iced tea," Ben said as he removed his straw hat to step inside. "We're all grateful to Bishop Tom for allowing the Witmers to air-condition their restaurant."

"Hear, hear!" Asa called out. "And we're grateful to Wyatt for feeding us in fine style."

"Sure beats sitting outside, even in the shade," Owen Coblentz agreed as he wiped his forehead on his shirtsleeve. "Local gals always provide *gut* food at our construction sites, but they can't cool us off in this heat. Feels like we're at the peak of Indian summer, hot as it is for September."

"Happy to make you men comfortable during your break," Wyatt said as he entered the café behind Rebecca. "Josiah's set aside the back dining room for us, and you're to fill as many plates at the buffet as you care to."

It was a sight to watch the crew of men heading toward the back of the restaurant, hanging their straw hats on wall pegs as they entered the room or headed toward the restroom. The savory aromas of grilled beef and pork mingled with the sweeter scents of cornbread, muffins, and the array of vegetables on the steam table. Pitchers of ice water and iced tea sat in the centers of the tables, which were built in a sturdy, rustic style that matched the simplicity of the building's interior.

Savilla came in from the kitchen rolling a cart of desserts. "We made these special for you fellows," she called out as the men eyed her pies, cakes, and platters of cookies. "I'll take whatever's left over, plus fresh pastries, to the work site for your afternoon break."

"You really think we'll have any left over?" Seth Brenneman teased.

The men's congenial laughter filled the room. As they headed for the buffet line, many of them shook Wyatt's hand and thanked him personally for providing them such a fine meal.

"I want you to come back to build the second barn—and stables and a house, eventually," Wyatt pointed out. "If there's anything more I can do for you, just let me know."

"I should be able to come back next week to get that second barn raised," Amos said. "All depends on the weather, of course, but I've blocked out some time on my calendar so your livestock buildings should all be completed by mid-October. I know you'd like to get your horses delivered and get your business up and running."

"I appreciate your doing that for me," Wyatt said with a nod. He smiled at Amos, admiring his sturdy, compact build and brown eyes that sparkled in a tanned, lined face framed by black hair and a beard shot with a little silver. "Rebecca has told me you and Owen are the best builders around, and she's absolutely right."

Amos chuckled. "Our women are usually right, ain't so?" he teased as he smiled at her. "Owen's been hounding me to get a website, even though word of mouth has kept us busy and fed since before he was born. I'll let you know if he talks me into it, Rebecca."

"Fair enough," she said. "Most Amish men can say the same thing, and you should do what you're comfortable with—and what your bishop allows."

"Bishop Vernon and your Bishop Tom go way back," Owen put in as he joined them. "I don't think it'll be a problem to get his permission—but Dat has a point. Doesn't make sense to advertise for work you don't have time to do right."

As he followed Rebecca through the buffet line, Wyatt knew a deep sense of satisfaction. He felt he belonged among these Amish, and he admired their work ethic—their down-to-earth methods of completing a task at hand. He smiled at the way Rebecca was selecting ribs, meat loaf, cheesy hash browns, and a variety of vegetables. Then she placed a square of cornbread and a banana muffin on top of it all.

"It's good to see a woman eat like she means it," he said softly. "And please don't interpret that as a put-down."

Rebecca's smile made Wyatt hold his breath. She'd removed her ball cap, so she had a slight ridge around her layered brown hair. Her blue eyes twinkled in a radiant face bronzed by the sun—no tanning salons for this young woman. "I don't think you have it in you to put me down, Wyatt," she said breezily. "Interpret that any way you care to."

With that, Rebecca plucked a biscuit from the buffet basket and started toward the back dining room, leaving Wyatt chuckling. She was right. He was attracted to her in so many ways, he couldn't leave her alone . . . and he didn't want to live alone much longer, either.

When he set his loaded plate on the table and sat down next to Rebecca, she was having an animated conversation with the Detweilers and the Brenneman brothers—all of whom joked and laughed with her as though they were quite comfortable with her living English despite being born into an Amish family. Wyatt found it refreshing that the men around these tables accepted Rebecca even though they would never allow their women to dress in shorts or sleeveless blouses.

He was also relieved that the unattached young men seemed to have no inclination to persuade her back into the Amish fold so they could marry her.

Everyone was eating heartily, with some men making their second trip to the buffet table, when Rebecca glanced toward the door. She sprang from her chair, rushing through the crowd toward a man with thinning brown hair and a pale, kindly face. When he opened his arms and Rebecca rushed into them, Wyatt knew a moment of mild envy.

Beside him, Ben Hooley smiled. "That's Rebecca's English *dat*, Bob Oliveri—the man who rescued her from the flooding river when she was a toddler," he explained. "I owe Bob a huge debt of gratitude for buying the previous café building for my Miriam when the bishop at that time was trying to weasel it away from her—back when he was dragging my reputation through the mud so she'd marry him instead of me."

Ben shook his head amiably as he recalled that time in his life. "Bob's been a real boon to our town. He's tickled to help us out from time to time, because he knows Rebecca's happiest living here near her *mamm.*"

Wyatt laid his cloth napkin on the table beside his plate. "Seems like a good time to make my presence known so Bob can size me up—and get used to me spending time with his daughter," he murmured. "Thanks for filling me in on who he is."

As he rose from his chair, Wyatt hoped his smile looked sincere rather than a bit nervous. It had been decades since he'd sought the approval of a young woman's father, yet he could tell by the way Oliveri was gazing at Rebecca that he was a man whose opinion mattered—a lot. He fought the urge to check the front of his shirt for barbecue sauce, focusing instead on the man who was perhaps ten years older than he was.

When Rebecca saw him approaching, she brightened. "Dad, this is Wyatt McKenzie—the man who's building that big barn you probably saw on your way into town," she said eagerly. "Wyatt, this is my father, Bob Oliveri."

Wyatt grasped Bob's hand with a nod. "It's a real pleasure to meet you," he said. "Ben was telling me about how you rescued his Miriam from a former bishop—and how grateful he is that you did."

Bob gripped his hand, laughing. "That bishop was a piece of work—eventually tinkered with Josiah's smokers behind Miriam's building and got caught in the explosion. From what I've been hearing from

Rebecca, you've been lighting a few fires as well, Wyatt."

Seeing the way Rebecca's cheeks were turning pink with pleasure—and a little embarrassment—Wyatt framed an answer that had nothing to do with his feelings for Rebecca. "Willow Ridge is the perfect place to ease away from Thoroughbreds and race-tracks so I can turn my efforts toward more practical animals," he said. "In your opinion, Bob, would I be smarter to raise Belgians or Percherons? I've met a lot more carpenters than farmers these past few weeks, so I haven't chatted with many who depend upon horses for their livelihoods."

Bob shrugged, appearing pleased to be asked. "All I know about horses is that the Amish are the most expert trainers you'll find," he replied. "I suspect they'll make do with smaller homes and fewer frills in order to afford the best horses to pull their buggies or their farm machinery."

Wyatt nodded. He liked knowing that Rebecca's dad wouldn't be horning in on his business decisions—and he liked Bob for other reasons as well. Any man who would raise a little girl to adulthood and so graciously accept her decision to live among her Amish relatives had a good, solid heart.

"Well, I'm going to scoot along home," Bob said, gazing from Rebecca to Wyatt. "I just returned from a cruise on several European rivers—I flew into Kansas City and drove the three hours from there, so I'm tired. Awfully nice to meet you, Wyatt. Rebecca's told me a lot about you."

Wyatt exchanged a few more pleasantries with him and returned to his dinner while Rebecca walked her dad to his car. He was guessing Bob had known to come to the Grill N Skillet because Rebecca had texted or emailed her location—which meant she might have engineered their introduction as well.

That's as it should be. It means she's close to her dad, and she's close enough to me that she wants me to meet him. It's all good.

As he sat down, Bishop Tom winked at him from across the table. "Looks like you've passed muster so far, Wyatt," he teased. "Bob appears mild-mannered and harmless, but he's a man to be reckoned with when he's upset—or when his daughter's welfare is at stake."

"*Jah*, Bob looks things—and people—over pretty closely rather than taking anything at face value," Ben put in as he picked up his dirty dinner plate. "And from what I could tell, he thinks your face has value."

The men around him chuckled, and Wyatt did, too. Once again he felt he belonged among these honest, honorable men—and the expression on Rebecca's face when she sat down told him she felt the same.

"You did good, McKenzie," she teased. "My dad thinks I should latch on to somebody younger and less likely to sway my opinions and affection with his money, but other than that he likes you just fine."

Wyatt laughed, extremely pleased with her candid remark. Rebecca was an independent young woman, but she was still her daddy's little girl. The future looked a lot brighter now that father and daughter were on the same page and were willing to write him into their story, too.

Chapter Twenty

As Loretta and her sisters sat singing the opening hymns on Sunday morning, they were in the center of the women's side, with the older women toward the front and the younger girls behind them. It was always a treat to attend services at Preacher Ben and Miriam's house, because the windows were spaced to allow a crosscurrent of the breeze from outside. When some interior walls were removed, the entire congregation could be seated in the main room at the front of the house—which also had a gas-powered ceiling fan to provide more comfort on a stuffy, humid morning.

Voices swelled in the final stanzas of the last hymn as Bishop Tom, Preacher Ben, and Preacher Henry emerged from the back bedroom where they'd held their usual meeting to determine who would preach. As Preacher Henry took his place among the men of the congregation, Tom and Ben positioned themselves on either side of Dat on the preachers' bench that sat between the men's and the women's sides. Bishop Tom handed Dat a piece of paper, which listed the Bible verses he was to read later.

As the last notes of the hymn lingered, Preacher Ben rose to begin the first sermon. He glanced at Dat with an expression that stilled Loretta's heart. Was he going to expound upon whatever wrongdoing he and the bishop had discussed with Dat when they'd come to the house? Bishop Tom's weathered face was composed yet taut, as though he was searching for words of wisdom—and maybe a warning—to share during the main sermon he would preach later.

"Our Lord Jesus, early in His ministry, chose twelve disciples who would carry on His work after His death," Preacher Ben began, "and those men were like us. Even after three years with the Son of God, they faltered, they went through times of doubt and disbelief about who Jesus was—and in the book of John, near the end of the sixth chapter, Jesus says, 'Have not I chosen you twelve, and one of you is a devil?'"

Loretta stopped breathing. Preacher Ben's accent on the word *devil* had jarred everyone from their usual Sunday morning sense of well-being. Dat's face went pale.

"We know that Judas Iscariot betrayed Jesus in the Garden of Gethsemane for thirty pieces of silver," Preacher Ben went on, "and shortly thereafter he hanged himself, so great was his guilt. We believe that Jesus knew all along that Judas would betray Him, yet He chose Judas to serve—perhaps hoping Judas would see the light of God and be made clean and whole instead of carrying out his loathsome mission."

Preacher Ben bowed his head as though his words weighed heavily on his soul. When he looked up again, he spoke softly, pressing his point in a way that forced folks to listen hard. "Judas' confession of sin and acceptance of God's love would have altered the course of history—but we won't go into that," he added with a sigh. "I wish to speak to the point that even those who are chosen by God to serve sometimes make grave mistakes and display poor judgment. And I'm hoping that we can cast out this demon before it drives the one in whom it dwells to commit further sins—or to go the way of Judas Iscariot."

Loretta's eyes widened as she looked at Rosalyn on her left and Edith on her right, grasping their hands. What could Dat possibly have done that Preacher Ben was apparently comparing him to the man who'd betrayed Jesus? Was Dat really in danger of being overcome by guilt and taking his own life? Suicide was a sin in itself, no matter what else he'd done to inspire today's ominous sermon.

Or is Preacher Ben warning all of us here that we, too, might be tempted enough by earthly gain to commit serious sins? It happens to every one of us, as he said. Maybe another member besides Dat has strayed from the path.

As the preacher continued, Loretta became aware that many in the room appeared uncomfortable—Preacher Ben had a way of making his sermons speak to each of them in ways they couldn't ignore. After about twenty minutes, he concluded by gazing at the congregation, slowly looking many of them in the eye.

"Each and every one of us possesses a Judas or two—demons that tempt us when we're so lonely or desperate that we can't see God right in front of us, trying to lead us into His light," Preacher Ben reminded them earnestly. "And each and every one of us is responsible for helping his or her neighbors in their hour of darkness, to extend God's love—or perhaps even to help those folks understand how their demons are leading them astray."

Preacher Ben smiled, yet he still appeared saddened by the hard truth he'd kept to himself. "It takes a lot of honesty and great faith to reach the level of love Jesus and our Father God intend for us to attain so we'll be fit to dwell with Him in heaven when He calls us home," he said, clasping his hands before him. "I pray that we'll all be vigilant and take our part in His earthly kingdom seriously. We don't know the day or the hour when He'll come again."

As he sat down on the preachers' bench, Bishop Tom rose to speak. "As we enter our time of silent prayer, let us search our souls and ask the Lord to help us find our way," he said.

Loretta went to her knees on the floor along with everyone around her. Folding her hands on the pew bench in front of her, she rested her head on them and closed her eyes. *You alone know what-all Dat has done that's displeased You,* she began, focusing on her prayer despite the fears that spiraled in her mind, much like dry leaves caught in a whirlwind. *If Rosalyn, Edith, and I can help set him straight, please show us how to do that, Jesus . . . because You know how Dat gets when we speak our minds.*

After several minutes, Bishop Tom's steady voice guided them back to their worship as a group. "Hear our prayers, oh Lord," he said reverently. "Incline Thine ear to us and grant us Thy peace."

As everyone rose to sit on the pew benches again, Loretta glanced at Dat. It was time for him to stand up and read the Scripture, and despite the breeze circulated by the ceiling fan, he appeared extremely uncomfortable. The men didn't wear their black suit coats in the summertime—only their long-sleeved white shirts with black vests and trousers—but Dat's face was flushed and sweaty above his beard as he glanced at the small piece of paper the bishop had handed him earlier. He nearly dropped the big King James Bible as he opened it.

"Our first passage is found in the fourth chapter of Ephesians, verses twenty-five through twenty-eight. Hear the word of the Lord," he said in a voice that sounded cautious and strained. He found his place on the page with his finger and began to read.

"'Wherefore putting away lying, speak every man truth with his neighbor: for we are members one of another,'" Dat said, reading more quickly than usual. "'Be ye angry, and sin not: let not the sun go down upon your wrath: Neither give place to the devil. Let him that stole steal no more,'" he continued with a nervous gasp, "'but rather let him labor, working with his hands the thing which is good, that he may have to give to him that needeth.'"

Loretta glanced at her sisters, whose eyes were as wide as hers. Was this their father, the deacon who normally read aloud from the Bible with gusto and exuberance? As he noisily turned the large, thin pages to find the next passage he was to read, he appeared pale—and he had to flip back and forth to find the correct place. Without looking up at anyone, Dat continued.

"From the book of James, chapter one, verses twelve through sixteen." He cleared his throat as though a large lump were lodged in it. "'Blessed is the man that endureth temptation: for when he is tried, he shall receive the crown of life, which the Lord hath promised to them that love Him. Let no man say when he is tempted, I am tempted of God: for God cannot be tempted with evil, neither tempteth He any man,'" Dat continued doggedly. "'But every man is tempted, when he is drawn away of his own lust, and enticed. Then when lust hath conceived, it bringeth forth sin: and sin, when it is finished, bringeth forth death. Do not err, my beloved brethren.'"

Dat closed the Bible with a loud *whump* and quickly returned to the preachers' bench. When he landed between Preacher Ben and Bishop Tom, he hugged the big book to his chest like a shield, as though he expected one of the men on either side of him to strike him. Folks in the crowd were shifting on the benches, wearing puzzled expressions. Not only had the passages seemed prickly, compared to their usual Sunday morning readings, but it was very obvious that they'd upset Dat in a way Loretta hadn't seen since Mamm had died. Had Ben and Tom chosen the verses because they would put Dat on edge?

As Bishop Tom rose to begin the main sermon, he glanced at Dat and then gazed at the congregation with an expression that made Loretta's pulse pound heavily. Was he going to speak more directly about whatever wrongdoing he and Preacher Ben had discussed with Dat when they'd come to the house?

"'Every man is tempted,'" the bishop said, echoing the words Dat had read. "Every one of us falls prey to Satan's whispers, whether the devil speaks to our need to own and conceal electrical devices our Amish faith doesn't allow, or he lures us to the refrigerator to eat more than we need, or . . ."

Bishop Tom paused to let his gaze linger on each side of the room. The congregation had become so silent that not even the brushing of women's aprons against their dresses could be heard. "And sometimes Satan convinces us that because we are one of God's chosen, or in a position of power, we can get by with a few little things, like spreading gossip—or big things, like stealing money, or shoplifting, or abusing

the wives and children He has blessed us with."
Bishop Tom inhaled deeply and released the air
slowly. "It seems almost ridiculous for James to tell us
not to err, for to err is human, *jah?* But in our hearts,
we know when we've crossed the line—when we've
cheated others, or cheated God, and then lied to
ourselves so we could go on as though we've done
nothing wrong."

Loretta swallowed hard. Folks were shifting nervously on the pew benches, some of them looking
down at their laps, as though to ask, *Is it I, Lord?* Even
the young children were wide-eyed and quiet, sensing
the bishop's serious tone. Dat was licking his lips,
brushing his hair back with a hand that trembled. As
the sermon continued, he appeared to be breathing
very shallowly so as not to draw attention to himself.
Beside him, Preacher Ben sat calmly, yet his usual
smile was missing as he occasionally nodded at points
the bishop was making.

"In closing, my friends," Bishop Tom said several
minutes later, "I will remind you that the antidote to
our sinful human nature is confession. When we
admit our wrongdoing—to God, and to those neighbors we have sinned against—we free ourselves of
a burden that's too heavy for us to bear alone. We
release our sin! We offer it up as testimony to our
weakness, and we can then dare to ask for understanding and pardon. We can beg forgiveness from
those we've wronged."

Bishop Tom took one more look around at the
crowd. "And then, my friends, we can follow Paul's
words to the Ephesians and work with our hands
toward the common welfare so that folks in need will
have enough to get by on—and to repay the debt we

owe. May God's love be in our hearts, and may His will be our guide, today and always."

The room seemed to exhale in relief as the bishop resumed his seat on the bench. Women began fanning themselves with stiff paper fans from the funeral home in New Haven or with folding plastic fans they pulled from their apron pockets. Some of the men glanced at one another as they blotted their foreheads with their handkerchiefs, questions in their eyes.

Loretta didn't dare whisper to her sisters, who appeared as chastised as she felt. Although everyone in the room was guilty of something, she had a pretty good idea that her *dat* had been the target of Preacher Ben and Bishop Tom's unusually heavy words. Was the bishop going to call a members' meeting after church and demand that Dat get on his knees and confess? As ominous as both sermons had sounded, she wasn't sure she really wanted to know how far her father had fallen or what he was expected to admit.

The service continued with a long prayer they read from a prayer book, the bishop's benediction, and a final hymn. As the final strains of the song died away, folks sat expectantly to see if Bishop Tom was going to call a members' meeting. He gazed around the room pensively. "If anyone cares to step forward and confess anything, now would be a *gut* time."

Everyone sat absolutely still and silent, only their eyes moving as they waited for someone to respond.

The bishop smiled sadly, as though he hadn't really expected any volunteers. "All right then, I for one am hungry for a simple meal and some fellowship," he said quietly. "And I bet you kids are ready to run outside and play for a bit."

With a whoop, Annie Mae Wagler's three little brothers ran for the door, followed by their young sister. The women quickly headed for Miriam's kitchen to set out the food they'd brought as the men went to fetch the long folding tables.

The talk was in loud whispers, and it rang with fearful curiosity. "What on God's *gut* earth is going on, that the sermons were about a demon among us?" Savilla asked as she handed food from the refrigerator to the women waiting nearby.

"I got the feeling that somebody's in deep trouble," Naomi Brenneman remarked softly. "Really makes me wonder what's happened."

Loretta busied herself carrying platters and bowls of food out to the tables the men were setting up, and her sisters joined her. Her conscience tingled as though *she* had committed the heinous sins hinted at during the sermons—but she wasn't about to mention Ben and Tom's visit with Dat, which had happened nearly two weeks ago. There would be no living with her father if she or Rosalyn spoke up, so they kept their knowledge under their *kapp*s. Sometimes it was just best to let God work things out His way.

Chapter Twenty-One

Drew smiled to himself as he and the other men set up the tables in Preacher Ben's front room. Some of them appeared very curious, while others were clearly concerned that the two sermons had been aimed at them. Cornelius had excused himself to use the bathroom—and Drew wondered if he would slip out the back door rather than remain for the meal.

Drew thought Ben and the bishop had done an admirable job of preaching about Cornelius's crime—and giving him a chance to voluntarily confess it—without naming him as the culprit in front of his neighbors. They had honored their part of the bargain by keeping his secret, but they had certainly made him sweat.

The men made small talk as they handled the tables, but with Bishop Tom and Preacher Ben working alongside them, they weren't going to speculate about the demon in their midst. Drew had heard rumors that a few of these fellows had been caught with televisions or radios hidden away in back rooms of their shops and plugged in to outlets attached to the solar panels on their rooftops. Rumor had it that

Atlee Glick was using a cell phone to conduct business at the sale barn he managed. Although cell phones without Internet connections existed for Plain people, Bishop Tom had encouraged Willow Ridge residents to keep using their phone shanties because a cell phone was only one step away from other worldly temptations that led English folks astray.

Finally, Adam Wagler spoke up. "Bishop, are you going to give us any idea about what—or whom—you and Ben were preaching this morning?"

Every man in the room got quiet.

After a long moment, Bishop Tom smiled. "It's always best for those who have sinned to confess of their own free will," he replied as he met their gazes. "If any of you feel Ben and I were talking about you, now's your chance to release your burden."

The men glanced around, but nobody replied. Drew wondered if they'd noticed how hastily Cornelius had left the room—or if they'd gotten ideas about his guilt while he'd squirmed and turned pale during the sermons or while he'd read the Scripture passages so nervously. As Loretta, Rosalyn, and Edith came from the kitchen with food, however, Drew's thoughts changed direction.

The worry on the Riehl sisters' faces stabbed at him. Drew felt sorry that he was keeping information from them—yet he still believed they'd be devastated to learn the full extent of their father's wrongdoing. He and Nora had agreed to let Bishop Tom handle this situation, so he was keeping his mouth shut.

His mission for the rest of the day was to make Loretta smile. And say *yes*.

Drew caught up with her before she returned to the kitchen, keeping his voice low. "I know you often sit with your sisters or the other women at the common meal," he began, "but I'd be tickled if you'd sit with me today. And after we eat, I'd like to go for a walk—or for a drive. Whichever you'd like best."

Loretta's face lit up with gratitude. "*Jah,* I'll sit with you," she replied happily. "And if we go for a drive, we catch a little more breeze than if we walk, *jah?*"

And we leave all the prying eyes behind faster, too. Drew nodded. "Soon as I've finished eating, I'll go hitch Raven to my rig and we'll be off. I've been cooped up long enough today."

"*Jah,* the room ran out of air during church," Loretta murmured sadly. "It'll be a treat to go for a ride."

A few minutes later, everyone was sitting down at the long tables and passing big bowls of potato salad, coleslaw, broccoli salad, and fruit gelatin and platters of sliced ham and sandwiches. The September weather had remained unseasonably warm, so the women had prepared food that didn't require running an oven. Drew was happy to eat fresh vegetables from his neighbors' gardens and sample salads that a single man didn't prepare for himself.

"What did you bring today?" he asked, leaning closer to Loretta. He enjoyed watching the color rise in her flawless cheeks.

"Rosalyn and I made the no-bake peanut butter cookies and the big blue bowl of potato salad," she replied, holding his gaze with her hazel eyes. "And what did you bring, Drew?"

He laughed—but being a bachelor didn't mean he couldn't contribute to the meal. He always felt that if you were going to eat, you should bring something, even if it was a bag of potato chips. "I grilled the chicken legs."

Loretta's eyebrows rose as she picked up the chicken leg on her plate. "You must've had to grill two or three batches, as many legs as are in that glass casserole," she said in an approving tone. After she bit in and chewed the chicken, she nodded. "You'll make some girl a lucky catch, Drew. These are seasoned well with just enough sauce, and they're cooked just right. I love cold chicken, don't you?"

His heart thudded hard. They'd tossed the subject of marriage around—indirectly—for a while now, and he hoped Loretta's remark meant that she was of a mind to accept his proposal. "Zook's Market had family-size packages of chicken legs on sale, so it seemed like an easy thing to cook for my supper last night and to bring today."

Loretta smiled again. "You're quite the meal planner. Most fellows don't have a clue about doing that."

Drew shrugged. "When you live alone," he said with a playful sigh, "you can't open cans of chili or boxes of mac and cheese every day, or exist on frozen pizza. Well, you could—but *yuck.*"

Her burst of laughter delighted him, even though it made a lot of people turn their way. Drew didn't care about that. He was pleased to have Loretta smiling and responding so well to him after her difficult morning—and he wanted folks to know that he and Loretta were a couple. When he saw Will smile knowingly from a table across the crowded room, he also noticed that Savilla was seated across from him. He was pleased that Gingerich had found somebody to spend his time with as well.

Drew cleared his plate and resisted the urge to refill it. "See you in a few," he whispered as he rose from the table.

Loretta nodded. "I'll be out front by Miriam's rosebushes. Ready to go."

It was all Drew could do not to run from the Hooley

home to the stable near Asa and Edith's house. "All right, Raven," he said as he quickly hitched his open rig to the Percheron, "today's the day, and you've got to help me get it right. We've got to strike while the iron's hot."

As he thought about that old saying, he realized it didn't quite fit his situation—but he laughed, because Raven wouldn't know the difference anyway. Everything delighted him today, and he prayed that the afternoon's ride would work its magic and that Loretta would be his fiancée when they returned to town.

His pulse was pounding as he drove to the intersection and turned onto the county blacktop, because Loretta was standing there waiting for him. She was rocking from heel to toe in her eagerness to ride with him, smiling brightly as she watched him approach— making him feel he could say or do no wrong. He hopped down to lift her into the rig, holding her gaze as he placed his hands at her waist.

"You make me so happy, Loretta," he said.

"I do, don't I?" she teased. "I don't care where we go, as long as we find some shady places to park along the way."

"I just happen to know of a few," Drew said, easily lifting her into the open buggy.

The easy banter they shared as he drove along the county highway seemed to foretell the marriage they would share, not just as husband and wife, but as good friends. They remarked about the huge red barn that had been completed on Wyatt McKenzie's property—along with the fancy double-wide trailer he was living in—and speculated about the other structures he might build.

"Do you suppose he'll build a house and hitch up with Rebecca?" Loretta asked.

"They seemed pretty chummy the day his barn was raised," Drew remarked lightly.

Loretta considered this for a moment. "That would mean her pretty brick house would be empty. Maybe up for sale," she hinted.

"Who knows? Her *dat* built that house, and he might have other plans for it," he pointed out.

Drew steered Raven toward Cedar Creek, because long stretches of the road were shaded by a canopy of trees growing along both sides. When they reached the first of these cooler areas, Drew slipped his arm around Loretta. "Just beyond this next bend, you'll see the old stone silo and the big white house that belong to Bishop Vernon," he said.

Loretta leaned forward in anticipation as the *clip-clop, clip-clop* of Raven's hooves resounded against the shady road. "Oh my, are those black cattle his, too? That's a pretty picture, with them grazing in the pasture."

"*Jah*, those are Black Angus, which he raises for their high-quality beef," Drew replied. "Just down the road, his nephew Abner runs a butcher shop, where a lot of the meat gets processed."

"Bishop Vernon's such a kind, levelheaded man," she murmured. "He was such a voice of reason and wisdom when we were figuring out Will and Asa's dilemma about who fathered Louisa and Leroy."

"He was," Drew agreed. It was too bad she'd mentioned the part of his past he wasn't particularly proud of, yet her tone held nothing but acceptance of the way Asa and Edith had taken Drew's children to raise as their own. "We're lucky Bishop Vernon and Bishop Tom are longtime friends who help each other out—and we're lucky that Nazareth and Vernon's wife, Jerusalem, are sisters, so we see him a little more often."

"Do you suppose Bishop Tom will consult with him about whatever Dat's been caught at?"

Drew pulled the rig over onto a wide spot at the side of the road and set the brake. From here, the silo, the big white house, and the black cattle dotting the lush green pasture made a picturesque backdrop— the perfect spot to take Loretta's mind off her troubles.

"I don't know the answer to that," he murmured as he pulled her closer. "Right now, your *dat* is the furthest thing from my mind."

Loretta giggled and reached for him as he went after the kiss he'd been craving all day. With her arms around his neck and her lithe body leaning into his, the moment ascended to a bliss he hoped to maintain for several more minutes—and for years to come.

Drew kissed Loretta again, praying the words came out just right—and hoping with all his heart that she would accept his offer. His heart was beating so fast and loud, she could surely hear it, but as he gently placed his hand on her neck, he realized her pulse was thrumming in time with his. There would never be a more harmonious, opportune moment, so Drew held her close.

"Loretta, will you marry me?" he whispered near her ear. "You're all I can think about, and it seems to me you feel the same—"

Loretta eased away to gaze at him with her vibrant hazel eyes. "I've been waiting for you to ask me," she murmured in a dreamlike voice. "I'd be pleased and proud to be your wife, Andrew Detweiler."

He didn't often go by his given first name, yet the

way Loretta said it made him feel ten feet tall. Drew hugged her close again, reveling in her immediate acceptance. "I love you so much," he said hoarsely.

"I love you, too, Drew. These feelings I have are so much different from when—well," she added with a little shrug, "I guess we've both been in love before, or we believed we were. With you, I feel like a completely different person than I did the last time I got engaged."

Drew closed his eyes, resting his forehead against hers. "Maybe because we both understand how it feels to move beyond our past feelings, we're better prepared to make it work this time," he suggested softly. "Your forgiveness of my relationship with Molly means so much, Loretta. *Denki* for understanding."

Her face shone like the sun as she smiled at him. "Who can regret Louisa and Leroy?" she asked sweetly. "You saw that they'd be raised with a *mamm* and a *dat*, at a time when Will couldn't possibly have cared for them."

"Ah, but your sisters got them through the toughest days," Drew countered. "Had Edith not stood up for them and expected me—and Will—to do right by them, where would we be?"

"And now we're a bigger, happier family," Loretta said with a nod. "Someday, we'll be an even bigger family, *jah*?"

Her teasing tone sent desire coursing through Drew's body. "So when would you like to be married? Bishop Tom will want to allow time for some instruction, even though we've both already joined the church."

Loretta considered his question. "Today's the eighteenth of September, so . . . sometime in late

October? As soon as Bishop Tom can perform the
ceremony? Rosalyn and Edith and I will need to plan
the meal and—"

"I'd be happy to spring for dinner at the Grill N
Skillet," Drew put in. "Edith's raising babies and you
and Rosalyn are busy with canning vegetables, so why
not let Josiah and Savilla cook?"

"And we'll ask Miriam to bake the wedding cake!"
Loretta said. "Her cakes are the prettiest I've ever
seen. And the ladies are all happy to bake pies, if we
ask them."

"Sounds like we have the day pretty well planned."
Drew smiled, feeling as though his world had expanded to the point that he was floating inside a
huge balloon filled with love, as happy as he'd ever
been. "If you want to, we can go back to the house
and ask Bishop Tom to announce our engagement.
That will set our plans in motion a little sooner."

"*Gut* idea! Let's do it!" Loretta hugged him hard
and then kissed him with excited fervor. "It's not as
though our news will come as a total surprise."

Drew disengaged the brake and took up the leather
lines. "Geddap, Raven," he murmured, steering the
Percheron in a wide circle to head back to Willow
Ridge.

Despite the afternoon heat, Loretta sat against him
as he wrapped his arm around her. If things went as
they'd planned, he'd be married to this delightful
young woman by the end of October, and his heart
skipped happily at the thought. There'd been a time
in his life when the responsibilities of marriage had
seemed heavy and onerous, but at this moment he
simply knew that Loretta was the woman he'd been
born to marry. He'd resisted moving to Willow Ridge
when Asa said it would improve business for their

furniture shop, yet now he could see that God's providential hand had been guiding him all along.

"Where shall we live, Drew?" Loretta asked softly. "Maybe if Rebecca takes up with Wyatt, she would rent us her house—"

"We can't assume that she'll do that—or that her plans will be on the same schedule as ours," Drew put in with a chuckle.

"I know there won't be time for you to have a house built—unless we wait," she continued pensively. "But then, maybe you don't have the money to do that—and it's okay if you don't. Honest."

"Money's not an issue," Drew assured her. "The furniture business has been brisk, and I've not been spending money for much except groceries." His thoughts began to spin as he mentally worded his reply to her original question.

"Or we could live with Asa and Edith," Loretta said. "They have plenty of bedrooms—"

"I thought we'd live at your place for a while," Drew said carefully. "Lots of couples stay with the bride's family until—"

"Absolutely not." Loretta straightened on the buggy seat to fix him with her intense hazel-eyed gaze. "I've spent my entire life wishing to get out from under Dat's thumb. Since Mamm's been gone, he's taken out his frustration and—well, just plain meanness—on my sisters and me, and I'm *tired* of it. And who *knows* what he's gotten himself into lately?"

Drew's heart clutched for a painful moment. Loretta wasn't accusing him, exactly, but he *had* withheld information about her father's activities—and that probably didn't seem fair to her. "I don't know all the details about your *dat*'s predicament, either," he hedged. "But—but I told Bishop Tom and Ben that I would move to your place so your *dat* wouldn't feel tempted to . . . backslide."

Loretta's eyes widened as she scooted away from him. "And you made these plans without asking *me*? Assuming I'd marry you and go along with whatever you'd decided?" she demanded in a hurt whisper. "Drew, you know how cranky and unreasonable he gets about every little—"

"If I'm living there, I believe he'll curb his tongue," Drew insisted quickly. "Your *dat* persists in his criticism because he knows you girls won't stand up to him. I *will*."

Loretta turned away from him, crossing her arms as waves of indignation stretched between them like an ocean. Drew steered Raven over to the side of the road again, fearing that even the canopy of shade wouldn't cool the mood Loretta was in.

And you put her in that mood, his conscience pointed out. *You assumed you were acting on her behalf, with the best of intentions, and now you've really stepped in it.*

"You're right, Loretta," he said softly. "I should have spoken to you first, but at the time—after Ben and Tom visited your *dat*, and Cornelius and I had our private chat during that difficult dinner at your place—I said I was going to keep track of his comings and goings. His trips to Kansas City haven't been for buying clock parts, Loretta. I'm sorry."

"Not half as sorry as I am," she retorted with a whimper. Still looking away from him, she wiped away tears. "For most things, I could go along with what you want, Drew—I could be an agreeable wife. But I promised myself long ago that once I married, I'd no longer be living at home."

She might as well have sucker punched him. Her words sounded serious. Final. "Well then, you made that decision without asking me about it, too, ain't so?" he asked quietly.

Loretta turned back around to glare at him. Her eyes were filled with tears, and a few of them ran down her flawless face. "That's different, and you know it."

With a sigh, he dared to ask the question that hung between them. "So you're saying that you won't marry me if we're going to live at your place?"

Loretta heaved a heavy sigh. "No, actually I'm saying it's probably best if I don't marry you at all," she replied in a quavering voice. "I thought you of all people would realize how unhappy I've been at home. We apparently don't know each other very well—and that's not a *gut* way to start out as husband and wife."

Drew nearly choked. "But—but we can talk this over," he protested. "Married people should state their opinions and listen to each other and—"

"Nope. Just take me back to Willow Ridge."

He felt as though Raven had kicked him in the chest, and for a moment he could hardly breathe. "Loretta, an engagement is the time for us to settle issues like this, and—and I'm willing to reconsider—"

"I don't think so. I'm too upset to see reason right now."

Drew stared blankly at Raven's muscled hindquarters. How had the conversation gone from the dizzying heights of her *yes* to this rock-bottom basement of her disappointment and his despair? In a matter of minutes they'd planned their wedding day, and within seconds Loretta had backed out.

He lightly clapped the lines on his horse's back. "Maybe tomorrow, after we've had a chance to think about it—"

"I'm finished thinking. I want to go home."

Drew immediately saw the irony in her statement, but he knew better than to point it out to her. The ride back to Willow Ridge felt hot and sticky with the day's humidity and Loretta's tears. He urged Raven into a faster gait, sensing that the young woman beside him would've walked home if they hadn't been more than a mile out of town. Anything to be away from him.

About twenty minutes later, the new barn at the McKenzie place came into view, along with the mill on the river. Drew cleared his throat. "I can either drop you at the Hooleys' place or at your house—"

"No, I want to get out right here," Loretta insisted. "I'll walk—"

"And have the men sitting in Ben's front yard speculate about why you're hiking down the road while I'm driving the rig?" Drew interrupted. "Sit right where you are. Neither of us needs their questions right now."

Loretta pressed her lips into a tight line, but she nodded. Rather than passing the gathering of men in lawn chairs, Drew steered Raven onto the road that went in front of Nora and Luke's house and the barn that housed Simple Gifts. He was searching for words to change her mind, to give himself a foot in the door to see her again, but as they drove past the Wagler home and followed the curve left to pass the Kanagy farm, he decided to leave things as they stood.

For all they knew, Cornelius was home. He'd apparently left Ben and Miriam's house before folks had even sat down, because he'd never shown up to eat the common meal.

She'll just have to deal with him. I offered to act as a buffer between her and Cornelius, but she turned me down.

A few minutes later they drove past Bishop Tom's dairy farm, where his black-and-white Holsteins were gathered beneath the shade trees in the pasture. The Hostetler place wasn't quite as picturesque as Bishop Vernon's, but the cows appeared contented—which was more than Drew could say for himself. When he eased the rig to a halt in front of the Riehl house, he sighed. "I hope you'll reconsider, Loretta," he said softly. "We can talk this over. I—I still love you."

Her wounded expression said more than words. Without waiting for him to come around and help her, Loretta hopped down from the buggy. Her stiff walk as she crossed the road stabbed at Drew's heart—but he'd done everything he knew to dissuade her from leaving things between them on a sour note. He watched her hurry up the porch steps and into the house. He drove slowly to the barn where he and Asa stabled their horses.

After he tossed some feed into Raven's bin and ran fresh water into the metal horse tank, he walked slowly back to his apartment above the furniture shop. From his bedroom and kitchen windows he could see the white Riehl house, and he'd often enjoyed imagining where Loretta might be inside it at any given time and what she might be doing. He'd also dared to dream of sharing a room upstairs with her after they married—

Better stop that, he told himself as he walked away from the window. *Loretta's shut you down, and now you won't be able to monitor Cornelius as you told the bishop you would, either. You're two shades of stupid for thinking you had this situation all figured out.*

Chapter Twenty-Two

As Rebecca set a foil pan of rhubarb crisp on the floor of her car, she was smiling, anticipating the expression on Wyatt's handsome face when she surprised him with it. He'd been at his New York horse farm earlier this week, and he'd called her every night he was away, sounding eager to return to Willow Ridge to see her. They had established a comfortable pattern of allowing each other space to work and tend to business, and it suited her. Wyatt teased about getting her into bed without pushing her—and that suited her, too. One of these days, when they'd committed to each other, sharing their innermost secrets would be the right thing to do.

Rebecca set a chilled bottle of white wine on the seat alongside her laptop, started the car, and backed out of her driveway. The cloudless evening sky vibrated with the day's last light and a heat that shimmered as it rose from the asphalt county highway. On this Friday night in September, it seemed right to celebrate the raising of Wyatt's second huge barn, which was scheduled for the next day. She'd updated his new website and wanted to show him how it looked now that it was live, anticipating the heartfelt appreciation he always expressed for her work.

She entered Willow Ridge, waving at her sister Rhoda, who was watering the flower beds that surrounded the clinic building, where she lived in the upstairs level with Andy Leitner and their kids. As Rebecca reached the intersection, she caught the aroma of Josiah's smokers, redolent with the seasoned beef and pork he was serving to the supper crowd. By the looks of the parking lot, the Grill N Skillet was packed.

Across the road from the café, Mamma and Ben were sitting in their porch swing with little Bethlehem. They waved cheerfully at her as well. She felt a little guilty for not stopping, but she was eager to catch up with Wyatt—and Mamma would understand about that. After her mother had met Wyatt and agreed to organize the break refreshments for his barn raisings, she'd invited him to dinner with Rebecca for the following Sunday so he could get better acquainted with the family. Mamma had also remarked to Rebecca that Wyatt was somewhat older than she'd expected, and in the next breath she stated that she and Rebecca's father, Jesse, had been years apart, too—and that the years between her and Ben made no difference in the love they shared.

As Rebecca passed the mill and crossed the river bridge, Wyatt's first barn rose into view. She drove past it nearly every day, yet its magnificence still amazed her. She slowed the car, carefully turned onto the packed dirt path that served as a road, and drove toward the luxurious trailer parked in the shade near the pond. When she saw lights through the windows, her heart beat faster.

Wyatt was home, and he would be so surprised that she was stopping by without calling—feeling comfortable enough with their relationship to just show up, as he'd done on occasion at her place. He'd teased her about being so formal, so now she was stepping outside the proverbial box and acting far more spontaneously.

Rebecca pulled up beside his Lexus and shut off the engine. She felt odd checking her makeup in the rearview mirror, yet she'd taken extra pains with it so Wyatt would see that she could rise above her hometown girl-next-door look to appear more sophisticated. She got out, smoothing the creases the safety belt had made in the paisley print top Wyatt always complimented. Taking a deep breath, she lifted the warm foil pan from the floor of her car and started for his door. The wine and the laptop could wait until she'd surprised him with a home-baked dessert.

A glance into the large front window stopped Rebecca before she stepped onto the deck. Wyatt was standing inside, a silhouette with a backdrop of lamplight. But he wasn't alone.

Rebecca gripped the pan of dessert, trying to believe what she was seeing. The other silhouette was shorter and thinner than Wyatt, and when it turned its head, Rebecca saw a sleek, distinctive topknot she'd stared at many times online.

It's that woman in the red dress—the Lexington socialite who's hanging all over Wyatt in the photos I've seen.

Rebecca forced herself to take a deep breath. Why on earth would that hifalutin, high-maintenance woman come to a tiny town like Willow Ridge? Had

Wyatt actually been in Lexington, spending time with the woman in red, rather than in New York?

When the woman placed her arms around Wyatt's neck and moved against him, Rebecca bit back a scream. She might be a hometown girl, but she knew what she was watching, and it was seduction. Apparently Wyatt wasn't happy waiting for *her*, so he'd brought along a willing woman from the other world he inhabited.

Rebecca's throat tightened, and she blinked back tears. She'd obviously misread and misinterpreted everything Wyatt had done and everything he'd said to her, thinking she *meant* something to him— believing he wanted to be only with her. Her first instinct was to slink back to her car and go home for a good cry, because compared to the wealthy, sophisticated peacock in Wyatt's trailer, she was a little wren pecking at the dust. She would simply not answer his calls anymore, would keep herself busy with her graphic design business, as she had before—

"Phooey on that!" Rebecca muttered. Keeping the solid front door between herself and the pair inside Wyatt's trailer, she stepped up onto the deck. Anger and frustration washed over her, and she pounded loudly on the door, ready to spit nails.

It took several moments for Wyatt to answer—time he'd most likely spent kissing his other guest before prying himself out of her embrace. When he opened the door and saw her, the startled surprise in his blue-gray eyes was that of a cornered animal.

"Rebecca! I wasn't expecting—"

"Yeah, I wasn't, either," she blurted out. "I thought we were *partners*. Equals. This is for you, *jerk*." Without a moment's hesitation, she placed her hand under the flexible pan and pitched it at his face.

Wyatt's stifled cry and the sight of rhubarb and crust splattering his head and silk shirt gave Rebecca a moment of vengeful triumph. She turned and ran to her car, however, too upset to stick around for an explanation. What could he possibly say to refute what she'd seen through the window? She raced away from the trailer and turned onto the county highway with squealing tires, so heartsick she could barely see.

By the time she'd reached the bridge and the mill, Rebecca realized she needed to slow down, to concentrate on driving safely, because Wyatt's betrayal wasn't worth having a wreck. She pulled into a parking space at the café, shaking badly and crying as she shifted the car out of gear. She leaned against the steering wheel to weep as only a brokenhearted woman could do.

A tap on the car window startled her. Nora and Luke were standing outside, appearing very concerned and gesturing for her to roll down the window. Rebecca sighed. The last thing she wanted was for word about her and Wyatt's confrontation to race along the local grapevine.

The window was only down a couple of inches when Nora asked, "Rebecca, what's wrong, sweetie? You look like you've lost your last friend."

"Can we buy you some supper and talk it over?" Luke added as he peered in at her.

Rebecca shook her head. "This is something I've got to handle myself," she insisted, sniffling loudly. "I'll get over it."

Nora pulled a facial tissue from her handbag and offered it to her. "We'll be home after we eat our supper—in case you don't feel like being alone."

"Thanks. You two are the best." Rebecca blew her nose loudly and dabbed at her eyes. "Don't let my crying jag keep you from taking your time to enjoy a nice meal. I'll be fine. Really."

"If there's somebody who needs a talking-to on your behalf, let me know," Luke said protectively. "I don't take it lightly when somebody upsets a *gut* friend like you, Rebecca."

His words warmed her heart, but she really just wanted the Hooleys to go into the café and leave her to her pity party. When they finally stepped inside, Rebecca backed out of the parking lot and drove slowly toward the county highway. She didn't need anyone else stopping to inquire about her anguish . . . yet she didn't feel like going home to an empty house, either. She wiped her eyes against her sleeve—and then, in the rearview mirror, she saw that she'd smeared her mascara and makeup so badly that her blotchy, tear-streaked face resembled a bad Halloween mask.

Laughing sadly at herself, Rebecca drove the short distance to Mamma and Ben's house and pulled into their lane. Sometimes a girl really needed her mother.

By the time she'd gotten out of her car, Mamma was crossing the wide porch to greet her. Bethlehem, now eight months old and sporting a halo of light brown curls, rested against Mamma's shoulder, peering curiously at Rebecca with a finger in her mouth.

When Mamma got a good look at Rebecca, she frowned. "What's happened, honey-girl?" she asked softly. "Not five minutes ago you were driving by as though you had a date with—"

"Should've called before I surprised him with some fresh rhubarb crisp," Rebecca muttered, shaking her head. "You might as well figure he's not coming for dinner on Sunday. It's over."

Mamma's expressive eyebrows rose. "I don't like the sound of this—or the look of your poor face," she added sympathetically. She turned to look at Ben. "Your little girl's due for some *dat* time while my little girl and I go to the kitchen for some talk and lemonade."

"I was hoping I'd get a turn with her," Ben said cheerfully. "Bethlehem's been telling me I need to practice on 'You Are My Sunshine' so I sing it just right for her."

Gratitude welled up inside Rebecca as she stepped up onto the porch. With a quick wave for Ben, who was already humming the tune when he took the baby, she preceded Mamma into the house. Toys were scattered in the front room, and the aromas of fried chicken and fried potatoes lingered in the air. She was surprised to see the supper dishes still on the table—but they gave her something constructive to do as she told her tale of woe.

"Bennie and I like to sit on the porch for a bit of an evening," Mamma said in explanation. She started scraping the plates, so Rebecca went to the sink to run dishwater. "I'm happy to get off my feet for a while after we eat, and it's not as though the dirty dishes will run off when we're not looking."

"The good fairies don't come and do them?" Rebecca teased. "When I was growing up with the Oliveris, that was the joke when I wanted to disappear after supper instead of helping."

Mamma's face softened with memories. "Rachel and Rhoda weren't keen on washing dishes, either, truth be told," she recalled, carrying the plates to the counter beside the sink. She set them down and slipped an arm around Rebecca. "Looks like you went to special trouble to look nice for Wyatt, but things didn't go the way you expected."

Rebecca sighed. "I'll be back after I wash my face. I look like a wreck."

When she stepped into the half bathroom down the hallway, she gazed sadly at her mascara-smeared face. "What a waste of makeup," she murmured as she turned on the water. She wet the oldest washcloth she could find in the vanity and pumped hand soap on it—not the ideal thing for cleansing her face, but it would remove all traces of her cosmetics.

Too bad it can't restore your soul and your hurt feelings, she thought as she closed her eyes and washed. After Rebecca dried her face, she spread some of Mamma's basic hand cream on it and removed the last traces of mascara from around her eyes. Her reflection showed a face in its plain state, as clean and fresh as her mother's—except that regret and worry didn't rim Mamma's eyes.

After she washed the makeup from the washcloth, Rebecca returned to the kitchen—and to her mother's inquisitive gaze as she turned from the lemonade she was pouring.

"Now your natural beauty shines through, child," Mamma said gently. "Care to tell me what happened?"

Rebecca swallowed half the glass of freshly-squeezed lemonade Mamma offered her. It amazed her how simple things like a clean face and a cold drink could restore her sense of perspective. "Mamma, I was taking a pan of rhubarb crisp to surprise Wyatt," she began softly, "but the surprise was on me. He—he was in his trailer with another woman."

Mamma frowned sadly as she reached for a tea towel. "Anyone we know?"

"I've seen her in pictures on his other websites.

She lives in Lexington—runs in the same high-dollar horse circles Wyatt does." Rebecca shrugged sadly and began to wash the dishes Mamma had set in the water to soak. "She's blond and thin and rich and beautiful—"

"And you're every bit the woman she is, because God made you that way, daughter," Mamma interrupted kindly. "No need to put yourself down on account of whom you assume her to be."

Rebecca's lips twitched with a half-hearted smile. Mamma had a way of getting straight to the details that really mattered. "But I saw her put her arms around Wyatt," she said in a thin voice. "I—I almost went back to the car with my tail between my legs, but I banged on the door instead. And when Wyatt looked startled to see me—looked guilty—I threw the pan of crisp in his face."

Mamma's eyes widened. "I hope he didn't get cut on the glass—"

"It was in a disposable foil pan," Rebecca explained. "Not that I wouldn't have thrown it anyway, mad as I was."

Mamma considered this as she dried a couple of plates. "It's not our way to succumb to a fit of temper," she reminded Rebecca with a wry smile. "Early on in my marriage to your father, however, he remarked that my piecrust wasn't as tender and flaky as his *mamm*'s. After he said it a second time, I told him he could go to his mother's to eat pie—and I threw the rest of that one at him before storming off to lock myself in the bedroom for a *gut* cry."

Rebecca's eyes widened. "From what I've seen since my return to Willow Ridge, I can't imagine you ever losing your temper, Mamma," she murmured.

Mamma chuckled. "Turns out I was carrying you

three girls at the time and didn't yet know it," she explained. "My condition didn't justify pitching a glass pie pan at Jesse, but I later chalked it up to roller-coaster hormones—and your *dat* didn't say any more about my crust, either. A lesson well learned."

Smiling, Rebecca scrubbed chicken grease from a platter. With her hands submerged in warm, soapy dishwater and the soothing sound of her mother's voice in her ear, she felt herself relaxing, returning to a rational state of mind. "Why would anyone think your piecrust wasn't wonderful?" she murmured. "You've surely baked a thousand pies in your life-time."

"*Jah*, that's true. But I only threw one of them," Mamma remarked. "Seeing cherry filling smeared all over Jesse's face and shirt felt pretty satisfying—until I realized I was the one who'd be laundering that shirt and having to live with him, beholden to him for his forgiveness. It was a waste of perfectly *gut* pie, too."

Rebecca nodded sadly. "Yeah, I put a lot of effort into that rhubarb crisp, and I didn't even get a taste of it," she murmured. "But what am I going to do? Wyatt's been coming on to me ever since we met, saying he wants to be with me—wants to start fresh in Willow Ridge instead of raising or racing his high-dollar Thoroughbreds," she added glumly. "But I know what I saw. She has her hooks in him, Mamma."

Her mother thought for several moments, her face still and her brown-eyed gaze clear and patient. Rebecca could only hope that as she matured, she would acquire her mother's quiet wisdom and her perpetual sense of peace.

"Sometimes our eyes and ears fool us," Mamma said softly. "We *think* we know what we see or hear, and yet we don't usually realize what remains unseen and unsaid. Every person we meet has lived a life we have no idea about—or carries secret burdens that would make us shudder if we knew about them."

Rebecca's first impulse was to refute her mother's statement—after all, Mamma hadn't seen those two entwined silhouettes inside Wyatt's trailer. But she bit back her retort, sensing the rest of the lesson was yet to come.

Mamma smiled at her, love shining on her face. "Sometimes the best tactic is to ask a man straight-out what's going on," she said. "If he squirms and dodges your question, you know he's hiding something. But if he has a plausible explanation, he probably deserves the benefit of your doubt—and if he's any sort of man at all, he'll work hard to remove your doubt altogether before you even ask your question."

Rebecca focused on scrubbing the skillet in which Mamma had fried chicken, scraping a stuck-on scrap with her thumbnail. "Wyatt's older than I am, so I realize he has some history with other women that I don't know about," she said with a sigh. "How on earth am I supposed to ask him about that woman— especially if she's still there?"

Mamma shrugged. "From what little I know of Wyatt, he's a shrewd businessman with a *gut* reputation—which means he knows how to deal with people," she said. "And I believe his intentions toward you are heartfelt and honest—he apologized to me for cutting three roses he took to you a while back, even though I'd never missed them."

Rebecca smiled at the memory of how Wyatt had punctured his thumb on the thorn of one of Mamma's beautiful roses.

"He told me he loved you, Rebecca," Mamma continued in a sentimental tone. "Most men don't go gushing to a young woman's mother unless they're sincere."

He told me he loved you.

Rebecca sucked in a deep breath, wanting to believe that statement. In her mind, however, she was still seeing Wyatt with that other woman. "You think he has a reasonable explanation for her?"

"If he does, wouldn't it be a shame to walk away based on a faulty assumption?" Mamma slipped her arms around Rebecca and hugged her close. "And if he's playing you false, it's better to find out now rather than after you've married him, *jah?*"

Rebecca found herself smiling in spite of her hurt feelings. Mamma's down-to-earth attitude—and her belief that Wyatt was worth a second chance—was settling her frayed nerves. She reveled in the warmth and pride that flowed from her mother, savoring her embrace. So much of the lifestyle and career Rebecca enjoyed flew in the face of Old Order beliefs, yet Miriam Lantz Hooley hadn't given up on her and would never, ever forsake her. Mamma's love was the biggest miracle in Rebecca's life.

So listen to her. She's wise. She wants all the best for you.

Rebecca kissed Mamma's cheek. "What would I do without you?" she whispered. "I'll think about this issue—pray about it—and reconsider my opinion of Wyatt."

Squeezing her again, Mamma eased away with a furtive smile. "I'll expect you both here for Sunday dinner—or I'll be waiting for a very *gut* excuse as to why you haven't put your relationship with Wyatt back in order."

Rebecca's breath caught at the thought of approaching Wyatt so soon after he'd crushed her. But there was no arguing with her mother. Amish folks believed that forgiveness should follow close on the heels of any perceived offense. Only backsliders allowed their anger to fester.

"All right, Mamma, for you I can do that," she said after a moment. "*Denki* for listening."

"It's a pleasure and a privilege to be a part of your life again, child," Mamma whispered. "God gave me a second chance to love you, so why would I want to do otherwise?"

After they finished putting the kitchen to rights, Rebecca chatted with Ben on the porch for a few minutes. She was delighted that little Bethlehem reached for her, babbling in baby talk, and by the time she was heading for her car she felt healed and restored.

The laptop on her front seat gave her an idea— and she wondered why she hadn't thought of it before. *Puh. You only had eyes for Wyatt when you did your previous Internet searches.*

On the table in her kitchen, Rebecca opened the computer and searched for the photographs of the woman who'd been in Wyatt's trailer. She navigated to the website for his Lexington horse farm, where several images of the chic blond appeared— most of them featuring her in the strapless red evening gown Rebecca envied.

"What's your name?" Rebecca muttered, trying to locate the information on the Internet. "Why hasn't Wyatt identified you on his site? Why doesn't he want people to know who you are?"

Doubt niggled at her as she continued to search— until she finally clicked on a Google image and found the woman who'd caused her such torment. "Vanessa Herriott," she murmured, and then typed the name into a slot on a website that listed addresses, phone numbers, arrest and law enforcement reports—all manner of information you could access about people for a membership fee. She used this service to check out her clients' backgrounds before she agreed to design sites for them. Why hadn't she thought to look up the socialite in the red dress before?

"Hmm. No record of criminal activity or delinquent taxes . . . thirty-seven years old . . . associated with Wyatt McKenzie," Rebecca read aloud.

That could mean several different things. Unless she wanted to endure a lot of questions from Mamma on Sunday about why she and Wyatt weren't coming for dinner, she needed to talk to him. Soon.

This isn't going to be easy, Rebecca thought with a sigh.

Chapter Twenty-Three

With the banging of hammers and the whine of drills filling the air around her at the McKenzie barn raising Saturday morning, Loretta gazed wistfully at a familiar, lithe figure. Drew and his brother were helping to raise a completed end of the barn—or at least its skeleton of studs and a truss—along with other men, as though they labored this way every day. Watching Amos Coblentz's skilled crewmen working alongside local volunteers was an inspiring sight—a study in true teamwork.

Loretta, however, felt left out. Alone. She and her two sisters had volunteered to serve sticky buns and other goodies, along with cold drinks, at the mid-morning break, which would be in about fifteen minutes. As Edith and Rosalyn playfully lifted the twins high into the air, making them laugh and kick delightedly, Loretta glumly wondered if she would ever have children . . . or appear as deeply happy as Edith.

Maybe I shouldn't have been so hasty to back out of my engagement, she thought for the hundredth time this week. *At least if I married Drew, I would stand a chance*

*of leaving home someday. I can't imagine he'd want to live
at our place long, crabby as Dat has been this week.*

To occupy herself, Loretta began separating the
large plastic cups and pouring lemonade into them
from the big, insulated cooler on the wagon. The
yellow liquid streamed from the spigot quickly, and
she soon began to fill other glasses with tea. As she
was adding ice from another big cooler so the drinks
would stay cold, Amos called out to his workmen to
take their break.

"You've been doing all the work, sister." Edith
smiled as Louisa babbled and reached for Loretta.
"Your niece is ready for somebody new to entertain
her, I suspect. She sees her *mamm* day in and day out,
after all."

Loretta found a smile for the little girl dressed in
pink, whose flyaway wisps of black hair framed her
pixie face. "More likely, Louisa will entertain *me*," she
said. As Loretta bounced the baby against her shoulder, Edith removed the plastic wrap from the trays of
sticky buns, cinnamon rolls, and brownies.

Rosalyn glanced toward the crowd of men approaching the wagon. As she placed the drinks on
trays, she said, "Do you suppose Drew will say anything today? Maybe ask you to talk things over?"

Loretta sighed. Rosalyn and Edith had been heartsick when they'd learned that Drew had proposed
and Loretta had backed out of the engagement
minutes later. "Why would he?" she murmured. "I'm
the one who walked away."

Edith slipped her arm around Loretta's shoulders.
"But Drew stands to lose out on a fine wife if he
lets you *get* away," she pointed out. "Asa and I are staying out of it. We know you two will do the right thing
without any meddling from us."

"Or from me," Rosalyn added with a shake of her head. "It's not as though your older *maidel* sister can offer any advice."

"Somebody wonderful will come along for you, Rosalyn," Edith insisted cheerfully. She strapped the twins into their carrier baskets sitting atop the wagon bed. "God just hasn't yet maneuvered him into the right place at the right time."

Loretta picked up a tray of baked goods and approached the men who were closest to the break wagon. She didn't care to discuss her derailed romance in front of these fellows—and for all she knew, Drew had spread the word that she'd walked away from his offer. "Seth, you and your brothers have surely worked up an appetite this morning," she remarked as she extended the tray toward the Brennemans.

Aaron snatched up a cinnamon roll and began to uncurl the outer layer. "At least it's not as hot this morning as it was at our last barn raising," he remarked.

"Amos brought along a few more fellows from Cedar Creek today," Micah put in as he chose a sticky bun. "Bishop Vernon brought along two cordless impact drivers. He and Bishop Tom seem to have a contest going to see who can drive the most screws the fastest."

Wyatt stepped up and selected a big brownie. "I was surprised to see Vernon's fancy tools. Didn't figure an Amish bishop would own such top-of-the-line equipment."

"Vernon's a cabinetmaker, so his work's easier with the right tools," Micah pointed out.

Seth chuckled. "If we're to build anything efficiently, it makes sense for us to work around our ban on electricity," he explained. "Can you imagine how long it would take to raise a barn with hand saws and basic old screwdrivers?"

Wyatt laughed, and then winced a little as he touched the bandage on his face. "You Amish men have a lot of fun on the job," he said before smiling carefully at Loretta. "When I heard that the women call their work gatherings *frolics*, I was impressed, too. Attitude makes all the difference."

"Many hands make light work," Loretta said with a nod. "What fun is it to labor alone?"

She didn't ask him about the bandages on one side of his face and neck, as she was barely acquainted with the newest property owner in town. The injury probably hurt, judging from the fact that Wyatt wasn't smiling as widely as he usually did.

Preacher Ben came up to take a cinnamon roll, glancing at Wyatt. "Did the razor bite you this morning?" he asked lightly.

Wyatt's blue-gray eyes lost their shine. "Got burned," he stated. "Need to keep the skin covered while I'm working in the sun."

Ben nodded as though he might know something he wasn't telling, but he moved on to take a glass from the tray Rosalyn was holding.

It occurred to Loretta that Rebecca wasn't on site with her camera today, as she'd been during the first barn raising. From what she'd seen and heard, Rebecca and Wyatt were spending a lot of time together whenever he was in town—and she'd clearly been smitten with him that day he'd first introduced himself in Nora's shop.

Has something happened between them this week as well? Rebecca was in a fine mood yesterday morning while she was putting together Nora's newsletter.

As Loretta considered this idea, she saw Drew in her peripheral vision—and he was making a point of avoiding her. He took a glass of iced tea from Edith's tray, appearing as tight-lipped as Wyatt, and then helped himself to a couple of fried pies from the tray on the wagon bed. Without a word to anyone, Drew took off toward town with a few other men who were probably heading to the restroom at the café.

Would it be so bad to live at home after we married? With another man in the house, maybe Dat wouldn't complain and criticize Rosalyn and me so much.

Loretta sighed, gazing at Drew's retreating figure. Last Sunday they'd been on top of the world, so happy and in love and planning their wedding . . . and it was her fault they weren't celebrating their engagement. Even as Drew had dropped her off at the house, he'd told her he loved her, and that they could talk about this housing issue.

Why hadn't she listened?

"How about if I take your tray, Loretta?" Edith asked softly. "I think you have something—or somebody—on your mind right now, *jah*?"

Loretta smiled gratefully at her insightful sister. Edith was the youngest of the three of them, but her heart had always reached out first when folks were hurting. "Something needs to be said, and I'm the one to say it," she murmured.

"I bet Drew's ready to listen, too. He looks every bit as miserable as you do." Edith squeezed her shoulder. "It'll all work out, Loretta. I just know it."

Inhaling deeply to steady her nerves, Loretta nodded. "You always get it right, Edith, so who am I to doubt you? It's me I wonder about sometimes."

With that, Loretta started toward the county highway and the river bridge, remaining a short distance behind another bunch of men heading in that direction. *You've got to help me, Lord, or I'll mess this up again,* she prayed as she walked past Luke's mill. *I really don't want to be a two-time loser.*

When Drew came out of the restroom situated between the Grill N Skillet and the Schrocks' quilt shop, he paused to inhale the mouthwatering aromas of the meats and side dishes Josiah and Savilla were preparing for the lunch shift. The café wouldn't open for another hour, but the Witmers had left a side door open so the work crew could come inside to use the facilities.

He stopped at the pass-through window to say hello to Savilla, who was taking bread from the oven—six loaf pans were positioned side by side on a wooden server she was holding with both gloved hands. "Wow, that's a great way to handle a lot of bread at one time," he remarked.

Naomi Brenneman, the carpenters' *mamm,* waved at him from a stove, where she was stirring sausage in a skillet. "We try to make things easier and more efficient," she said cheerfully. "Savilla's a whiz when it comes to making a lot of food in a short time."

Savilla laughed. "We'll be feeding a multitude again today," she put in. "It's in my best interest to have plenty of everything for you fellows who're raising Wyatt's barn. Running out of food is the ultimate sin when you're running a restaurant."

As Drew looked at all the lidded metal pans that would soon hold food in the buffet's steam table, he couldn't imagine the Witmers running short—but in a couple of hours they'd be open for their usual lunch business, as well as feeding Wyatt's workers.

How Savilla and Josiah estimated the amount they would cook and serve each day was beyond him.

"I'm looking forward to a really *gut* meal," he said. "*Denki* again for taking care of us in such fine style."

When Drew stepped away from the serving window he stopped suddenly, swallowing hard. Loretta was sitting at the table nearest the side door. He couldn't possibly leave the building without walking past her. Speaking to her.

Here's your chance to make another offer. Don't blow it, his inner voice warned.

Drew focused on her, taking in the tightness of her face and the stiff way she sat in the sturdy wooden chair. When Loretta looked up and saw him gazing at her, she sat straighter—as though she didn't know whether to stay or to rush out the door. Dozens of times since Sunday, he'd thought about walking over to the Riehl place to talk to her, yet his pride had prevented him from being the one to speak first. She'd wounded him, after all.

It had been the longest, loneliest week of his life.

Drew headed for the table where she sat, his heart pounding. Smiling nervously, he sat down across from her. "Loretta, I've been meaning to—"

"Drew, I've been a stubborn fool and—"

"—suggest that we could maybe live—"

"—I'll be sorry for the rest of my life if I don't—"

"—in my apartment instead of at your house."

"—reconsider your offer to . . ." Loretta's eyes widened. "What did you just say?" she whispered.

Drew laughed at the rapid-fire conversation that had just cleared the logjam of their tangled emotions. He reached across the table. "I said we could live in my apartment—if you don't mind having to fix it up some," he added, clasping her small, sturdy hands between his. "Why didn't I think of that last week when we argued?"

Loretta heaved a sigh of relief. "I've missed you so much this week, I don't really care where we live," she murmured. "I just want to be your wife, Drew. I'm sorry I was so hardheaded about not living with Dat."

He smiled all the way down to his soul, feeling as though this pretty young woman had just saved his life. "I can certainly understand why you feel that way, sugar," he said softly. "If it means that much to you, we'll live across the street—"

"And we could keep track of his comings and goings from your upstairs windows," she said as the realization dawned on her. "Or Rosalyn could let us know if he was planning to be gone. But then Rosalyn . . ."

"*Jah*, that's the way I see it. Although, at the end of the day," Drew said as he gazed into her hazel eyes, "your *dat* is responsible for keeping his promise to Bishop Tom. Either he'll repay his debt—straighten up and fly right—or he won't. I really doubt that my living in his house to act as his watchdog will make much difference."

Loretta gripped his hands, pausing to think about what he'd said and to consider the consequences of moving to Drew's apartment. "You're right," she said softly. "Dat got himself into serious trouble— whatever it was—and only he can dig himself out of it. I'm really surprised the bishop didn't call him out . . . didn't have him confessing on his knees after church last week."

"Bishop Tom and Preacher Ben lit a fire under him with their sermons and gave him every chance to come clean," Drew pointed out. He studied Loretta's face, sensing some hesitation behind her happiness. "What else is on your mind, pretty girl?"

Loretta sighed. "I guess now that I have a choice of places to live after we marry," she began, "I'm thinking about what it'll be like for Rosalyn if I move out and she's the only one at home with Dat. Day in and day out, that'll be really hard on her. *I* certainly wouldn't want to be in that position."

Drew nodded. "There's that. And my suggestion to live at your place, at least for a while, still stands," he said, holding her hands in his. "We can live wherever you think is best, Loretta."

The clouds left her eyes and she beamed at him. "You're a brave, generous man, Drew, and I love you for the way you're willing to step in for us girls and deal with Dat."

Drew shrugged a little awkwardly. Loretta's compliment filled his soul. Considering the way he'd deceived his brother and Edith before they'd married, it still felt like a miracle that Loretta loved him and wanted to be his wife. "I love you, too, Loretta, and I'll do all I can to make you happy," he murmured as he rose from his chair. "Right now your *dat* is the furthest thing from my mind, though. Come here."

His heart turned a cartwheel when she sprang into his arms and met his mouth with her soft, eager lips. Drew pulled her close, kissing her thoroughly before whispering, "Does this mean you'll marry me after all? For sure and for certain?"

Loretta laughed. Her expression, filled with longing and love, was all the answer he needed. "I will, Drew," she replied breathlessly. "I promise not to be so hardheaded about wanting things to go my way."

"And I promise to love you always," he murmured before kissing her again. "I feel so much better now."

"*Jah*, let's decide right this minute not to fight after we're married," she said earnestly. "It's too hard on my heart when we disagree."

He held her close before releasing her. "I'll go talk to Bishop Tom—tell him we're ready to set a date," he said.

"Let me be the first to congratulate you!" Savilla called out from the steam table across the room. "I, um, couldn't help overhearing your *gut* news."

"You'll be cooking our wedding meal, too," Drew said happily. "It's going to be a mighty special day— probably in late October. We'll get back to you soon with our plans."

"We'll be happy to host your dinner," Savilla said. "Josiah and I love weddings."

Drew took Loretta's hand and tucked it into the crook of his elbow. "Shall we go? I think we'll make a lot of people happy with our announcement."

Loretta grinned. "I know *I'm* happy!"

"That's all that matters," Drew said as he opened the side door. "If you're happy, everything else will fall into place and life will be *gut*."

Chapter Twenty-Four

From the side of the road, Rebecca peered through the long lens of her camera, zooming in on Wyatt's face as he chose a brownie from the tray Loretta was holding. Why was he wearing bandages on his face and neck? Had the rhubarb crisp still been hot enough in the center to burn him?

She let out a long sigh and sank back against her car seat. She hadn't intended to injure him. Her first priority should be an apology, before she asked him point-blank about that woman in his trailer.

Just then the sleek socialite stepped outside onto the deck of the double-wide. She stretched languidly, as though she'd enjoyed sleeping late and had then taken a leisurely shower, unaware that a work crew had been erecting a large barn while she lounged.

Or maybe she was watching them through the window. Maybe she has a thing for muscular men wearing tool belts.

When Wyatt had teased Rebecca about watching the men work, she'd thought he was funny—but she wasn't laughing this time. Maybe the blond she-cat on the deck had eyes only for Wyatt.

Rebecca's stomach churned. She should've shown

up earlier, maybe taken Wyatt aside, even if the men would speculate about their conversation. It seemed that if she was to speak with Wyatt now, his other woman would be present—and she would probably do a lot more than speculate. She might tell Rebecca to hit the road and not darken Wyatt's door again—especially if she'd burned him with her crisp.

If she does that, and Wyatt goes along with her, you have your answer about him, don't you? Then you can tell Mamma you tried to make amends, but the truth about him has set you free, so to speak.

Pulling off the shoulder where she'd parked and back onto the county highway, Rebecca steered her car toward the packed dirt pathway that led to Wyatt's trailer and the work site. She felt nervous and inadequate and outclassed, but it was time to have this conversation. As she parked near the wagon with the coolers and snack trays on it, most of the men were ambling toward the Grill N Skillet's restroom. She set her camera in the passenger's seat and opened the car door, prepared to be scorned and raked over the coals of Wyatt's displeasure.

Ben waved from the other side of the wagon and approached her. "*Gut* to see you, Rebecca," he called out. When he reached her, he lowered his voice. "Are you responsible for those bandages on Wyatt's face? All he's saying is that he got burned."

I could say the same thing, she mused. "I don't know, but I'm about to find out and apologize, if I need to," she murmured, watching as Wyatt chatted with Adam and Matthias Wagler before they, too, walked toward town. "Has he said anything about that blonde who's stepping off his deck, walking toward him?"

Ben turned, his gaze lingering on the woman's hot pink short shorts and the faceted belt that sparkled in the sunlight as she walked. "Not a word. But I can see why you'd be upset, honey-girl," he murmured. "This doesn't look too promising, even to a fellow who tries to see the *gut* in everyone and every situation."

Rebecca smiled, grateful for Ben's appraisal. "I'm not looking forward to it, but I've come to speak with Wyatt—as Mamma suggested. I wasn't counting on having a stranger listening in."

Ben removed his straw hat and smoothed his sweat-dampened brown hair. "Want me to come with you?"

Rebecca wanted to kiss him. Was it any wonder Mamma was so in love with this caring, compassionate man? "I really appreciate your offer, Ben, but I'm a big girl, and I should handle this myself," she said. "What can Wyatt—or that woman—do to me out in the open where you and Bishop Tom can watch?"

Ben's hazel eyes lit up with soft laughter. "You've got a lot of your *mamm* in you. You'll be fine, Rebecca."

With a nod, she walked around the flatbed wagon, steeling herself for whatever Wyatt might say. *You've got a lot of your* mamm *in you* echoed in her mind like a mantra. What would Mamma do right now?

When Wyatt caught sight of Rebecca, his steely gaze gave her pause. He crossed his arms and seemed to plant himself more firmly where he stood—which made Edith, Rosalyn, and Bishop Tom turn to see what he was staring at. The sight of his two large bandages sent a shiver of guilt through her.

But she still deserved the truth.

Clasping her hands to keep them from shaking, Rebecca approached him. Her throat was so dry she wasn't sure the words would come out, but it was her place to speak first. As though they sensed they shouldn't intrude, Edith and Rosalyn wiggled their fingers at her and then busied themselves with picking up the used plastic cups the men had left behind. After Bishop Tom waved at Rebecca, he joined Ben with the last of the crewmen who were heading toward the café. Only Wyatt and That Woman remained in place, watching Rebecca take the last few steps toward them.

Wyatt's lips lifted. "Rebecca, I'd like you to meet my sister, Vanessa Herriott," he said simply. "Vanessa, this is Rebecca Oliveri, my website designer—and the light of my life."

"Your *sister*?" Rebecca blurted out. Images of two entwined silhouettes and a sleek socialite in a red gown whirled in her mind as disbelief nearly choked her. "Why, of *course* that's what I should've assumed when I saw her putting her arms around you last night," she added with a cynical frown.

Vanessa laughed and jabbed Wyatt with her finger, as though the joke was on him. "Wyatt's invited me to visit his new place a dozen times, and on the spur of the moment, I decided to see what the excitement was about," she said in a husky voice. "Never dreamed I'd be driving him to the emergency room."

Rebecca heard the words, but they still didn't make sense. Vanessa's voice and manner fit her socialite looks—and it didn't help when she placed her arm around Wyatt's waist.

"You bake a *mean* rhubarb crisp, Rebecca," Wyatt put in, slipping his arm around Vanessa. "We managed to salvage some of it and enjoyed it with ice cream after we got back from the hospital in New Haven."

What's wrong with this picture? These two are acting like

last night's incident was a big joke—and they're standing way too close for my comfort.

Rebecca took a step back, shaking her head. It was too late for her *What would Mamma do?* approach, because Mamma would surely be baffled—and suspicious—about the smiles on the two faces before her. Faces that resembled one another around the eyes and chins, she noticed.

"You—you never mentioned a sister," Rebecca rasped after an uncomfortable silence had passed. "I've seen her on your website, all dressed up—"

"Photos from a charity Christmas ball we attended in Lexington," Wyatt explained. "Vanessa is widowed, and I'm often at a loss for a date to attend such functions, so we go together."

"Neither of us are all that wild about gala balls," Vanessa added with a shrug that made her faceted belt shimmer. "But we figure if we're expected to write a big donation check, we might as well go for dinner and drinks." She elbowed Wyatt. "Nice job, not bothering to mention me. Maybe you deserved to have a pan of rhubarb crisp thrown in your face."

Rebecca blinked. Vanessa seemed sincere—more down-to-earth than she appeared—and Wyatt displayed no signs of deception. Even though his arm remained around his sister, his blue-gray eyes held Rebecca's gaze steadily, imploring her to believe his story.

Sometimes our eyes and ears fool us. We think we know what we see or hear, yet we don't usually realize what remains unseen and unsaid.

As Mamma's words rang in Rebecca's memory, her shoulders relaxed. It occurred to her that Wyatt's introduction had disarmed her fear and doubt before she'd had a chance to demand an explanation about the chic blonde who'd been wrapping her arms around him. The image still unsettled her, but maybe her imagination had rendered the scene more romantic than it really was.

"I'm sorry, Wyatt," Rebecca murmured. She stepped up to him and gently turned his face to get a better look at the bandages—even though Vanessa remained in place, watching her. "It wasn't my intention to burn you—"

"And I didn't intend to burn you, either, dear heart," he interrupted sadly. "I really should've told you I was bringing Vanessa back with me. What you saw last night must've looked awfully incriminating."

"I travel a lot to oversee my late husband's businesses," Vanessa explained, "so on the rare occasions when Wyatt and I see each other, we hug a lot. We lost our parents when we were very young, and if it hadn't been for Wyatt's watching out for me, Lord only knows where I might've ended up."

"Vanessa has agreed to manage my horse farms in New York and Lexington," Wyatt added with a smile. "I've told her to do whatever she wants with them, because I'm devoting myself to this new venture in Willow Ridge. I'll devote myself to you, too, Rebecca—if you'll still have me."

The intimate timbre of his voice and the look in his eyes melted her. When Rebecca leaned in to him, Wyatt wrapped his arms around her and hugged her close before seeking out her lips with his. The rest of the world disappeared as she got lost in his embrace—although she realized he was wooing her in front of Vanessa and whoever else happened to be around without any sign of embarrassment.

When she finally eased away from Wyatt, she realized that they were standing alone. Everyone else had seemingly found somewhere else to go.

"Vanessa couldn't stand the heat," he said with a chuckle. "She's been very curious about you, knowing how finicky I am about women. I hope the two of you can become friends despite the awkward way you met."

Rebecca smiled. "Mamma's still expecting us for dinner tomorrow, so I'll tell her to set a place for Vanessa, too," she said. "It won't be a fancy meal, because Amish women don't cook much on Sundays. That's considered work."

Wyatt smiled. "No matter what's on the table, we'll be delighted to come. I think it's fabulous that Amish women don't spend all day fussing over a Sunday dinner that gets eaten in a matter of minutes."

Rebecca nodded. "They have the right idea about Sunday being a day of rest. And if your sister gets a taste of Mamma's hospitality—our family's happiness when we're all together," she added brightly, "maybe she'll feel better about you leaving your other life to settle here."

"I'll tell her to wear something other than those shorts," he said with a wink. "Vanessa has had some serious doubts about my Willow Ridge adventure— but you know what? Although her opinion matters to me, she doesn't control what I do."

Rebecca glanced away, grinning. "You could say the same thing about me, right?"

Wyatt laughed and wrapped his arm around her. "You have more control over me than you know, sweet lady. Why not drive me over to your mom's place, and we'll tell her we'll definitely be there for dinner tomorrow. All the draft horses in Willow Ridge couldn't keep me away."

Rebecca laughed as they walked toward her car. *Mamma's not going to believe the way this turned out.*

Chapter Twenty-Five

As Loretta helped her sisters set the table for the noon meal on Sunday, it felt good to be working together in Edith's large, sunshine yellow kitchen. Leroy and Louisa faced each other in windup swing sets at one end of the room, laughing and kicking as their swing seats nearly touched when they moved toward each other. They were such happy, beautiful children, and Loretta dreamed of having her own laughing babies someday soon.

And every time she looked at the beautiful table and chairs Asa had bought for Edith, Loretta secretly hoped that someday she would be setting such a fine table of her own—even though she had decided to delay the day when she and Drew would settle in their own place.

"When Drew and I announce our wedding date today," she said softly, "we'll also be telling Dat that we plan to live at home for a while. I didn't want you to be surprised when we said that."

Edith and Rosalyn immediately came to stand on either side of her so Dat wouldn't overhear them as he sat in the front room talking with Drew and Asa.

Edith's brow furrowed. "But Loretta, ever since we were wee girls, you've dreamed of the time when you could move out with your husband," she pointed out with a puzzled frown. "You've always been more . . . challenged by Dat's moods than Rosalyn and I."

"And that day you stood up to Dat, saying you wished we could live in a happy, peaceful home again," Rosalyn recalled. "I had my doubts about that wish ever coming true—much as I hoped it would. I can't imagine Drew really wants to start married life down the hall from his crotchety, cranky father-in-law."

"This is your chance for happiness, Loretta," Edith insisted. "I think you should have a place of your own, if that's possible."

Loretta wrapped her arms around her sisters, loving the way they were sticking up for her—and saying exactly what she'd expected. As they stood in their huddle, she realized how different their lives had become since Edith had moved across the road, and she knew that her marrying Drew would change the family dynamic yet again.

"Drew and I have talked about this, and he's willing to live wherever I want to be," she said, glancing first at Edith and then at Rosalyn. "I want to live with you, Rosalyn. I can't think our home will ever be happy knowing you have to deal with Dat all by yourself—not to mention tending the garden and the chickens, and delivering the eggs to Luke, and—"

Rosalyn waved her off. "That's not a very daughterly sentiment, Loretta," she said with a rueful smile. "I've known ever since you and Drew started dating that I would someday be the last one of us to live at home. Don't you think Mamm would've wanted one of us to look after Dat?"

"No!" Edith whispered quickly. "She would've expected Dat to get on with his life and find another wife, rather than having one of her girls forfeit having a family of her own." She glanced away, as though appealing to Mamm for help expressing her thoughts. "As I get older, I suspect Mamm sacrificed her happiness to keep peace in the family—to keep Dat from losing his temper—more often than we realized."

Loretta sighed. It made her sad to think their mother hadn't lived long enough to see any of her girls married—and it bothered her that Edith had stated a truth they didn't often discuss. Their mother had constantly acted as a buffer between them and Dat's moods or changed her plans so Dat's temper wouldn't ruin everyone's day. In the end, Dat usually got his way because the women in his life had been taught to obey him.

"Loretta does have a point, though," Edith said after a few moments. "I can't imagine being the last daughter at home, trying to measure up to Dat's idealized memories of Mamm. And with this mysterious money trouble he's gotten into, I suspect he'll only get crankier as time goes by."

"Drew and Asa will stand with us," Loretta said with a nod, "but we girls have to stick together on this, no matter what comes of the trouble he's gotten into. Things between him and Bishop Tom may get worse before they get better."

Rosalyn glanced toward the front room. "I wish we knew exactly what he's done so—"

Dat burst through the doorway, glaring at them. "Are we ever going to eat, or are you three going to spend the day whispering in the kitchen?"

Loretta's pulse raced. Had he been listening at

the doorway? Or was he just edgy? She glanced at the clock on Edith's wall. "It's only eleven thirty, Dat, so—"

"What's so hard about putting cold, already prepared food on the table?" he demanded stiffly. "Are you so inflexible that we can't eat earlier?"

The sisters exchanged a guarded gaze. "I'll pour the water," Rosalyn murmured as she headed toward the refrigerator.

Loretta hesitated to confront her father, but she was tired of biting her tongue. "You know, Dat, when we're at Edith's house, she's the one to decide when we'll—"

"Edith knows better than to keep her *dat* waiting," he countered smugly.

Edith crossed her arms, which were trembling slightly. "We'll eat in ten minutes," she announced in a taut voice. "We have some important matters to discuss today, Dat, so please figure on staying with us for a while instead of hurrying home to—"

Drew's timely arrival in the kitchen made them all look toward the doorway. "Say, Cornelius, did I see Bishop Tom carrying something long and white away from your place a couple of days ago?" he asked as Asa came in behind him.

"*Jah*, Drew and I thought it looked like one of those fancy air conditioners that fastens to the wall instead of being hung in a window," Asa remarked with a purposeful smile.

Dat's face turned as red as a raw steak. "What business of yours is—how would you know anything about—?" he blustered. "How do you get any work done if you're constantly spying on me?"

"If the bishop confiscated an air conditioner because you wouldn't take it off your shop wall," Drew said breezily, "there's no reason for you to hurry home—especially on Sunday—ain't so? We've got wedding plans to make!"

"And the sooner we get out of the girls' way, the sooner we can eat," Asa pointed out, nodding toward the front room.

Dat glared at the twin brothers as though he were planning a retort for their ears alone, and then he stalked out of the kitchen. "Carry on, ladies," Asa murmured as Drew blew them all a kiss.

When the men had left, Loretta and her sisters all stood near the refrigerator as Rosalyn took out bowls of macaroni salad, coleslaw, and carrot salad. "An air conditioner?" Edith demanded in a shocked whisper. "Since when—"

"I have no idea," Rosalyn murmured.

"Well, that might explain why Dat has been spending so much time in his shop this summer," Loretta said in a huff. "It was fine for us girls to be running the canners, working in all that heat, while *he* was as cool as a cucumber—"

Edith gently squeezed her shoulder. "Apparently Bishop Tom has handled it," she pointed out softly. "Think of the ruckus we would've caused had one of us discovered that air conditioner."

"*Jah*, and we might not like it that Drew knows more than we do about Dat's fall from grace," Rosalyn said, "but he's the better person to hold his information over Dat's head, because he's a man and he doesn't really answer to Dat. I like that," she added, smiling gratefully at Loretta. "If you and Drew really want to live at home, I thank you from the bottom of my *maidel* heart."

Loretta was about to remark that Rosalyn would surely find her own husband someday, except Dat walked into the kitchen and took his usual place at the head of the table—even though it was Asa's table. She exchanged a resigned glance with her sisters and carried the bowls of salad to the table while Edith wound the twins' swings so they would keep the babies occupied for a while longer.

Loretta sighed. No matter how badly she yearned for happiness and peace among her family members, there were things—and people—she was simply unable to change.

As all heads bowed around the table, Drew observed Cornelius through partially open eyes. The man was a bundle of nerves now that he and Asa had exposed the secret air conditioner and the fact that the bishop had confiscated it. The girls' startled expressions had confirmed Drew's suspicions: their *dat* was dead set against confessing even the most minor of his mistakes to his daughters.

But now he realizes that I might know a lot more than he'd originally figured on, Drew thought smugly. *And except for the exact amount of money he's gambled away, I believe I do.*

When Asa cleared his throat to end the silent prayer before Cornelius could do it, Drew smiled to himself. He'd told his brother about the magnitude of Cornelius's misbehavior, and Asa had agreed that those details should remain confidential, because Bishop Tom and Preacher Ben were ultimately in charge of the deacon's discipline. But Asa was incensed enough not to put up with any more of his father-in-law's bullying. It could only be good for the Riehl sisters that two more men had joined their family.

Cornelius shot Asa a sour look but said nothing

about him usurping the power of ending the prayer. He scowled at the platter of cold grilled chicken in front of him and then at the sliced ham, the various bowls of salad, and the basket of bread. "For this, I've waited all morning?" he grumbled as he reached for the chicken. "Same stuff we had for dinner nearly every day this week."

"And for that which we are about to receive, Lord, we are truly grateful," Drew intoned as he picked up the nearest bowl of salad. "Cornelius, maybe if you told us why you're so impatient and critical today, we could relieve you of your emotional burden."

"A burden shared is a burden halved," Loretta quipped quickly.

Drew winked at her, pleased to see she was rising above her father's persistent rancor.

"Maybe if you'd mind your own business and leave me alone, Detweiler, we'd all be better off," Cornelius shot back.

Drew took his time spooning carrot salad onto his plate, determined not to give Loretta's *dat* the power to shut down their dinner discussion. "All right," he said after a few moments, "the rest of us will continue talking as though you're not here. Feel free not to respond while we go about our business and leave you alone."

Edith's dark eyes sparkled as she accepted the platter of cold grilled chicken from her father. "A little bird tells me there's to be a wedding in the near future," she said happily, "but I'm waiting to hear a date. Weddings are such happy occasions—and we could all use one of those."

"That's not news," Cornelius muttered under his breath.

"Chirp, chirp!" Loretta teased, ignoring her *dat*.

"A lot of folks have been assuming Drew and I would get hitched, but right after he proposed the first time, I backed out because I didn't want to live at home anymore," she explained lightly. She made a point of looking at everyone except her father. "However, after a deeper discussion of the subject yesterday, I've seen the wisdom of Drew's desire to live at our place for a while after we're married—so I said yes again, and this time it's going to stick! It's in a woman's best interest to listen to her man, and to share his beliefs, after all."

Cornelius's eyes widened as he gripped the bowl of macaroni salad he was holding. "Since when do you listen to anything a man says?" he demanded tersely. "Detweiler told me he was moving in with us if you'd marry him, but that was just an idle threat. He's said and done a lot of things to play people false, after all."

Drew returned the radiant smile Loretta was sending him from across the table as though her father weren't present. He was glad to see the sisters having a little innocent fun.

"I'm still waiting to hear a date," Rosalyn chimed in, assuming her sisters' light tone. "I hope I can squeeze your wedding into my jam-packed social calendar, Loretta."

Everyone except Cornelius laughed, Rosalyn loudest of all. Cornelius set the bowl of macaroni salad on the table with a loud *thunk*.

"Thursday, October twentieth," Loretta said sweetly. "That gives us three and a half weeks to prepare the celebration and gives Drew and me time to complete our counseling sessions with the bishop."

Edith rose from the table and went to the calendar on the wall. She grabbed a pen from the drawer beneath it, lifted the page for September, and sketched the outline of a heart around the third Thursday of October. "It's official!" she declared. "Congratulations, Loretta and Drew!"

"*Jah*, welcome to the family," Asa teased as he pumped Drew's hand. "I guess that means you'll soon be my brother-in-law as well as my twin."

"Marriage complicates a lot of relationships," Drew shot back with a laugh.

Cornelius grunted. "Got that right."

"But I hope to un-complicate our wedding day by holding the dinner at the Grill N Skillet, as we did for you and Edith," Drew continued without so much as a glance toward Loretta's *dat*. "Josiah and Savilla put on such a fine spread for your wedding—"

"Twice," Asa put in with a chuckle.

"—that I thought we'd go with the same arrangement this time," Drew continued.

"You won't get a tastier wedding cake than Miriam makes," Edith reminded them. "And I'm appointing myself the gal in charge of asking our neighbor ladies for pies."

"I volunteer to call our friends in Roseville and the far-flung family in Indiana and Ohio," Rosalyn said eagerly.

"Why do we want to see those people again?" Cornelius muttered. "They were just here in June."

"And if you want to hold the wedding here at our place," Asa said, "we have all the space we need when we take down the two interior walls to expand the front room."

"Oh, think of the cleaning and furniture shifting that would save at our house," Rosalyn murmured.

"*Jah*, when you got married, the pew benches fit just right here, to give the bishop and the preacher and Deacon Cornelius plenty of space in the center of the room while they read the Bible and delivered their sermons," Drew recalled. Then he raised his eyebrows. "Too bad your original wedding day got waylaid by some guy with a huge chip on his shoulder and a bottle of sleeping pills."

"It all worked out, brother," Asa insisted immediately, clapping Drew on the back. "I've never let those peanut butter and jelly sandwiches come between us."

"Your mistake," Cornelius retorted under his breath.

The kitchen got very quiet. Even the twins were still as they sat in their wound-down swing sets. "Beg your pardon, Cornelius?" Asa demanded. "Did you say something?"

"We were leaving you alone, as you asked, Dat," Edith said in a deceptively calm voice. "But when you question the way Asa forgave Drew for what he did, I draw the line at remaining silent. Drew confessed, and he's been forgiven. From what I've heard, you'd do well to follow his example."

Drew's eyes widened. It still meant a lot to him every time Edith insisted she'd forgiven him for pretending to be Asa at her wedding and for slipping sleeping pills into Asa's sandwich on the previous evening. It meant even more that Cornelius's youngest daughter had dared to speak so boldly to her father on his behalf.

Cornelius's face was turning red again as he glared at Edith. "Marriage seems to have made you forget your place," he muttered, appearing ready to launch into a sermon about children honoring their parents.

"And while you're at *our* place," Asa said, leaning forward to gaze directly at Cornelius, "you'll do well to remember that we Detweilers don't tolerate unjust criticism or men who expect the women in their family to act like doormats."

"But that's the Old Order way of things!" Cornelius lashed out. "God put Adam in charge over all His other creations, and He declared that wives were to obey their husbands!"

"And He created women because He knew we men would make a mess of things, too," Drew said lightly, although he was totally serious. It was time for Cornelius to get a taste of how life would be different— very different—after he moved into the Riehl home.

"It's also the Old Order way of things to confess our sins and to ask forgiveness," Drew continued firmly. "Confession has made a better man of me, Cornelius, and I hope the same transformation will take place in your life when you admit to the extent of your wrongdoing during all those trips to Kansas City. It *amazes* me that Bishop Tom and Preacher Ben have allowed you to remain the deacon of our church district. Shall I say more?"

Cornelius paled and clapped his mouth shut.

The kitchen rang with tense silence for a few moments, until Rosalyn shook her head.

"What did you do, Dat?" she whispered. "All my life I've believed you were the authority on right living, and that as a pillar of the church, you were to help shepherd folks who'd wandered from the path to salvation. Is it worth risking your own salvation to keep such a serious secret?"

"I don't have to listen to this, you den of vipers!" Cornelius stood up so suddenly that his chair flew back and clattered against the kitchen floor. He strode from the kitchen and, seconds later, slammed the front door behind him.

Startled, Louisa began to cry in her swing, and

Leroy joined her. For the next few minutes Edith and Asa focused on comforting the little twins with bottles of goat's milk that Edith had been warming in a pan of hot water on the stove. Rosalyn appeared stunned by the vehemence of her father's outburst, while Loretta's hazel eyes remained wide with surprise.

"That settles it," Loretta said as she reached for Rosalyn's hand. "I'm not leaving you to live with Dat all by yourself."

"And when the day comes that we move into our own home, you'll have a room there, Rosalyn," Drew said.

Rosalyn sighed sadly. "He's getting worse, isn't he? The depression and grief have been eating away at him until—"

"*Jah,* he's still hanging on to his grief—and manipulating it to get his own way," Asa interrupted tersely. "But his *guilt*—his secret—is digging a hole so deep that it's become an emotional grave. Cornelius knows that confessing is the right thing to do, yet he refuses to submit to the ways of our faith."

"One of these days his transgressions are going to catch up to him," Edith predicted softly. She cradled Louisa in the crook of her arm as she held the baby's bottle. "We can only pray that his misbehavior won't drag a lot of other people down with him."

Drew sighed to himself. He had a feeling that Edith might be right—that Cornelius's situation might get worse before it got better, and that when the truth came out, it might shake Willow Ridge like a major earthquake.

As the five of them finished their dinner and enjoyed the cherry and pineapple fried pies Rosalyn had brought, Drew's thoughts turned toward making his fiancée glad she'd agreed to marry him. Cornelius wasn't the only man who had a few secrets—but the treasures Drew had hidden in the back room of the furniture shop would be a surprise Loretta could enjoy for years to come. He was waiting for the right time to show them to her.

While the sisters cleared the table, Drew and Asa carried the little twins into the front room and placed them in the playpen. Drew was amazed at how fast his children were growing—their little faces and bodies appeared different nearly every time he saw them. Lately he'd noticed how they resembled Molly Ropp around their eyes and noses, but he kept such observations to himself. One of the things he looked forward to most when he married Loretta was watching her grow round with his children.

And who would've believed you'd be thinking that way? his thoughts teased him. Just a few months previously he'd been skulking around Willow Ridge as he spied on Asa and Edith, envious of their courtship. Now he wanted to be settled in a home with a wife and children—and it seemed that God's plans for him and Loretta were finally lining up that way.

Chapter Twenty-Six

As Wyatt entered Ben and Miriam's front room on Sunday, he was surprised to hear so many voices and conversations coming from the kitchen when his car was the only vehicle in the driveway. "Good to see you, Ben," he said as they shook hands. "This is my sister Vanessa, visiting from Lexington, Kentucky—"

"*Jah*, so I heard," Ben said with a chuckle. He extended his hand toward her as well. "We're mighty happy to meet you, Vanessa. Welcome to our home."

Vanessa's eyes were wide as she glanced back toward the noisy kitchen. "Sounds like you have a large family," she said a little nervously.

"It's the usual crowd here today. With you folks, we'll have fifteen adults, a couple of kids, and three wee ones—and we don't expect you to remember everybody's name," he added with a boyish grin. "Ah, here's Rebecca. I'll let her make the introductions."

Wyatt's mouth almost dropped open. Rebecca was dressed Plain, wearing a dusty blue dress and a white apron, which fell to midcalf. With her hair pulled back beneath a pleated white prayer *kapp* and no makeup on her radiant face, she bore little resemblance to his tech-oriented website designer.

"Wyatt and Vanessa!" Rebecca said, reaching for their hands. She chuckled at their expressions. "Sometimes I dress like my sisters because even though we grew up apart, we're very close now. It's a triplet thing."

For a moment, he'd feared her attire might indicate her desire to become Amish, which would render her off-limits to a thoroughly English man. *And what does it mean that you want her right this minute because that dress and* kapp *make her look so innocent and untouched?*

His thoughts stopped wandering when two young women identical to Rebecca emerged from the kitchen wearing dresses and *kapp*s of the same style and color. When the three of them linked arms, grinning mischievously, Wyatt laughed. "Oh my," he said, shaking his head as he studied the three of them closely. "If I didn't know Rebecca was in the middle, I couldn't tell you apart."

"I bet you ladies get a lot of enjoyment out of that," Vanessa said as she, too, looked them over in amazement.

"This is Rachel," Rebecca said, holding her fingers in rabbit ears behind one of her sisters' heads. "She lives across the road with Micah Brenneman and baby Amelia, in the big white house that sits a ways behind the café. And Rhoda—"

Rebecca hugged the sister on her other side as Rhoda waved at them. "Rhoda is married to our local nurse, Andy Leitner, and her little Aden is two months old now. They live in the upstairs apartment above the clinic."

"And we have Andy's kids, Brett and Taylor, as well

as his *mamm*, Betty, living with us," Rhoda put in. "I was the wicked sister who fell in love with a divorced English man. But he joined the Old Order to be with me—and the folks in Willow Ridge have welcomed him as though he's been Amish all his life."

"We're blessed to have somebody with Andy's medical knowledge in town," Rachel remarked with a nod. "And the way I hear it, we're blessed to have *you* here, Wyatt, wanting to raise draft horses."

"*Jah,* I already know some men who're interested in your horses," Rhoda chimed in.

"My Micah, for one," Rachel said quickly. "The horses available at the sale barn between here and Morning Star have mostly been for pleasure riding lately—not sturdy enough for pulling wagons."

Wyatt was listening carefully, pleased with what he heard—and noting that the triplets even sounded alike as they wove their sentences together. "Micah was on the crew that helped raise my barns," he recalled. "I'll be happy to talk about horses whenever he's ready. And I'll have some Thoroughbreds retired from racing that will make nice buggy horses once they're trained."

"Come on in!" Rhoda said, gesturing for them to follow. "Everybody's ready to sit down at the table and get to know you two."

Although Wyatt had met and worked with most of the men around town, it was an odd sensation to be the only male in the kitchen without a beard, suspenders, and a solid-colored short-sleeve shirt. Miriam was making her way through the group of women who were placing dishes of food on the table, wiping her hands on a tea towel.

"Wyatt, it's so *gut* to see you—and Vanessa, we're all so pleased you've joined us today! I'm Rebecca's *mamm,* Miriam," she said as she clasped Vanessa's hands. "We're a rowdy, noisy bunch at times, but you'll not hear a cross word or see any signs of a mean streak among us."

"*Jah,* Miriam told us we had to be on our best behavior today," Luke called out from across the room.

"She threatened to withhold dessert if we didn't play nice with you," his brother Ira added.

Wyatt laughed along with everyone else, relieved to see some familiar faces in the largest kitchen he'd ever entered. As folks began taking seats at a table that filled the center of the room, Ben suggested that Wyatt sit to his right and that Vanessa could be between Miriam and Rebecca at his left.

"We'll have a few moments of silent grace," Ben told him. "Then we'll pass the food and make the other introductions."

"There'll be a quiz at the end of dinner to see how many names you remember," the dark-haired fellow sitting down beside him teased. "I'm Andy Leitner, Rhoda's husband, and I know exactly what you're going through today."

The divorced English guy who turned Amish, Wyatt recalled as he bowed his head along with everyone else. *If he can win this family's acceptance and respect, I surely stand a chance.*

As silence filled the kitchen, Wyatt was amazed that even the three babies he'd seen in carrier baskets on the floor near their mothers were absolutely quiet during the prayer. On a whim, he glanced across the table to enjoy the sight of Rebecca, who appeared downright angelic with her eyes closed and her head bowed—until she peered back at him and winked. Wyatt bit back a laugh, determined not to be the one who broke the prayerful silence.

"Amen," Ben said as he raised his head. "Wyatt, we generally grab what's in front of us and pass to the left. You'll notice we put the sliced ham, potato salad, and grilled chicken near you so you'll get a chance at them."

"*Jah*, those Hooley brothers and my two kids have been known to clear a platter in a matter of seconds," Andy remarked with a laugh. "Brett and Taylor, this is Wyatt McKenzie and his sister, Vanessa. The lady beside Taylor is my mom, Betty Leitner."

As the kids and Betty greeted him, Wyatt noticed they were dressed in Amish attire, except that Betty wasn't wearing a *kapp* covering her snow-white hair.

Brett focused on Wyatt, his eyes sparkling. "So is it true that those bandages on your face are where Rebecca threw a hot cobbler at you?" he asked mischievously.

Rhoda scolded the boy, but Wyatt had to chuckle as he touched the large bandages. "Yes, that's how it happened," he replied, winking at Rebecca. "We had a little misunderstanding—"

"But we've settled our differences," Rebecca put in firmly. "And we're happy that Wyatt's sister, Vanessa, has come to visit with us today."

"Vanessa's the best sister ever, too," Wyatt said as he smiled at the pretty little girl beside Brett. "I hope you and Taylor will grow up to be close friends, the way we have."

As everyone nodded and kept passing bowls of food, Ira leaned forward to address Wyatt. "This beautiful lady is my wife, Millie," he said, gesturing across the table. "You've probably not seen her around, as she spends a lot of time helping at her grandparents' place."

"Those would be the Glicks, our neighbors to the

east," Ben clarified. "Gabe and Wilma are Nora's parents—"

"And Millie is my daughter," Nora said as she put her arm around Millie's shoulders. "Not that we resemble each other."

Wyatt laughed. With her red hair and freckles, Millie was probably the spitting image of Nora when she'd been in her early twenties.

"Sometimes Tom and Vernon join us," Ben put in, accepting the platter of ham from Wyatt. "They're married to my two aunts, Nazareth and Jerusalem— but they're visiting at Vernon's place in Cedar Creek, because their district doesn't have church today, either."

"Our three-hour services are so long, we take a Sunday off between them to recuperate," Ira explained with a laugh.

As he spooned potato salad onto his plate, Wyatt had so many names spinning in his head he was pretty sure he'd get them wrong until he got to know his new neighbors better. He was also thinking that half the people of Willow Ridge must be related to the Hooley family. It impressed him that the men at this table owned the local mill, the cabinet shop, the blacksmith service, and the clinic—and that Nora owned the town's very successful consignment shop. He'd heard that Miriam had once operated the bakery café the Grill N Skillet had replaced, as well.

"Penny for your thoughts, Wyatt," Ben said jovially. "But you can pass the chicken first."

Had his thoughts been wandering? Wyatt noticed that, along with the grilled chicken, a bowl of sliced cantaloupe and a large tossed salad were awaiting his attention. "I was just realizing that I'm among some of the foremost CEOs of Willow Ridge—walking in tall cotton, as they'd put it in Lexington," he said.

Down the table, Micah's brow furrowed. "What's a CEO?"

"It stands for 'can't eat onions'!" young Brett blurted out.

Wyatt laughed loudly. Considering that he'd spent most of his adult life vying for prizes and special honors, competing against other breeders to beat out their pedigreed horses at the track, it was refreshing to be in the company of breadwinners and businessmen who didn't engage in such superficial, exclusive pursuits.

"A chief executive officer is the top dog of his company," Wyatt explained, smiling at Brett.

"The CEOs I know from overseeing my late husband's companies can be a stuffy bunch," Vanessa remarked wryly. "They spend a lot of time sitting around big tables in fancy boardrooms in skyscraper penthouses, mostly deciding how to spend or invest other people's money."

"Hmm," Ira said as he took a large serving of slaw. "I guess our mill is the tallest building in Willow Ridge, so the upper level—where Will lives now— must be the penthouse. We should charge more rent!"

"But the only money we spend is the income from selling our grains and the cage-free eggs the Riehls and our other farmers provide us," Luke pointed out in a more serious tone. "If we go under, we won't take anybody down with us."

"No, but our farmers and suppliers would take a hit," Ira pointed out softly.

"If you go under," Nora teased, pointing her fork at her husband, "you will *not* be spending *my* money! But I would be happy to support you, dear."

The men around the table chortled. "We Amish believe the family business is the backbone of a district's economy," Ben said as he buttered a fluffy dinner roll. "We Hooley brothers are a fine example of learning to diversify when there are too many sons in a family to survive on the family farm. I left home in my late twenties and roamed the Plain countryside as a farrier until I happened into Willow Ridge during a thunderstorm. Miriam felt sorry for me and married me last year, on New Year's Day."

"And before Nora set me straight last summer," Luke continued, "I was a freewheeling single man who was a pretty fair farmer without a farm. Ira here—"

"Didn't have two nickels to scrape together until Ben suggested Luke and I come to Willow Ridge," Ira said with a wide smile. "We had no idea a gristmill that processes specialty grains would be such a huge success. We have fifteen area farmers raising popcorn and grains for us. And we're planting a vineyard next spring on property we bought earlier this year."

Wyatt took in all of these accomplishments, impressed that the Hooley brothers had prospered so quickly after they'd arrived in Willow Ridge. "Anybody in your family good with horses?" he asked on a sudden inspiration. "Seems to me you Hooleys have a real knack for relocating and establishing your businesses. Although I plan to live in Willow Ridge full-time, I really need a man who specializes in training the Belgians and Percherons I'll be handling. They're a lot different from Thoroughbreds."

"*Gut* choices," Ben said with a nod. "Around here, one fellow prefers a Belgian while his neighbor swears by a Percheron."

Wyatt took a mouthful of creamy potato salad,

savoring the bits of onion, celery, and hard-boiled egg that complemented the tender cubed potatoes. When he glanced up, he noticed that Luke and Ira were gazing at each other as though the same idea had occurred to each of them.

"Marcus," Ira stated matter-of-factly.

"*Jah*, that would be our cousin Marcus from Bird-in-Hand—that's out east, in Lancaster County," Luke explained in a voice rising with excitement. "Now there's a fellow who could train a horse to stand on its head, if you paid him enough."

Ben's hazel eyes lit up. "Marcus did some black-smithing with me when he was a kid," he said enthusiastically. "Handled the horses like a pro before he was even a teenager, but his true calling is training rather than farrier work. Last I heard, though, he'd jumped the fence and taken up with some English gal—"

"But we could call his cell phone and find out if he'd be interested in coming," Luke said, gazing at Wyatt. His lips curved. "A fellow who's jumped the fence has left the Amish faith, so some folks think he's a lost soul and they want nothing to do with him unless he comes back to the fold. Marcus has a cell phone and a computer—all the modern stuff Amish folks aren't supposed to own."

Ira laughed. "But considering how Luke and I—and even Bennie—were way up in our twenties or early thirties before we stopped running around," he put in, "there's hope for Marcus. He must be about twenty by now, *jah?*"

Ben shrugged. "There were so many boys in Uncle Felty's family, I could never remember who came when," he admitted. "Since I've moved to

Missouri, I've lost track of how old they all are. We've got nothing to lose by calling him, though."

Wyatt felt a big smile on his face. He sensed he'd come to exactly the right place to seek help with his horses—and it couldn't hurt that Marcus Hooley would answer to his older male kin if he came to Willow Ridge.

"Let's talk to him after we take our time over this fabulous food," he said, smiling at Miriam. "It would be a sin to hurry through this wonderful, home-cooked meal."

Miriam waved him off, her cheeks turning a delicate shade of pink. "I know you English folks usually have a big hot meal on Sunday, so this isn't much—"

"Don't believe that," Vanessa insisted. "Summer days were made for cold meals, and this one's unlike any I've ever tasted. So many flavors and textures to enjoy."

"We should probably invite you back sometime when Mamma fries chicken and makes biscuits and gravy to go with it," Rebecca murmured playfully.

"You're on!" Wyatt said before he even thought about it. He realized how comfortable he felt with these salt-of-the-earth people, and he was glad he wouldn't just be an English stranger who'd built big barns and white plank fences up the hill from his Plain neighbors.

The meal proceeded at a leisurely pace, with all the platters and bowls being passed around again as everyone ate an amazing amount of food. Wyatt figured these folks kept fit by doing a lot of manual labor rather than depending on farm machinery or household appliances—yet he had no sense that they begrudged him such luxuries as his silk shirt, or the fact that he already owned two horse farms and was investing a huge amount of money to start up a third one.

During a lull in the conversation, Miriam gazed from Vanessa to Wyatt. "Not my intention to be nosy, understand," she began, "but Rebecca mentioned that you two lost your parents when you were kids. I'm guessing your grandparents or an aunt or uncle's family took you in?"

Wyatt watched his sister's reaction to that question. He and Vanessa didn't often discuss their difficult growing-up years—few of their friends in the breeding and racing business knew all the details of their past. When he met Vanessa's gaze, her nod told him she felt comfortable enough around these Amish folks to answer Miriam's question—and that she wanted Wyatt to do the talking.

"We were in a tricky situation," Wyatt began in a pensive tone. "Our parents died when the small plane Dad was flying went down in the ocean—or that's the best conclusion the adults in our lives could piece together," he added softly. "Their bodies and the wreckage of Dad's plane were never found."

"Oh, my. I'm so sorry," Rebecca whispered as she put her hand on Vanessa's arm.

Vanessa sighed sadly. "We'd been staying with Mom's sister Natalie while our parents were on their trip. We learned about their deaths when Aunt Natalie called a family meeting with Mom's other sister, Patricia—as well as with Dad's parents, whom we'd never met, because Dad was estranged from them."

She looked down at her half-eaten dinner, as if she were reliving that horrendous day. "The adults sent Wyatt and me to the kitchen for a snack while they were deciding what to do about us," she continued, shaking her head. "Somebody who thought we weren't listening suggested that the plane didn't really go down—and that our parents had conveniently disappeared to escape some legal and financial issues."

Miriam's eyebrows shot up. "Who would do such a thing—and leave behind their young children?" she murmured. "That's unthinkable!"

"Does *estranged* mean your *dat* had no contact with his family?" Ben whispered in disbelief. "How does that sort of separation happen? Even though we Amish shun folks when they break the rules of our faith, we do all we can to encourage them back into the fold, to keep our families together."

In the world Wyatt came from, such solidarity sounded like a fairy tale that was too good to be true. "I was about seven and Vanessa was only four when our parents died," he explained, "so we don't know all the details—"

"Our parents had never spoken about the McKenzie side of the family," Vanessa put in firmly. "Our mom's parents had passed away, and so we only knew about Aunt Natalie and Aunt Patricia—neither of whom wanted to raise two kids who'd put a crimp in their social lives," she added a little bitterly. "The McKenzie grandparents claimed their health wouldn't allow them to raise us. Not that they were interested in the kids of a son they'd apparently disowned."

Everyone around the kitchen table had grown quiet with disbelief. Beside Wyatt, Andy wore a glum expression. "I've heard of similar situations on my ex-wife's side of the family," he said softly. "The self-interest of the wealthier siblings overrode the welfare of family members who really needed their help."

Wyatt nodded. "Because our parents died without wills—and without naming anyone to become our guardian in the event of their passing," he went on, "our aunts turned us over to a social service agency to be put into foster care. We really lucked out. Nelson and Suzanne Carneal, a childless couple in Lexington, fostered and then adopted us—"

"Which is how we came to be associated with the Thoroughbred breeding and racing world," Vanessa said, continuing their story. "Our adoptive dad owned the farms in Saratoga Springs and Lexington, which had produced a few notable horses. Nelson groomed Wyatt to run the business from an early age, and Suzanne raised me with all the expectations and privileges that go with being a daughter of Southern society." She smiled at the folks around the table, who were drinking in her story. "Considering what most foster kids endure, we landed in the lap of luxury with a couple who gave us every advantage as we grew up."

"God was watching out for you," Miriam murmured. "He knew what you—and the folks who took you in—needed to make your lives worthwhile and purposeful."

Wyatt paused, considering her assessment. He suspected that many people in Willow Ridge would consider the world of horse breeding and racing excessive and extraneous because it was all for show. "I appreciate the gracious, optimistic way you phrased that, Miriam," he said. "We're not churchgoing people, but I've always believed that if Providence and the Carneals hadn't stepped in, my sister and I might have fallen through the cracks in the child welfare system."

"Do you hear from your aunts or grandparents?" Ben asked. "Seems the least they could do would be to keep in touch, since they turned you away."

Vanessa shook her head. "Wyatt and I have come

to suspect that our original parents left a lot of debt, and that Mom's sisters held it against us because they had to clean up the financial mess," she explained. "We've lost all contact with them. The Carneals were older when they took us in, and they're gone, too. So Wyatt's all the family I have."

Miriam's dark eyes clouded over as she grasped Vanessa's hand. "Well now," she murmured, glancing toward Rebecca, "if my brother was all I had to call family, I'd hug him every chance I got."

Wyatt saw a flicker of understanding on Rebecca's fresh, clean face. It meant a lot that her mother was speaking about his and Vanessa's relationship in such a positive way.

"The English world would be a better place if our society had passed along the values you Amish folks still hold sacred," Wyatt observed with a sad smile. "In an earlier time, our families were our top priority, too, but that's changed. It makes me sad and concerned about the sort of world we're creating."

"*Jah*, we Amish try real hard to keep our families close—physically and emotionally," Ben said with a nod. "We don't forbid the use of electricity just because it's modern and convenient. We know the sorts of troubles and temptations that enter a home through televisions and the Internet, and we believe these devices distract us from having *gut*, solid relationships with our family and church members."

"We Mennonites allow the use of technology," Nora put in, "but we still believe in the core values that God and our families must be our first priorities. And we believe it's our mission to assist our Amish neighbors with our computers and motorized vehicles and tools. We're all in God's world together."

"And then there's our cousin Marcus," Ira said with

a chuckle. "It'll be interesting to see what he's doing these days. Even as a kid, he resisted—resented—the yoke of Old Order beliefs."

"I think that's a hint to start passing the desserts so you can call him," Millie said as she rose from the table. "The more you say about Marcus, the more I want to meet this guy."

Wyatt wanted to meet Marcus, too—but the phone call could wait until they'd enjoyed the tempting assortment of desserts Millie and her mother were handing to folks at the ends of the table. "I see three pies, a pan of brownies, and a coconut layer cake. How am I supposed to choose just one?" he murmured.

Ben laughed, playfully punching Wyatt's shoulder. "Just one? Man's not supposed to live by bread alone," he quipped. "We've got to have cakes and pies and other goodies to help us get by! Dig in, Wyatt. You don't want the ladies to think you don't appreciate their efforts."

After Miriam and Nora scraped and stacked the dinner plates and Rebecca passed clean plates for their dessert, Wyatt accepted the glass pan Andy handed him. He gazed at a custard pie that was three inches thick and filled with coconut. "I see what you mean," he said as he lifted a small slice from the pan. "I love coconut, and I can't turn down chocolate—"

"And we've heard you have a taste for rhubarb, too," Luke teased from the other end of the table. "Here's the pie you'll want to try, because Miriam's rhubarb cream pie is the absolute best—not that Rhoda's fresh peach pie won't tickle your taste buds as well."

"If anyone wants ice cream on their pie, we have that, too," one of Rebecca's sisters said.

After all the desserts had made their way around
the table, Wyatt gazed at his plate and wondered how
he was supposed to eat the wedges of coconut custard
and rhubarb pies as well as a thick frosted brownie
with nuts on top. He noticed that Vanessa was facing
the same situation, although she'd taken half-slices of
the peach and rhubarb pies.

It's a good problem to have, he told himself as he
closed his mouth over his first bite of creamy, coconut-
filled custard. *We won't need any supper tonight.*

After they'd all scraped their dessert plates clean,
the women began clearing the table. Wyatt felt bad
that they would be washing seventeen people's plates,
serving dishes, and utensils by hand, considering that
he or Vanessa would've loaded them into an automatic dishwasher. Didn't washing all those dishes on
Sunday count as work? He didn't understand the ins
and outs of Amish beliefs, but it wasn't his place to
question them—especially because the men were all
leaving the kitchen as though their exodus was part
of the routine.

"Shall we call Marcus on my cell phone or from
your phone shanty, Ben?" Luke pulled his cell phone
from his pocket, as though he had a preference but
was allowing his older brother to decide.

Ben shrugged and pulled the chain on the front
room's ceiling fan to make it run faster. "Guess I
don't see the use in all of us hanging around the
shanty—especially if Wyatt wants to talk to him," he
replied.

Luke grinned and began running his finger along
the face of his phone. "Let me just find Marcus's
number . . . had it when we moved to Missouri. Ah!
Here he is." He pressed on the phone and held it to

his ear as Ben gestured for the men and Brett to make themselves comfortable on the couches or in the upholstered chairs. Luke plopped down in the center of a sofa, between Wyatt and Ira.

After a moment, Luke chuckled with anticipation. "*Jah*, is this the Marcus Hooley who spends his time taming wild women and horses?" he teased. "It's your cousin Luke, calling from Missouri."

Wyatt chuckled along with the other men in the room. From Luke's expression, he surmised that Marcus had replied to Luke with a similarly raucous statement.

After he'd exchanged a few other pleasantries, Luke said, "We've got a proposition for you. An English neighbor of ours is looking for somebody to train Belgians and Percherons at his new horse farm, and you were the first guy we thought of. Think you might be interested?"

Wyatt watched Luke's handsome face for any sign that Marcus had turned him down without even hearing any details. Instead, Luke was nodding as he listened for a few minutes—and then he smiled at Wyatt, raising his eyebrows. "His name's Wyatt McKenzie and he's right here," he said. "You want to talk to him?"

When Luke handed him the cell phone, Wyatt thought quickly about what he wanted to say. With so many of his neighbors listening, he didn't want to talk about money yet, and he wanted to make a positive impression on this young man. "Hey there, Marcus, this is Wyatt McKenzie," he began smoothly. "You come highly recommended by your cousins here in Willow Ridge. Any chance you'd be interested in joining them, to work for me?"

There was a pause on the line. "So . . . why would I want to do that?" Marcus asked. He didn't sound insolent, exactly, but his attitude was noticeably different from that of his kinsmen.

Wyatt thought about his reply. He reminded himself that he needed this young horse trainer a lot more than Marcus needed him. "Well, you'll have the chance to set up your own training program in a brand-new, state-of-the-art facility," he began in a low-key voice. "I'll provide you with comfortable living quarters—"

"Sixty-inch flat screen TV? New computer? Gaming system?" Marcus fired off. "And don't go thinking I'm a horse and buggy man, so I'll need a garage—and maybe even a new car—"

"Hold it right there," Wyatt said coolly. He changed gears mentally, to deal with a young man who would obviously be a high-maintenance employee. "Luke and Ira have told me you've jumped the fence, and I'm fine with that. But I'm the owner, and you'll be the employee—*if* you can provide me with three references this week, and if you prove during your trial period that you're as good with horses as your cousins claim you are. Then we'll negotiate for some of those perks you want."

Marcus fell silent.

Ben and the other men were watching Wyatt's reaction curiously, wondering what had prompted him to speak so sternly to their cousin. He waited a few moments before he went on. "What kind of work are you doing now?" he asked Marcus. "If you need to give your supervisor notice that you're leaving—"

"Working at an auction barn," the kid replied in a dull tone. "The boss has me bring the horses onto the sale floor because I can make them stand tall and hold their heads just right while prospective buyers look them over."

Wyatt wondered if Marcus tended to exaggerate his expertise with horses—but if he could truly improve the stance and performance of a horse in the short time it was at the auction barn, he had a real talent. "How do you do that, Marcus?" he asked. "I'm guessing you handle a lot of horses during an auction, and you don't spend much time with any one of them."

"I know how to talk to them. How to touch them."

Wyatt blinked. He'd heard of "horse whisperers," but they were rare—and he wondered again if this young man was overstating his abilities. "Okay," he said, thinking quickly, "if you're that good with horses, why don't you have your own business? Living there in Lancaster County, you could make money hand over foot training horses for the Amish."

Another long pause made Wyatt wonder if Marcus had hung up—until the young man cleared his throat. "It seems my ability to manage money doesn't measure up to my talent for training horses," he said snidely. "My um, ex-girlfriend kicked me to the curb because I tend to spend more than I make."

"And you were spending her money, as well? Without telling her?" Wyatt asked before he could catch himself.

Marcus let out a short laugh. "You got it."

"And you've racked up a lot of credit card debt?"

Marcus cleared his throat again. "Yup."

Wyatt paused. His immediate impulse was to write the kid off, because Marcus's attitude and spending habits were two strikes against him before they'd even met. Wyatt knew a lot of spoiled young men in the

Thoroughbred world who habitually spent more than their wealthy fathers' generous allowances and then expected their dads to bail them out of their credit messes. He didn't need the headaches that would go with keeping track of Marcus's irresponsible spending behavior—or his sense of entitlement.

Yet he reconsidered. He really wanted an Amish trainer, even if Marcus had rebelled against being baptized into that faith. Deep down, Wyatt knew a lot about Marcus's mind-set, because he'd created some similar financial disasters when he'd been Marcus's age. If Nelson Carneal hadn't cut off his allowance and made him work for a salary—and if one woman and then another hadn't kicked him out for using her credit cards on the sly—he wouldn't have shouldered his responsibilities, wouldn't have attained his current comfortable position in life. Nelson had made it clear that Wyatt wouldn't inherit the two horse farms if he continued on the crash course he'd navigated in his twenties. His adoptive father had probably saved him from ruin, in more ways than one.

Wyatt refocused, choosing his words carefully. "Marcus, maybe you're due for a fresh start where you can earn a decent, steady wage," he suggested. "If I talk to your creditors and set up a repayment program you can handle, we can get you out from under that debt and establish a positive credit history. But you'll have to work for me—and work with me," he added firmly. "Nothing's free in this world, Marcus. A real man pays his way, and he pays it forward."

Marcus laughed derisively. "Yeah, well—"

"But if you don't think you can behave like a real man, working on my terms," Wyatt continued, "we'll just end this call and neither of us need waste any more time talking about a job you can't handle."

Marcus exhaled harshly. "Let me talk to Luke."

With a tight smile, Wyatt handed the cell phone back to Luke. "Your cousin wants a word," he said.

Luke put the phone to his ear, scowling in disbelief at what Wyatt had been saying. "What's going on out there, Marcus?" he demanded. "Wyatt's offering you a first-rate opportunity—"

Wyatt couldn't understand every word of Marcus's rant, but his belligerent tone came through loud and clear. Marcus didn't realize that a roomful of local men had heard Wyatt's side of the conversation and that they all wore wary expressions as they watched Luke's brows pucker.

"That's just nuts, man," Luke blurted out. "Wyatt's not expecting any more from you than any other employer would. Quite frankly, as I listened to what he was saying, I wondered if I'd steered him wrong by recommending you." After a few more minutes of listening to Marcus, he turned to Wyatt, placing his hand over the speaker end of the phone. "What do you need from Marcus to consider his application?" he whispered.

"Three references this week. If those folks confirm his ability, I'll pay his way to come out for a personal interview."

"More than fair." Luke removed his hand from the phone. "All right, here's the deal, Marcus. You email me three names and phone numbers tomorrow— men who know your work with horses," he said brusquely. "If they say you're the best trainer they've ever met, McKenzie will pay your way out here for an interview. And quite frankly, if you're not willing to straighten up and fly right, we don't want you here.

Ben and Ira and I have worked for every nickel we've earned, and we don't plan to bail you out of your money problems. Got it?"

When Luke hung up a few moments later he was shaking his head in exasperation. "I'm not even believin' this," he muttered. "How could a guy Marcus's age have already made such a mess of his life?" He looked at Wyatt. "After having this conversation, I won't blame you if you want nothing to do with our cousin. I'm sorry I got your hopes up about his talent with horses."

Wyatt shrugged. "The ball's in his court. If Marcus doesn't respond with those phone numbers, we'll have our answer, and I'll look elsewhere."

Ben leaned forward in his chair, his expression somber. "Are you telling us Marcus was using some gal's credit cards? And that he's up to his ears in debt?" he asked softly. "I can't imagine what Uncle Felty and Aunt Edna must be going through."

Luke slipped his phone back into his shirt pocket. "I got the distinct impression that Marcus is no longer living with his parents or answering to them," he said. "For all we know, Uncle Felty told him the same thing you did—to get his act together or get out. He's never been a man to tolerate the sort of nonsense we've heard about these past few minutes."

As the other men in the front room murmured about Marcus's apparent falling-out with his parents, Wyatt recalled the times he'd let Nelson Carneal down with his bad habits—and how his adoptive father had always loved him enough to offer him another chance anyway.

"All right, let's see a show of hands," Wyatt said as he gazed at the others. "How many of us heard advice or instruction from our dads about good money habits and blew them off?"

Wyatt raised his hand, smiling as every one of his companions did the same. "And how many of us filched a little—or a lot—of money at some time or another, thinking we'd never get caught at it?"

Again his hand went up, and so did a few of the other men's as they shook their heads, recalling what they'd done.

"And how many of us took advantage of a young woman's affection for us? Did her wrong in some way?" Wyatt asked, keeping his hand in the air.

Luke sighed. "I see what you're saying, Wyatt. You think we should give Marcus a chance to grow up— to pay off his debt and someday pay it forward, as you put it."

"If we don't, who will?" Wyatt challenged. "If he comes here, and he gets into trouble, I'll take full responsibility for—"

"No, you won't," Ben interrupted. "It's our job to be this young man's role models—and it's our way to forgive his past mistakes as we guide him forward." He let out a sigh. "I know of a man much older than Marcus who's recently made some serious mistakes with money, and we've given him a chance to come clean. We can do no less for Marcus—if he's smart enough to accept your offer, Wyatt."

"At least we know up front what we'll be dealing with when Marcus shows up—if he does," Luke remarked. "With all of us keeping tabs on him, I'm guessing he'll either get with our program, or he'll bolt."

"*Jah*, we've all made similar choices," Ira said. "And we all have family members and friends who steered us right when we wanted to stray. God already knows how this'll turn out, and He's counting on us to play our part with Marcus."

As the men asked Wyatt about when his fences and buildings were to be completed, he was amazed—and gratified—that every one of them offered to help with those tasks. They were excited about the prospect of having locally bred and trained draft horses and were genuinely interested in his plans for the tract of land he'd bought. By the time he and Vanessa were heading to the car to leave, Wyatt thrummed with the enthusiasm his neighbors had generated.

"You've got an interesting smile on your face, Wyatt," his sister hinted as he backed the Lexus down the lane.

Wyatt chuckled. "I had my first chat with the young horse trainer the Hooleys are recommending, and if Marcus comes, he's going to be a challenge," he explained. "As soon as the other men heard about some of his shenanigans with credit cards, they immediately stepped up and agreed to help me get him into shape. I have a support system in place, and I didn't even have to ask for their help. It was an amazing conversation."

Vanessa squeezed his arm. "I think you're going to do just fine here, Wyatt. These people are the most helpful, kindhearted souls I've been around in a long while." She glanced out the passenger-side window, a secretive smile on her face. "The women were asking questions of Rebecca and me, hinting about what the future holds for the two of you."

Wyatt focused on the road. He and his sister were close, but he wasn't keen on saying things to her before he'd discussed them with Rebecca. "What do you think of her?"

Vanessa laughed out loud. "I liked her from the moment she pitched that pan of crisp at you," she replied. "With Rebecca—and these other folks—what you see is what you get. Considering some of the crowd we've run with in the Thoroughbred world, I find Willow Ridge a tremendously refreshing little town. A good place to call home."

Wyatt let out the breath he'd been holding. As he turned the car onto the dirt path leading into his property, his sister's words felt like a blessing on this new adventure he'd undertaken. "Thanks, Nessa," he murmured. "I'm sorry you're leaving tomorrow, and I hope you'll come back now and then to see how things are going."

"I wouldn't miss it for anything."

Chapter Twenty-Seven

Loretta wanted to stop time, to allow this long-awaited wedding moment to shimmer blissfully in her memory for the rest of her life. How the past few weeks of preparations had seemed to drag—and how every other wedding she'd ever attended felt halting and slow, by comparison to her own! As she and Drew stood before Bishop Tom to repeat their marriage vows, it struck her that suddenly, in a few moments, she would be Mrs. Andrew Detweiler.

There would be no going back. Not that she would want to.

Focus forward, she thought fleetingly. *Today's the first day of a whole new life, when you stand a chance for the happiness and peace you've wished for.*

As Bishop Tom said the introductory words of the age-old ceremony, Loretta reminded herself to breathe. She glanced at Rosalyn and Edith, who beamed at her from the side-sitters' bench on the front row of the women's side. She felt the weight of Dat's sullen stare as he sat on the preachers' bench behind the bishop, but instead of making eye contact with him, she gazed up at Drew. He stood beside her as steady as a rock, dressed in the new white shirt, black vest, and black trousers she'd sewn for him after she'd made her royal blue wedding dress. His violet eyes expressed desires and promises Loretta dared to believe would finally come true in a very short time.

"Drew and Loretta," Bishop Tom said as he gazed solemnly at each of them, "the sacrament of marriage is a holy bond, not to be entered into on a whim or without absolute certainty that this relationship will thrive and prosper until death parts you. Do you understand this?"

Loretta nodded, breathless. Drew did the same.

"Likewise to the rest of us here," the bishop continued in a louder voice as he looked out over the crowd that filled Asa and Edith's front room. He also turned to look briefly at Dat. "We are to honor this union and to encourage these young folks as they embark on the journey of their life together. If anyone knows of a reason that this man and this woman should not marry, speak now or forever hold your peace."

Loretta's heart raced as she imagined her father rising from the preachers' bench to protest the marriage—if only to keep Drew from living in his house.

But Dat remained seated, exhaling impatiently.

"All right then, we'll proceed." Bishop Tom's weathered face relaxed into a smile as he led them in their vows.

Loretta listened carefully, praying she was repeating the bishop's words in a clear, confident voice—because for a breathless moment she felt as though she'd separated from her body and was observing the ceremony from somewhere near the ceiling.

Was Drew experiencing the same sensation as he repeated the same vows? He faced her fearlessly, all signs of his roguish, rule-breaking side replaced by a gaze of utmost love and devotion. When she saw herself reflected in his bottomless, midnight blue eyes, Loretta fell in love all over again.

When the bishop pronounced them husband and wife, the room filled with applause and cheers. Drew pulled Loretta close for a kiss that made her tingle all the way to her toes.

When she came to her senses, Will had risen from the side-sitters' bench on the men's side and was standing before her to clasp her hands. "Loretta, I wish you and Drew all the happiness your hearts can hold," he said as he smiled brightly at them. "*Denki* for enduring all that emotional stuff I put you through earlier and for standing by me as I recovered."

"Hey, we're glad you made it through the valley of the shadow and could stand up with us today," Drew said as he pumped Will's hand. "We want all the best to happen for you, too."

Will's smile suggested he knew things he wasn't yet ready to share. "I'm working on it," he murmured, glancing up at Luke and Nora as they came over. "I have a lot to be grateful for, and my job farming for Luke is one of them."

"Happy to have you, Gingerich," Luke said as he approached and clapped Will on the shoulder.

"And *I'm* glad that, for the time being, Loretta will continue working at Simple Gifts on Tuesdays and Thursdays—and that she'll be spending her Saturdays with you now, Drew," Nora added as she slipped her arms around Drew and Loretta's waists. "You're a wonderful husband to allow your bride to keep her job."

Drew nodded as he chuckled at Loretta. "*Jah*, I'm

wonderful," he teased. "And I know my wife gets a lot more than a paycheck while she's working for you, Nora."

"Simple Gifts is such a fun place to work," Rosalyn said wistfully as she, too, came to stand with them. "I've been thinking—if you'd want me to, Nora—that I could cover the Saturday hours Loretta used to work, and maybe another day during the week—"

"You're on!" Nora exclaimed. "I could really use your help as we get closer to Christmas."

"That's a wonderful-*gut* idea," Loretta said as she hugged her sister. She glanced around the crowd and saw their father chatting with Adam Wagler. "Does Dat know yet?"

Rosalyn's cheeks turned pink as she shook her head. "He won't be happy. He'll give me that same lecture about dutiful daughters obeying their fathers—but it's my way of finding a little of that happiness and peace you've been wishing for, Loretta. If I don't seek out my own satisfaction, how will I find any?"

For a moment everyone who'd gathered around them gazed at Rosalyn in admiration. "Well said," Nora put in with an emphatic nod. "Seek and ye shall find."

"And if Dat gives you any flack about that," Edith put in as she joined them, with little Louisa balanced on one hip, "I'll tell him it's time I started bringing the twins over for visits while you're working. How could he not be a happier man if he spent more time with his grandchildren? We could put their playpen in the shop while he tinkers with his clocks."

Louisa's loud squawk of laughter made everyone else join in her merriment. As Loretta hugged more of the guests and accepted their congratulations, she felt pleased that Rosalyn had decided to spend some time in Nora's store, where her efforts and the wreaths she made would be appreciated. If she and Rosalyn alternated their work days, one of them would be at home with Dat, so it wasn't as though he'd go without his noon meal or be otherwise inconvenienced.

Josiah and Savilla worked their way through the crowd to shake Drew's hand and hug Loretta. "We're on our way over to set up the steam tables," he said so everyone could hear him. "Give us about ten minutes, and we'll be ready for you."

Lots of folks applauded and expressed their readiness to feast at the Grill N Skillet. Bishop Tom returned from chatting with Drew's parents, a wide smile on his face.

"If you newlyweds and side-sitters will sign the marriage certificate that's on the kitchen table, we'll have the formalities taken care of, and the rest of the day is a party," he suggested as he handed Drew a pen. "Does my heart *gut* to be performing so many weddings of late and to have so many folks your age deciding to settle in Willow Ridge."

"Asa and I are pleased to be here," Drew remarked as he led the wedding party toward the kitchen. "I'm not sure how much longer our furniture business could've been profitable in Clifford."

"And we met up with some mighty fine women here," Asa chimed in, elbowing his brother. "Our lives have been *Riehl* happy since we came."

Loretta couldn't stop smiling as she watched Drew sign his full name on the certificate. When he handed her the pen, she paused, considering her words. "If you've signed but I don't," she teased, "will that mean I'm not bound by our marriage vows?"

Drew's lips curved as he gazed at her with shining

eyes. "It means *I* will have all the say, and *you'll* not be getting any of those marital privileges you've been so eager for," he murmured playfully. "Such as sleeping in that bed I refurbished for our room."

As their side-sitters and the bishop chuckled, Loretta felt her cheeks prickle with heat. It was a bit embarrassing that Drew was hinting about private passionate encounters in front of other folks—but only a bit. She snatched the pen from him and signed her name with a flourish before handing it to Edith. "Sleeping," she said under her breath, "is highly overrated."

A few minutes later, when she and Drew were headed toward the Grill N Skillet, the cool October breeze felt good after spending the entire morning in a crowded house. A few orange and yellow leaves drifted from the maple trees in Asa and Edith's front yard, the first signs that autumn was coming to Willow Ridge. Their friends and family members ambled down the lane and along the road ahead of them, flowing like a lazy stream to the meal everyone would linger over for most of the afternoon. The sight filled Loretta with a rare excitement, because this time the Witmers' bountiful buffet table was serving the dinner to honor her and Drew—to celebrate their union, their future together.

"We're going to take a little detour about now," Drew whispered as he steered her toward the Detweiler Furniture Works building. "Nobody will even notice we're not at the café yet—unless *you* make us late, sugar."

Loretta felt a rush of goose bumps. "Why are we going to your shop? You surely don't intend to work on our wedding day."

"Trust me. You'll like this detour."

Loretta couldn't miss the mischievous glint in his eyes as he opened the metal building's back door. The stairway was too narrow for them to climb it side by side, so Drew gestured for her to go first. As her footsteps echoed in the stairwell, they masked the pounding of her pulse, for Drew's apartment had been forbidden territory when she'd been a single girl. Now that she was his wife, however, a whole new world awaited her—and after she opened the door at the top of the steps, she paused to take it in.

"It's nothing fancy," Drew said as he entered the simple kitchen behind her. "As a bachelor, I didn't require much—just a basic fridge, an apartment-sized stove, and a sink. But I thought you and I could transform it into our . . . little hideaway. A more private place when we'd like some time alone."

Loretta's eyes widened with comprehension. "That's a fine idea," she whispered. "I really love the bedroom set you and Asa refurbished for our room at home, but when I slept there last night, I noticed a lot of creaks and noises."

"It's old. Probably dates back to the nineteen twenties," he said with a nod. "But I can tighten it up and wax some of the joints to make it quieter. I um, thought of you sleeping there last night and couldn't seem to fall asleep myself."

Loretta's heartbeat raced as Drew took her in his arms. "You'll probably be so tired you'll have to leave the wedding party to take a nap this afternoon," she teased.

"Will you come with me?" He pulled her close against him, gazing intently at her. His mouth found hers for a thorough kiss that hinted at anything but an afternoon snooze.

Loretta's cheeks tingled. "But everyone will know what we're doing if—"

"So?"

Her thoughts whirled wildly. More than once she'd made her desire known to him, yet now that Drew was tempting her, daring her to respond to his brazen idea, she felt pulled between behaving like a proper bride and flaunting her wayward desires in front of their guests.

"We wouldn't be the first newlyweds to slip away from their festivities, you know," he murmured alluringly.

Loretta nipped her lip. "We'll see."

Drew smiled and kissed her temple. "All right, we will. And before I get so carried away that we don't show up for dinner at all, I'll give you a quick tour of the rest of the place."

Loretta loved the way his large hand enveloped hers as he gestured toward the sofa and coffee table before leading her down a short hallway and past a basic bathroom. The other end of the apartment was a large bedroom with simple furnishings. She was impressed with how neat and tidy the apartment appeared as she gazed at a low bed in a style she'd never seen.

"That's a king-size platform bed with a water mattress. Found it at an estate sale," Drew explained. "It's a lot easier to make because once the fitted sheet's on, you don't have to tuck anything under the mattress. I hope you'll like it."

Curious, Loretta walked over to the bed and pressed her hand into it. Beneath the simple quilt, she felt the mattress shift slightly under her palm. "There's water in there?"

"Yup. It's kind of like floating on an air mattress on a pond—except you can't roll off and fall in," Drew added with a laugh.

"Oh my," Loretta whispered as she pressed harder and felt the movement beneath her hand. "That might take some getting used to."

"Stretch out on it," Drew suggested playfully.

Loretta turned away from the large, low bed to challenge him with a direct gaze. "You'd like that, wouldn't you?" she challenged him. "But we're leaving for the Grill N Skillet right now, before everyone speculates about where we've gone and what we're doing."

Drew shot her a knowing smile. "We should fortify ourselves. For what comes later," he added quickly as he held out his hand. "I hope you won't make me wait much longer, Loretta."

As they descended the stairway from the apartment and stepped outside again, Loretta felt a surge of powerful happiness. She felt blessed to be married to a man who respected her wish to work a while longer and whose sense of humor and keen desire complemented hers. Sometimes at work frolics she'd heard hints from married women who felt they'd forfeited their innermost emotional needs or who seemed burdened by always submitting to their husbands' wills.

Mamm lived such a life, Loretta thought suddenly. *But you don't have to.*

"Penny for your thoughts," Drew murmured as they reached the road. "I hope I haven't pushed you past your comfort zone or—"

"Oh, no," Loretta assured him. Seeing that they would soon be inside the noisy café, surrounded by well-wishers, she stopped at the side of the road to face him. "I was just thinking how lucky I am—how very blessed—that you consider what I'd like, and that you want to make me happy, Drew," she said, caressing his cheek. "I feel like all my heart's desires—all the birthday wishes I've ever made—have come true today because you've married me."

Drew blinked. "Wow."

"*Jah*, wow," Loretta murmured as she smiled up at him. "We'll share a fine life forever if we aim for *wow* every day."

Please turn the page for an excerpt from
a very special new Amish romance by
Charlotte Hubbard!

A Mother's Gift

As Lenore Otto sat on the bed with Leah, wistfully watching the November dusk fill her daughter's room, her heart was torn. The two of them had shared this evening ritual of talking and praying since Lenore's husband, Raymond, had died last year. It had always brought her a comforting sense of peace, along with the certainty that she and her daughter would move forward with the plans God had for them. After all the cleaning they'd done and the preparations they'd made to host Leah's wedding festivities the next day, she was ready to relax—but she needed to speak the words that weighed so heavily on her heart.

Tomorrow, when Leah got married, their lives would follow separate paths. Lenore knew she would be fine remaining on the small farm alone, making and selling her specialty quilts. She supposed some of the qualms she had about her daughter's marriage plagued every mother . . .

Lord, I wish I could be sure my Leah is reaching toward happiness rather than heartache.

Before God's still, small voice could respond to

Lenore, Leah let out an ecstatic sigh. "Oh, Mama, it's a dream come true," she murmured. "Starting tomorrow, when I marry Jude, my life will finally be the way I've always wanted it. My waiting is over!"

Not for the first time, Lenore sighed inwardly at her daughter's fantasy. As she returned Leah's hug, savoring these precious moments in the room where her little girl had matured into a woman of twenty-eight, she didn't have it in her to shatter Leah's dreams. No mother wanted her daughter to forever remain a *maidel*, yet during these final hours before the wedding, Lenore thought she should try once again to point out the realities of marrying Jude Shetler. Jude was a fine, upstanding man any parent would be pleased to welcome as a son-in-law, but as a widower, he carried a certain amount of . . . baggage.

"Leah, when you marry, your life will change in ways you can't anticipate," Lenore began softly. She rested her head against the headboard, grasping her daughter's hand. "When you move into a man's home—"

"Oh, Mama, you've already told me what to expect in the bedroom," Leah interrupted with a nervous giggle. "It's not as though I haven't seen the deer and the horses mating."

Lenore closed her eyes, praying for words that would gently pierce the balloon of maidenly naïveté in which Leah seemed to live. "There's more to marriage than mating," she whispered earnestly. "You'll be moving into a home where Jude and his kids have established their routine. We've both heard the rumors about how young Alice and Adeline might be behaving inappropriately during their *rumspringa*—"

"They're sixteen, and they're very pretty," Leah quickly pointed out. "Twins are inclined to get into double trouble as part of their nature at that age. *I* certainly found mischief during my running-around years."

Lenore sighed again. She wished Raymond were here to help her with this difficult discussion. "Sweetheart, I doubt you were ever out of your *dat's* or my sight for more than an hour at a time. The pranks you used to pull at sale barns when you were helping Dat with the livestock were nothing compared to the way I've heard Alice and Adeline run the roads with English boys in their cars."

"I rode in a few cars—and pickups—you didn't know about," Leah shot back. "It's not as though I spent my time hanging around with *girls* at the auction barns, you know."

Squeezing Leah's fingers so she'd focus on the matters at hand, Lenore held her daughter's gaze in the dimness. "I probably should've insisted that you learn to cook and sew and keep house instead of tending the animals with your Dat," she murmured. "But you were a tremendous help to him—and you were the only child God blessed us with. More than anything, I've wanted you to spend your life doing what makes you happy."

"And I *am* happy, Mama!" Leah said blissfully. "I make a *gut* income selling my dressed chickens and ducks, my goat's milk, and raising deer—the same way Dat did. If I hadn't spent so much time in the sale barns around Jude, he would never have come to know me—or love me."

Lenore paused, searching for another conversational path. She had no doubt that her daughter's love for Jude was sincere, and that Jude loved Leah, too, but it took more than shared affection to make a marriage work and keep a household running smoothly.

"And, Mama, if your quilts don't sell—or if you want to stop working so hard on them," Leah said tenderly, "you know I'll help you out with money so you can stay here at home. I know how much you and Dat have always loved this place."

Tears sprang to Lenore's eyes. Once again her daughter spoke with the utmost sincerity, unaware that Jude might have different ideas about Leah's income—or that he might insist that she give up raising and selling her chickens, ducks, and goats. He might also be reluctant for his wife to raise deer that were destined to stock hunting lodges, even if he admired Leah's way with those animals.

"*Denki* for thinking of me, dear, but we're talking about you now," Lenore insisted gently. "I'm concerned because Jude's *mamm*, Margaret, also lives with Jude and the twins—not to mention Stevie, who seems rather immature for five. Margaret will have her way of doing things, because she took charge after Frieda died. And with Stevie still missing his *mamm*, you'll have a lot of little-boy emotions to deal with as you prepare him to start school next year. Most new brides only have a husband to get used to until the babies start coming."

"*Jah*, but with Margaret running the household and tending the three kids—especially Stevie—their routine can remain uninterrupted," Leah pointed out. "That will give Jude and me time to adjust to being husband and wife, and it'll mean that meals are put on the table and the laundry and cleaning will still get done. From what I know of Margaret, she'll have instructed Alice and Adeline about doing their part, too."

From what I know of Margaret, Lenore thought sadly, *she'll be snipping at you every chance she gets, calling you a slacker—or worse—because you're not assuming the traditional role of an Amish wife.*

Lenore stared at the far wall, sensing that whatever she said would go unheard. "Just be ready for your plans to be changed, Leah," she warned gently. "Spending most of your time with Jude at auctions, or in the barnyard tending your animals, might not work out the way you've imagined. Margaret will be a woman with a plan, too, you know."

Leah leaned her head against the wooden headboard, closing her eyes. "I'll cross that bridge when—or if—I get to it, Mama. Tomorrow's my big day, and I know it'll be just perfect, because Jude's sharing it with me. The light in his eyes when he looks at me is all I need to see to believe he'll love me forever and ever."

Lenore looked out the window at the half moon, which shone brilliantly in the night sky. *Bless your heart, Leah, I wonder if you still believe the moon's made of green cheese, as Dat and I teased about when you were a child,* she thought with a sinking heart. *We probably should have done a lot of things differently as we were raising you . . . but it's too late to change your way of looking at things.*

"I wish you all the best as you start your new life, Leah," she said softly. With a final squeeze to her daughter's hand, Lenore rose from the bed. "You'll always be in my thoughts and prayers—and I'll always love you. *Gut* night and sleep tight."

"You can sleep for me, Mama. I'm too excited to close my eyes."

Lenore paused in the doorway of the unlit room for a last glance at her giddy daughter. *Bless her, Lord, and hold her in Your hand,* she prayed. *At this point, only You can keep Leah's happiness from turning into a disaster.*

More by Bestselling Author
Hannah Howell